THE LIBRARY OF ATHENA, BOOK TWO

# THE ANKH OF ISIS

# CHRISTINE NORRIS

Pennsville, NJ

PUBLISHED BY
Paper Phoenix Press
A division of eSpec Books
PO Box 242
Pennsville, NJ 08070
www.especbooks.com



ISBN:  978-1-956463-73-6
ISBN (eBook): 978-1-956463-72-9



Cover Image and Design: Mike and Danielle McPhail, McP Digital Graphics
Basilisk model by Summoner.

Interior Design: Danielle McPhail, McP Digital Graphics

Shutterstock images - www.shutterstock.com

Greek pattern. Roman ellipse frame. Outline greece border isolated on white background. Round greec boarder for design prints. Circular ancient ornament. Fret rome key stripes. Vector illustration © Omeris

Goddess Athena © Masterlevsha

Olive tree vector illustration design © Hisyam arib herli u

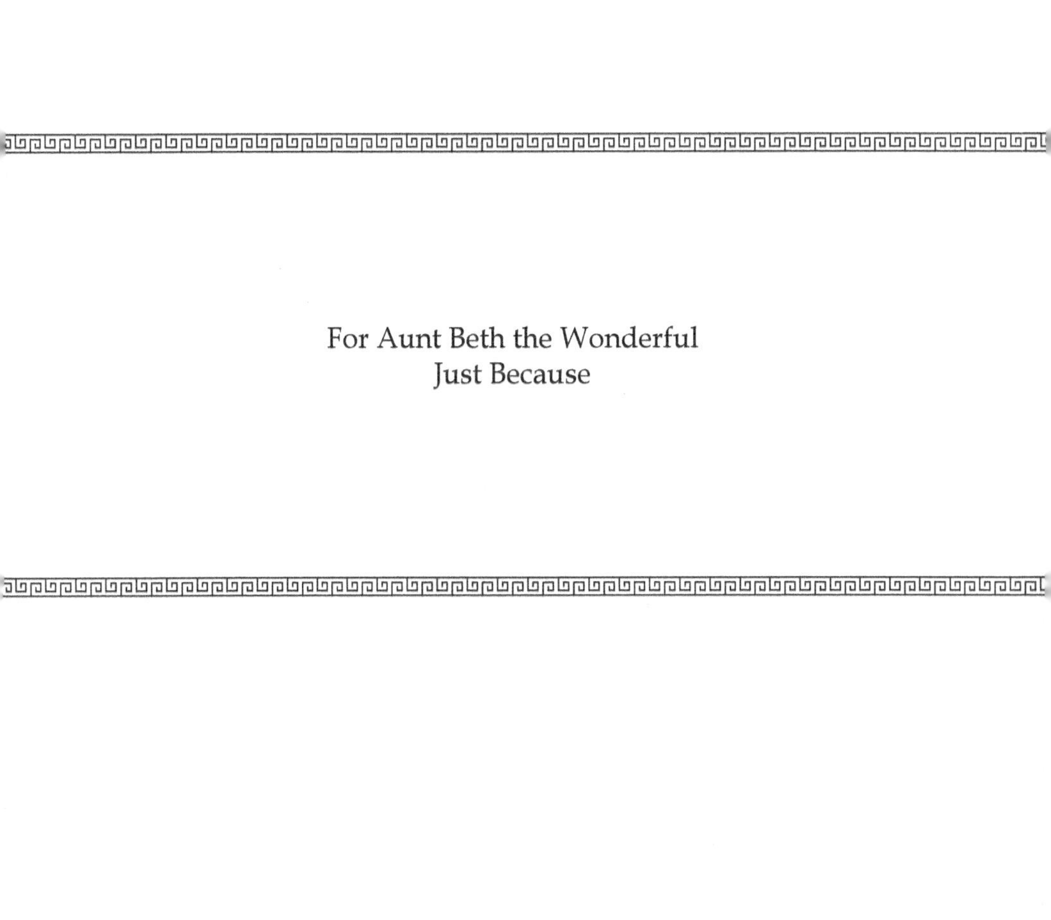

For Aunt Beth the Wonderful
Just Because

There is no Frigate like a Book
To take us Lands away
Nor any Coursers like a page
Of prancing Poetry —
This Traverse may the poorest take
Without oppress of Toll —
How frugal is the Chariot
That bears the Human soul.
— Emily Dickinson

# CHAPTER 1

*Spring Break Comes with a Surprise Guest Star.*

MEGAN STUMBLED THROUGH THE FORMAL DINING ROOM, STILL HALF-asleep, and kicked the stand of a tall Oriental vase.

"Ow!" She cursed as pain shot up her leg, hopping up and down, her foot in her hand.

*That's the third time this week. Stupid thing. I need to ask Bailey to move that.*

Toe throbbing, she limped from the dining room, through the door, and into the hall behind it, before pushing open the swinging door to the kitchen. She was greeted by a warm, brightly lit room and the smell of baking. Maggie, the plump Irish woman who cooked for Megan and her father, was busy preparing breakfast.

"Good morning, miss," Maggie said cheerfully. She poured water into the coffeemaker and turned it on, then reached into the refrigerator and pulled out a jug of orange juice. "What are you doing up so early? It's the first day of the holidays." She set the jug on the counter.

Megan sat on a stool in front of the kitchen's center island and rubbed her sore foot.

"I'm not awake on purpose. Miranda woke me up while she was making the fire in my room." She picked an apple from the bowl on the counter and took a bite. "It's all right, I have some things to do today anyway."

"Don't talk with your mouth full," Maggie chided. "What kind of things could you have to do today, child?" She bent and pulled a tray of fresh rolls from the oven, then tossed her mitts on the counter. "Surely, your professors didn't give you homework over the break, did they?"

Megan swallowed and rolled her eyes at the painful reminder.

"Of course they did. Rachel is coming over today. We're going to work on our history papers and maybe go into town to do some shopping this afternoon." Rachel Cuthbert was Megan's best friend. They were both in third year at St. Agatha's College for Girls, a much tougher school than her old school in New York—where Megan had lived until seven months ago—could ever dream of being.

Megan and Rachel were both in the same academic House—Whitmore—and on the House hockey team. One girl rarely went anywhere without the other. Megan had wanted to go riding today, but Rachel, for some reason, insisted she wanted to get some work done.

"Ah." Maggie nodded with a look of mock seriousness. "Important things, I see. Well, breakfast is almost ready. I think there's enough time for you to get yourself back upstairs to wash and dress before your da comes down."

Megan pushed out her lower lip. "But it's vacation. If I have to do homework, why can't I bum around in my PJs for a while?"

Maggie cocked an eyebrow, wearing a familiar expression meant to inflict an overwhelming sense of guilt.

"It's not very ladylike, traipsing around in your pajamas. If you're going to be about in the house, you should go and get dressed."

Megan's mother, Gwen, had died in a car crash four years earlier, leaving Megan and her father alone. Since they'd moved to The Parthenon, a huge manor house in the English countryside, the cook had become something of a surrogate.

"Fine." Megan, feeling sufficiently scolded, turned to go back upstairs when she heard her father in the dining room. There was a *thump* and a loud curse. She gave an evil grin. Not only wasn't she the only one who had a sore foot, she was spared the rest of Maggie's lecture.

"Too late, sorry." Megan dashed out the door. She heard Maggie's tongue cluck in disapproval just before the kitchen door swung shut.

Megan finished up her apple as she left the kitchen through a different door than the one she'd used to enter and crossed into the solarium. It was smaller than most of the other rooms, with a terracotta tiled floor, and the east wall, which faced outside, covered in squares of thick glass. She and her father took most of their morning meals in this bright, cheery room. He already sat at the small, round table, perusing the newspaper.

"Morning, Daddy." Megan gave him a peck on the cheek and sat in the chair opposite him. Her father was an investment banker based in London. He worked so hard, sometimes long hours, and she was busy with school. Breakfast and dinner were practically the only times they saw each other. Sometimes not even then.

His eyes never left the paper. "Good morning, Megums," he mumbled. "Ready for school?"

Maggie came in with a tray of rolls, a pitcher of orange juice, a cup of coffee, and a small pot of steaming tea. She glanced at Megan as she set the tray on the small table, shook her head, and left without a word.

"Dad, I'm off all week," Megan said in a gentle tone meant to remind. She reached for the basket of rolls. "It's Easter holiday. You know, like Spring Break. How could you forget?"

He folded down the top of the paper and looked across the table. "Is it?" He shook his head and took a sip of coffee. "I'm sorry, Meg. I've been so busy with work these last few weeks that everything else has just gotten pushed to the back of my brain."

Megan poured herself a glass of orange juice. "Problem with a client?" Troublesome clients always seemed to make him lose track of everything else. "Who is it — Mrs. Sanderson again?"

Mrs. Sanderson was seventy-two years old, very wealthy, and hard of hearing. She also thought everyone was constantly trying to rip her off. Whenever she called, Megan's father had to put everything else on hold until the old bat was satisfied.

Her father folded the paper in quarters and set it beside his plate. "Nope, not Mrs. Sanderson, thank goodness. This one is still only a potential client. He's a very wealthy man. Old money, but he's successful on his own too. I've been trying to get him to sign with us for weeks."

He picked up his knife and focused his attention on slathering a roll with Maggie's special honey butter.

"I'm thinking about bringing him here for a day or two. You know, wine and dine him a bit, show him how serious we are about having his business."

Megan raised her eyebrows, shocked at the idea. "Bring him here? Why in the world would you want to bring him here — we live in the middle of nowhere."

"Why? The English countryside, of course. Fresh air, country living." He laughed. "Actually, Meg, he's an archaeologist. Curator of some museum in Berlin. I think he's a fan of Sir Gregory's." He slurped up the last of his coffee.

"He's hinted to me and Mr. Baird that he wants to come here, and if that will seal the deal, I'll be happy to have him."

*Huh?* It seemed like an odd request, to ask to spend time at a complete stranger's house, even if it was the former home of someone you admired. It struck her as… well, rude.

"Whatever. It's not like we don't have the room. It could be fun, I guess, to have a guest." She finished the last bite of her breakfast and decided to drop the subject. It was just an idea, no sense in talking about it.

"Glad you think so, because he's coming tonight."

Megan's jaw dropped. "Wait, what? I thought it was just an idea?"

"I wanted to break it to you gently." Her dad took a bite of his roll and washed it down with a swig of coffee.

"Okay, I guess? Couldn't give me a little warning?"

"What? I gave you a whole day. He called late last night and said he would be in London today on other business, so I offered. You just said you're off from school, so it all works out well."

Megan sighed her most dramatic teenage sigh. "Fine, I guess. Rachel's coming over, so I have to get ready."

"Make sure you're here when our guest arrives, okay?"

Megan paused at the solarium's door. "Sure thing. I'll see you later. Have a nice day, Dad."

She walked back through the dining room, carefully avoiding the vase, crossed the drawing room, then the lounge with its big leather armchairs in front of a gray stone fireplace. As usual, all was quiet here at The Parthenon, which was the odd name given to the enormous manor where Megan, her father, and a small household staff were the only residents. The Montgomerys had moved here from New York after her father's firm gave him a promotion that forced her to leave the only home she had ever known.

Maggie and the rest of the staff had been here when Megan and her father moved in. All of them had worked and lived at The Parthenon for many years, most hired by the builder and previous owner of the house, Sir Gregory Archibald.

Megan, in her slippered feet, slid across the black-and-white polished marble floor of the cavernous entrance hall and up the sweeping grand staircase in the center. On the landing stood an impressive eight-foot-tall marble sculpture of the Goddess Athena. In one hand she held a long spear, while the other arm reached out toward the front door. On the hand perched an owl.

The staircase split at the landing, each branch leading to a different wing of the second floor. Megan turned left, passing the portrait of a man in his thirties with brown hair, eyes of brilliant green, a long nose and a rakish grin. This was the aforementioned Sir Gregory, a man who had described himself more as an adventurer than an archaeologist.

Megan had taken a liking to the portrait. Sir Gregory was what might be described as dashing—he reminded her of Indiana Jones. He was also a mysterious man who'd had many secrets, as Megan had discovered soon after moving in. Not the least of which was that he spent much of his life collecting mysterious artifacts many people thought did not exist.

At the top of the stairs, Megan walked down the hall, her feet silent on the thick Persian carpet runner. She padded past a series of identical closed oak doors with brass knobs that led to unoccupied bedrooms. Halfway down, she stopped at her own door and went inside. It was gigantic, easily half the size of her entire apartment in New York. It even had its own walk-in closet and luxurious bathroom.

She flopped on her queen-size four-poster bed and closed her eyes. Because she had been rudely awakened so early, there was still plenty of time before Rachel was due. More than enough for a quick nap.

A nearby buzzing woke Megan with a start. She reached over and grabbed her cell phone, nearly knocking over the silver-framed photo of her mother in the process. It took a moment for her bleary eyes to clear. There were four texts from Rachel. Megan looked at the phone's clock.

*An hour and a half?* She had fallen asleep for an hour and a half! Rachel's texts said she was on her way over, and then three wondering why Megan hadn't replied.

She typed a hasty text, then jumped up, grabbed her robe, and ran to the bathroom to take the fastest shower of her life. After scraping the gunk from her teeth, she ran to the closet and pulled out some jeans, a tee-shirt, and a hoodie and threw them on.

The doorbell rang just as she wrangled her damp auburn curls into a ponytail. By the time her feet hit the last step of the grand staircase, Rachel was already inside.

"Hello, Bailey," Rachel said to the dour-faced butler. "How are you today?"

"Good day, miss." Bailey closed the door behind her. "I am fine, thank you." His words were polite, his tone all business as usual. The butler rarely displayed emotion. Megan could count on one hand the time she had seen him smile.

"Thanks, Bailey," Megan said. "I would have gotten it myself."

"It is my duty, miss." Bailey gave a stiff bow and walked toward the back of the house.

"Hi, Rach."

Rachel gave a cheery wave. "Ready?" She wore jeans that accentuated her slim, athletic figure, and a long-sleeved red shirt. Her hair, dark as raven's feathers, hung in a braid down the center of her back, and her school bag was slung over one shoulder. She shook out an umbrella.

"It's raining?" Megan asked. As if in answer, a rumble of thunder echoed through the cavernous house. "Do you remember the last time we actually saw the sun?"

Rachel giggled. "Come on, Meg. It's not that bad. This is England in spring, after all. You'll get used to it."

"Well, it's not good for people to have so little sunlight."

"Ha-ha. Can we get some study fuel?" Rachel shifted her bag from one shoulder to the other. "What's my girl Maggie got that we could nick from the kitchen?"

With glasses of iced tea and a platter of sandwiches secured, the girls went upstairs to Megan's room. She opened her laptop and logged into her school account, then did a quick search for the guidelines that Professor Livingston, their world history teacher, had given them for their project. Professor Livingston was also their Head of House, and one of Megan's favorite teachers, but she was tough. Her projects were notoriously complicated, asking for tons of references that demanded hours of research.

Megan turned to Rachel, who sat on the bed eating. Her bag was on the bed, closed, her laptop nowhere in sight.

"Uh, Rach? The bag works better when you open it. That thing there? It's called a zipper."

Rachel gave a small, furtive smile that made Megan nervous.

*I don't like that look. That look always means trouble.*

"I have a better idea. Let's go down to the Library."

"Why do you want to go there? It's kind of stuffy and the chairs aren't really comfortable. I mean, we can see if there are any books to help us with our project, but I don't want to work down there all day."

Rachel gave her a meaningful look. "Not that library, you dolt. The other library. *The Library.*"

Megan raised her brows. "Oh, *that* Library."

Sir Gregory Archibald was a man with many secrets, several of which they had learned when they had discovered his diary hidden in Megan's room. But the biggest was that his house sat above a huge library called The Library of Athena, that housed a very eclectic and strange collection. The only reason Megan and Rachel even knew about it was because they had accidentally found it. And then they had been sucked into one of the books and had to fight their way through monsters and magic to get home again.

"I don't know, Rache…" Megan hadn't been down there since they had returned from their "adventure," as they called it. Even though she had the key and was technically in charge of the gigantic collection.

"Oh, come on, Megan. You get to go down there whenever you want. I don't."

"But I thought we were working on our papers?"

"There might be some really interesting books we could use. Pleeaasse?"

Things were starting to make sense. "Is that why you came over?"

Rachel had the good sense to look shocked. "I'm a little insulted you would think that." Her shoulders dropped and she let out her breath in a *whoosh.* "I mean, I would have come over anyway."

Megan picked up a pillow and threw it at Rachel, laughing. "Brat."

Rachel caught it and hugged it to herself. "We have loads of time to work on the paper. Let's go exploring instead."

Megan inhaled and held her breath, as if she were still deciding, but really, she was just making Rachel wait a bit.

"Oh, all right."

Rachel giggled and clapped her hands like a child. "Yay. You're a love."

Megan pulled open the top drawer of her dresser. Rachel looked over her shoulder. "You keep the key to a secret magical library in your underwear drawer?"

"Can you think of a better place? Nobody goes into it except Lilly, who does the laundry, and sometimes Miranda. And she just puts everything on top and shuts the drawer."

Megan dug to the bottom of the drawer and pulled out a long, old-fashioned brass key. "Not that anyone knows I've got the key, except you, Claire, Harriet, and Bailey. I'm not even sure the rest of the staff knows."

Megan had found the key, a cryptic poem, and a small journal in a secret compartment beneath one of the hearthstones of the fireplace in her room. According to Bailey, Sir Gregory had believed that whoever found it, and the library, would be the new guardian of the Library of Athena. So Megan was now the Librarian. It was a pretty easy job, considering very few people knew it even existed.

She stuffed the key in her front pocket and shut the drawer.

"Let's go."

# CHAPTER 2

*Research Sometimes Requires Sacrifices. Hopefully Not the Human Kind.*
*Chances are Low But Never Zero.*

MEGAN AND RACHEL STOOD SIDE-BY-SIDE ON THE LANDING, IN FRONT OF the statue of Athena. The manor was quiet, except for the steady beat of the grandfather clock in the lounge and the rain as it tapped against the windows in a counterpoint rhythm to the clock.

Athena was Sir Gregory's patron goddess, which was why the manor was named after her temple in Athens. She was the Goddess of Wisdom, something with which Sir Gregory apparently identified deeply. The statue guarded the entrance to the Library of Athena. Which, when Megan thought about it, was kind of obvious, but only if you knew her secret.

Megan reached up, grabbed the head of the owl that sat on Athena's hand, and pulled it so the owl, along with Athena's hand, spun completely around. There was a tiny click from somewhere nearby as a hidden mechanism opened a door in the wall behind the statue.

"Come on." Megan turned on the flashlight she had taken from the hall cupboard and pushed the door open. Behind it was a dark, winding stone staircase that led deep below the house. Megan descended, and Rachel followed.

"Have you been down here, since our… trip?" Rachel asked.

"Twice," Megan replied. "Over Christmas break."

"You didn't go into any of the other books, did you?" The Special Collection room was full of enchanted books, where "falling into the story" became frighteningly literal. Megan and Rachel, along with two of their other friends, had found that out the hard way when they were accidentally sucked inside one and transported to a fictional version of Ancient Greece. The books, created by Sir Gregory, were actually clever hiding places for his collection of magical artifacts. In order to get out, they had to find the Crown of Zeus, the legendary headpiece of the Greek god that granted all knowledge to the wearer.

Megan put her free hand against the wall to brace herself — the stairs were slippery. "Absolutely not. I just looked through the books out in the main room. There are some really cool ones down here. I found a spell book that's three hundred years old. It was pretty awesome, actually."

The enchanted books were but a small part of the library's vast collection. Many of the books in the Library of Athena were magical how-to books—spell books, potion books, books about fantastic creatures like dragons. Sir Gregory had spent much of his life collecting them from all over the world and using them to teach himself magic. There were also rare and unusual books, some of which no one knew existed. For example, when the four girls first discovered the library, their friend Claire had found some unknown writings of Leonardo da Vinci, while Rachel had stumbled across notebooks of sonnets apparently written in Shakespeare's own hand.

"Spell books? You've been looking through those, have you?" Rachel asked in a not-trying-to-pry-when-she-really-wanted-to-pry tone. "You haven't… tried any of them, have you? Spells, I mean."

Megan laughed, the sound bouncing off of the stone walls. "No. I'm not about to, either. I just found them… interesting. I was bored. It was too cold to go out and ride, Dad was working, and you were away somewhere. Visiting your great-aunt, I think."

"And Bailey doesn't mind?" Rachel said. "I would think he would have a fit if he knew you were down there, messing up his library."

"I didn't mess it up," Megan said. "No, he doesn't mind, because technically it's not his library. He's the caretaker. I'm the Librarian, remember?" She affected the butler's accent and stiff demeanor. "You should remember, however, that you are now accountable for the Library and all it contains. That is a great responsibility."

Rachel giggled and gave her a look. "Do you suppose having guests down is responsible?"

"It doesn't matter," Megan said as her foot hit the bottom step. "You've already been here. It's not like I've taken an ad in The Sunday Times and sold tickets."

The stairs ended in a small, stone anteroom. Megan trained the flashlight on the floor until she came to a particular stone. She pressed it with her foot. There was a loud pop, and gas-powered torches sprang to life. They illuminated the anteroom, the single arch that led from it, and the next room.

The girls passed beneath the arch and into a huge empty space, carved out from solid rock. Inside was a perfect replica of a Greek temple, forty feet long. Twenty-foot-tall white marble columns stood at intervals along the outer edge and reached up to the smooth, flat ceiling of the cavern. The ceiling was carved with symbols—Greek, Egyptian, Cabalistic and several others Megan didn't recognize.

The temple was beautiful and exceptionally detailed. It took Megan's breath away every time she saw it. She imagined the labor of love it had been for Sir Gregory to build, although she had yet to figure out how he'd built it so far underground, and alone.

Rachel must have read Megan's thoughts. "I rather like this temple. It's got a certain mysterious charm to it."

"I'm surprised you like anything that reminds you of ancient Greece," Megan said with a teasing smirk. She wrapped an arm around her friend's shoulders. "I would think you'd had enough of it."

Rachel put a hand to her chest. "I can't imagine why you would say such a thing. I mean, I only helped you cut off a Gorgon's head. Then I was forced to fly on the back of some mad mythical horse."

"His name is Pegasus."

"Whatever, it was perfectly terrifying. Then I was almost captured by some bull-man creature and eaten—"

"Minotaur."

"—and had to face a Sphinx who threatened to eat me if I didn't answer her silly riddles." She took a deep breath. "It doesn't make the temple any less interesting."

Megan snorted a laugh. "I guess it doesn't."

Tucked into the far corner, in the shadow of one of the columns, was a plain oak wooden door with a brass knob. Megan pulled the key from her pocket and unlocked the door. She swung the door open and allowed Rachel to enter.

Rachel's voice echoed in the dark. "Brr. I'd forgotten how cold it is in here."

"Bailey says it's climate-controlled," Megan explained. She flicked a switch, and torch-shaped electric lights came on to chase away the gloom. "The cavern keeps the books at precisely the right temperature and humidity levels to preserve them." She picked up two pairs of white cotton gloves from a holder on the wall next to the door. She handed a pair to Rachel. "If you're going to touch the books, put these on."

"Why?" Rachel took the gloves. "We didn't have to before."

"We didn't know any better last time. They keep the oils on our hands from damaging the paper."

Rachel pulled on the gloves and took a few steps into the oak-paneled room three times the size of the temple outside. Polished wooden floors reflected pools of light. A wide, carpeted aisle ran down the center of the room and away into the distance. On either side stood row upon row of bookshelves, filled with more books than one could hope to read in three lifetimes.

Above them arched an elegant, domed plaster ceiling. Today the dome looked like a perfect spring day—robin's-egg blue with white fluffy clouds floating across it. It was enchanted to work as a sort of timepiece. The ceiling would change as the day wore on. The light would shift and the clouds fade, the sky darkening until it was a deep, midnight blue spattered with golden stars. When Megan had asked, Bailey had said that Sir Gregory had done it so he wouldn't lose track of time down here, since there were no windows, and he often forgot to wear a watch.

The Library of Athena.

There was something solemn, something sad about this huge, quiet room. At the same time, it was, if Megan had to admit, just a *little* exciting. How many other people had their very own library full of books about magic? How many people actually believed in magic? Anyone who came down here would probably be more interested in the scrolls or the rare first editions… or only editions, in some cases.

Megan hadn't believed in magic herself before her first-hand, near-death experience with it. Now she was a true believer, and she took her job protecting the Library seriously. It was up to her to be responsible, to care for the Library as best she could.

Rachel walked slowly down the aisle, stopping to read the cards mounted in brass holders on the end of every case. The handwritten cards indicated what was shelved there.

"I don't know what's down here that we could use for our papers," Megan said.

Rachel reached the fifth set of shelves, turned right, and disappeared down the aisle.

"Rachel…" Megan said, her tone a warning. She pulled the door shut and followed her.

Rachel hadn't gone far. Megan found her in front of a set of shelves halfway down, scanning the titles.

"Looking for something in particular?" Megan asked, her suspicion reflected in her voice.

Rachel picked three books from the shelf. "I'm doing my paper for Livingston's class on ancient Egypt," she said. She tucked the books beneath her arm and walked away from Megan, through the stacks.

Megan chased after her. "I think we should be careful about using books from here…"

Rachel shot a look over her shoulder. "Come on, Megan. They're way better books here than at the school's library, or even the library upstairs. Who am I to pass up a great resource?"

The stacks emptied into a narrow open area with several reading tables. Rachel pulled out a chair from beneath the nearest one and sat. She opened her pack and retrieved a notebook and pen from inside.

"I don't want to turn in the same old boring paper everyone else does."

Megan sat next to her. "Um, well, I guess you can look. Like I said, I don't know what you can actually use. Some of these books you'd have a hard time explaining in the bibliography." She picked up one of the books. "Like this one—Secret Spells of Ancient Egypt: A Translation of a Papyrus Found Buried Beneath the Temple of Osiris."

"What's wrong with that?" Rachel said. She opened her notebook and started writing. "It's not like hieroglyphs are some big secret. Everyone knows the Egyptian priests used their own brand of magic. If you're worried about me telling where I got it, I'll just say I found a copy online at the British Museum or something."

"No, you can't lie. Livingston will see right through you. And I'm not worried about that. This copy is handwritten, by Sir Gregory, from a manuscript he personally discovered." Megan said. She laid the open book down in front of Rachel.

She pointed to the title page. "Look here, it says it was translated in nineteen-thirty-six, by Sir Gregory Archibald." She scanned the translation. "I'd love to see the look on Livingston's face, but how would you explain it?"

Rachel's face fell. "I see your point. Not that one, then."

Megan picked up the next book.

"But you could probably use this one. A Guide to Egyptian Gods and Goddesses." She flipped through the book quickly. "I recognize this one; it's just a reference book. There's another one like it upstairs." She handed it back to Rachel. "It's a little on the old side, but I think you can get away with it. If Professor Livingston asks, you can tell her you borrowed it from me."

Rachel flipped through the book but didn't really look at it. "I wonder what it's doing down here, if it's not that special?"

"I guess even Sir Gregory needed a handy reference book or two," Megan said with a shrug. "Down in the potion section I found three books on herbs. Nothing super special about any of them, they were just about how to grow them and what they look like. Of course, there was also a book from seventeen-thirty-five detailing many useful potions containing hemlock and wolfsbane."

Rachel's eyebrows went up. "Really?"

Megan nodded. "You wouldn't believe some of the things they used it for. Poisons, medicines... a potion to turn someone into a brown toad."

Rachel knit her brows together. "You're serious."

"Oh, yeah. I mean, that's just what the book said. I didn't try it or anything." She gave Rachel a sidelong glance. "Although I'm pretty sure there's some wolfsbane in the storeroom."

The look on Rachel's face made Megan laugh out loud. "I'm kidding, I'm kidding. Sometimes you make it way too easy. Besides, I don't know how to get into the storeroom. It's in the vault, remember? Only Bailey can get in there."

Rachel set the reference book aside and picked up the third one she had selected. It was a large ring-bound volume with an odd-looking hard cover.

"I picked this one up because it just looked so cool." She ran her fingers over the front of the book. "It feels like it's embossed." The face of the book was covered with columns of hieroglyphs. In the center was a large scarab sporting a pair of wings and a ring around its head, like a halo.

Megan looked over Rachel's shoulder, then reached around and rapped her knuckles against the book. "It's not embossed, it's carved. The cover's wood."

Rachel laid the book open on the table. The pages were smooth light-brown paper. Each was filled with hieroglyphs, and drawings of Ancient Egyptians, like the slides Professor Livingston showed during her lecture on pyramid art.

Megan's eyes went wide as she rubbed a page between her fingers. The paper was so thin. "This book is cool. I wonder what kind of paper this is."

"Maybe it's papyrus or something," Rachel said. "Look here." She pointed to a small piece of paper taped inside the back cover. Megan recognized the handwriting as Sir Gregory's.

"'*The Book of the Dead*'," Rachel read. "'Funerary Spells of Ancient Egypt'."

Megan was intrigued. "Awesome. I'll bet Archibald probably found it in some musty old tomb during one of his expeditions." She turned one of the pages. "I wonder if it was exciting, like in the movies? Booby traps and ancient curses."

Rachel turned to look at her, serious. "Do you really have to ask?"

"I mean, like in real life. Not the magic kind. That really wasn't an expedition either, was it."

"No, it wasn't. More like an accidental quest." Rachel looked at the book again, turning back to Sir Gregory's inscription. "*Book of the Dead*? So, if I read this, can I bring some mummy back to life?"

Megan gave her an ominous look. "I don't know. Maybe we should read it and see."

She couldn't keep a straight face — she covered her mouth as she giggled. "Sounds ridiculous, doesn't it? Are you sure you don't want to borrow it?"

Rachel shut the book and pushed it away. "No, thank you. You can never be too careful. I've seen what's in some of these other books. I've been in one of the other books. I'll take my chances with this nice safe reference, if you don't mind."

The two girls spent the afternoon pulling out books and flipping through them, taking notes. They amused themselves by having a friendly contest to see which of them could find the strangest non-enchanted book in the Library. Megan, who had an advantage of having been there much more often than Rachel, won by a landslide when she emerged from between the shelves with a huge book called Sixty-Five Ways to Spot a Werewolf in Your Village.

Megan looked up and realized the light in the dome-sky above them had shifted and looked at her watch.

"Wow, I didn't realize it was that late. Come on, we've got to go. I need to get cleaned up before my dad and his guest get here." She had explained to Rachel earlier about the conversation with her father.

The girls returned all their books to their places. Rachel shoved the reference book into her pack, and they left the library, making sure to shut off the lights and lock the door.

When they reached the top of the stone staircase, Megan put out a hand to pull the door open.

"Shh." She held up her other hand to stop Rachel. "Don't say a thing. Someone's out there." The door was open a half-inch, and voices floated to them through it.

"Who is it?" Rachel whispered. "Bailey and one of the maids, maybe?"

Megan shook her head. "There are definitely more than two people out there. I hear at least three, I think." She put her ear to the door and listened for a few moments. "Shoot, it's my dad. He must have taken an earlier train. I don't recognize the other voice. It must be the client he told me about." She listened again. "I don't hear the third person now, but I know I did. I wonder who it is."

"It's probably Bailey," Rachel said.

"Maybe. He doesn't usually say much in front of guests, though."

The familiar roar of Megan's father's laughter echoed across the entrance hall, followed by the sound of footfalls on the steps. They stopped on the landing, right in front of Athena. Megan held her breath, even though she knew no one could see the hidden door from where they stood.

"What a beautiful statue," said an unfamiliar, deep voice. "An unusual one for such a home as this, is it not?" The speaker's voice had an accent—not British, and not American. Megan's father hadn't indicated where the client was coming from, but he wasn't local. His words were clipped, and he pronounced the word 'what' as 'vat'.

Megan heart galloped as she stood there, not breathing in case anyone heard. She said a silent prayer that they wouldn't notice the statue's hand was upside down. It stayed that way until the secret door was closed, and the mechanism reset itself. *My own stupid fault, I didn't make sure the door was shut all the way.* She could practically hear Bailey now, calling her careless in her duty.

"Sir Gregory had… eclectic tastes," Megan heard her father say. "If you like this one, you'll really love the reflecting pool out back. Come, this way, Bailey will show you to your rooms, and then I'll be happy to give you the whole tour."

Megan listened as they continued upstairs, exhaling quietly as their voices faded. "That was close." She pulled the door open all the way and stepped into the tiny space behind the statue. "Good thing my dad is loud, or they might have heard us."

Megan's father did not know about the Library. It wasn't that she didn't want to tell him, but she had sworn to Bailey when she took the job as Librarian that she wouldn't tell anyone else, including her father. For all she loved and trusted him, her father was a very down-to-earth man, his eye always on the bottom line. She couldn't risk his wanting to have the contents of the Library appraised or put on display, or even that he would ask his employer, who technically still owned the house, about it.

Sir Gregory had been a client of the firm her father now worked for, and a friend to its founder, Mr. Baird. When Sir Gregory died with no family, he left the house to Mr. Baird with the stipulation it was never sold. Sir Gregory's wishes were honored, but as far as she knew, none of the Baird family ever knew about the Library.

There was more than one reason to keep the secret from everyone else. Bailey had told her and Rachel that, before the Library was even thought of, someone sent a burglar to try and steal the Crown of Zeus. He never learned who'd hired the unsuccessful thief, but whoever it was had known about the crown's power. It had crossed Megan's mind on more than one occasion that someone might still be after it, or any of the other artifacts. The world was full of untrustworthy people.

She peeked from behind the statue.

"The coast is clear." She waved Rachel out, and Rachel closed the secret door without a sound.

"I'm going to go," Rachel said. She hopped down the stairs and walked to the front door. The rain had stopped, and weak sunshine came through the windows to fall on the entrance hall floor. She tapped her backpack. "I'll bring this back soon, all right?"

Megan nodded. "Want to go riding tomorrow? We could, you know, enjoy a little of our holiday?"

"Oooh, that's tempting, but I should really get started on this paper."

"Aw, c'mon, it's vacation. I'll call Claire and Harriet. We'll all go. You can start on the paper tomorrow night."

Rachel closed her eyes and dropped her head back. "All right. I surrender to temptation. Put it on the group chat. Claire might be up for it, but Harriet's out of town, remember?"

Megan thought for a minute. "Oh, that's right. She went with her parents to Paris, right? Shopping trip or some such thing."

Rachel nodded, then opened the door and gave Megan a quick wave. "I'll see you."

"I'll text you later," Megan called after her. When the door closed, she turned and walked up the steps to the hall. Bailey walked toward her.

"Good day, miss," he said in his usual dry tone. "I trust you and Miss Rachel had an enjoyable day?"

"Yes, thank you," Megan said.

"I also trust you left the Library as you found it?"

# CHAPTER 3

*The Surprise Guest Brings a Plus One, But You're Not Even Mad About It.*

MEGAN'S HEAD SNAPPED UP, AND SHE MET THE BUTLER'S RESERVED, unwavering gaze. "You always know. How do you always know?"

"It's my job to know, miss."

Megan tried to read his expression. Nothing, as usual. Just once, she wished she could figure out what he was thinking.

"Yes, Bailey, the place is in perfect order." It was technically true. Megan just didn't feel like dealing with the look she would get if she told him she had let Rachel borrow a harmless reference book. She was barely able to contain her eye roll, but was sure it was evident in her tone. She put her hand on the knob to her bedroom door. "If you see my dad, please tell him I'll be down in a little bit. I need to clean up and change."

Bailey bowed, and Megan could swear she saw a smile skirt the edges of his mouth. "Yes, miss."

He hurried away down the hall toward the stairs. Megan went to her closet. Rifling through her clothes she picked out a crisp light blue blouse and a pair of khaki pants, suitable for meeting new people. Well, for meeting new adults, anyway. After a quick scrub of her face and a check of her hair, she got dressed and dashed downstairs to look for her father and his guest.

After a brief search she found them in the parlor. The silver tea set sat on the coffee table, along with a plate of shortbread cookies. Her father sat in one of two overstuffed chairs, sipping tea and munching on a cookie while nodding to the two people who sat on the blue velvet-covered loveseat on the opposite side of the table.

*Two people? I thought Dad said there would only be one guest.*

The person on the left looked to be in his mid-fifties, with short salt-and-pepper hair and a well-groomed mustache. Ice-blue eyes peered from behind round wire-framed glasses perched on the bridge of a long, thin nose, centered in an angular, lined face. He said something to Megan's father, and Megan recognized his voice—it was the one she had heard on the landing while she and Rachel were hiding behind the secret stairs.

Beside him sat a boy about Megan's age. His hair was dark, a bit longer than the man's, his face thin but not pinched. He'd inherited his eyes and nose from the older man. The boy held a teacup in one long-fingered, well-manicured hand, a look of polite boredom on his face.

Megan realized she was staring at him and looked away. She shuffled her feet and cleared her throat to announce her presence. Her father turned his head and smiled brightly.

He finished his cookie and waved her over. "Ah, there you are. This is my daughter, Megan. Megan, this is Herr Josef Hemmlich, and his son, Diedrich. Diedrich is also on a school holiday, so Herr Hemmlich asked if it was all right if he came along. I figured you'd be able to show him around."

Megan gave Diedrich another quick appraisal. *So, here's the third voice. Not an unpleasant surprise. I can totally live with it. Having a guest or two might not be so bad after all.*

She gave the visitors a small wave. "Hello. It's nice to meet you."

"We are most happy to meet you," Hemmlich the elder said in his accent that Megan now recognized as German. He set his cup down on the table. "You have a beautiful home. Such a lovely country, too — my son and I had no idea it was so…" He waved one hand in small circles, searching for the right word. "Quaint."

Megan sat in the empty chair next to her father. "Uh, thank you."

Mr. Hemmlich continued, "I was just telling your father that I am most interested in the history of your home. He tells me that it has been an asset of his firm since Sir Gregory's death. It has an odd name, don't you agree?"

Megan took a cookie from the plate on the table and slowly prepared herself a cup of tea. Her father had said Mr. Hemmlich was a fan of Sir Gregory's, but the question still surprised her.

"Yes, I guess," she said, and took a sip of tea. "But Sir Gregory liked ancient Greece, so then again, I guess not."

"No, I suppose not," Mr. Hemmlich replied with a thin smile. "Your father doesn't seem to know much about Sir Gregory beyond what is public knowledge."

Her father laughed; it was what Megan liked to call his 'business' laugh. "I'll readily admit it. I don't have much time for leisurely pursuits.

I sleep, eat, and spend the occasional day in my home office, but otherwise I'm in the London office, doing my best to keep my clients happy."

Megan gave her father a look that said *Subtle as a brick, Dad.*

Her father took another cookie and pulled the conversation back to the house. "Megan is here by herself most of the time. Well, her and the staff, of course. And her friends, they practically live here. So I guess she's really never alone." He chuckled.

Mr. Hemmlich fixed Megan with a pointed, piercing gaze. "Do you know much of Sir Gregory, Miss Montgomery?"

Megan tried not to choke on her tea. "Uh, not really." She reached for a napkin. "I know a little more than my father, that I learned from the servants and books. He was a prominent archaeologist in the thirties and forties. He also loved antiques and was an avid art collector. The big painting in the entrance hall, for example. The one by the front door, of the ballerinas? That's an original Degas. He found it in a small curio shop in Paris."

The elder Hemmlich cocked his head to one side. "How do you know that? Sir Gregory's personal art collection is well documented, so I know the piece. I don't recall ever hearing anything about how he acquired it, however."

Her father looked puzzled. "Yes, Meg, how do you know? I don't remember hearing that before either."

"Uh, Miranda must have told me." Megan stuffed the rest of the cookie into her mouth and chewed, hoping to cover her stupid mistake. Miranda *had* told her the painting had been Sir Gregory's favorite, but not where he had found it. That bit of information she'd discovered in Gregory Archibald's own journal, hidden with the key and poem beneath the hearthstone in her room.

Mr. Hemmlich nodded. The light reflected off his glasses, throwing little beams around the room.

"Those firsthand accounts are always the most rewarding. They have that little bit of personality that makes them so much better than reading about things in books." He gave Megan a look that for some reason made her nervous. "Perhaps the servants would be willing to regale me with their tales sometime during my visit?"

"I'm sure they would," Megan's father said.

Mr. Hemmlich continued to give Megan that strange look, and Megan tried not to squirm beneath his gaze.

Megan's father appeared not to notice. "I'll arrange it myself, later in the week. You can interview them in the lounge." He pointed to Diedrich, who had put down his cup and now sat comfortably with his long legs crossed. "Diedrich here is just about your age, Meg. He also likes horses."

Diedrich gave Megan a humble look and a shrug. "I ride at home, to relax." His voice was rich and warm, and his accent was not as pronounced as his father's.

Mr. Hemmlich finally broke eye contact with Megan. "Don't be so modest." He patted his son on the knee. "Diedrich is a dressage champion. He is an outstanding rider, the best at his school."

"*Pater*, please," Diedrich said, and blushed. "It is a hobby, nothing more." He turned his blue eyes up to meet Megan's green ones. They were the same color as his father's, yes, but unlike the older man's, they held a warmth his father's did not have. She suddenly couldn't remember what she'd been going to say.

"Um… uh…" she stammered. When her tongue finally unlocked, she said, "Sure, we can go riding. There are plenty of trails, and our horses are very, uh… gentle."

*Smooth, Megan, very smooth. You sound like an idiot.* She didn't know what had gotten into her. It wasn't like this was the first boy she'd ever talked to.

Diedrich's gaze held steady. "That would be lovely." He said with a crooked smile that lit up his whole face. Megan thought she would melt through the floor right there. Surely everyone in the room could hear her heartbeat pounding like a bass line.

The awkward silence that followed stretched out for what seemed like an eternity but was probably only a few seconds. Megan pushed a curl behind her ear and searched for something incredibly witty to say. She had just opened her mouth when Bailey strode into the room.

"Dinner is served." He turned on his heel and left.

Megan's father stood. "Come, I'll take you to the dining room. Wait until you taste our cook's food, it's fantastic."

Mr. Hemmlich also stood and straightened his dark-gray suit coat. "I'm sure it will be quite acceptable." He joined Megan's father, and they walked toward the door. "Come, Diedrich, don't dawdle."

Diedrich hesitated just a moment before standing, bending slightly to offer Megan a hand up. "It would be rude to leave without waiting for our hostess."

Megan's cheeks felt like she had suddenly developed a terrible sunburn as she tilted her head way back to look up at him before quickly lowering her eyes to her lap. He stood taller than his father! And the warmth of his gaze… She couldn't stand, because she was sure her legs had been replaced by gelatin.

"Um, you really don't have to wait for me. I'll be there in just a sec."

Diedrich still held his hand out to her. "I won't hear of it. It would be my pleasure to escort you to dinner."

Megan balled her trembling hands into fists to stop them from shaking. She took a deep breath, which she let out slowly, then reached up and slipped a hand inside his.

"Thank you." Her voice shook and her face flamed.

Diedrich helped her stand and led her toward the door where the two older men waited.

"All set, then?" her father said, and Megan caught the stifled laugh in his voice, though she was almost sure neither of their guests did. The quick scowl she gave him was as sharp as Athena's spear, and he wiped the look of amusement off his face. "Let's go eat."

Dinner was Maggie's best roast chicken with all the trimmings. After the crepes-and-cream dessert, Mr. Hemmlich insisted in his charming, off-handed-yet-insistent way that Megan and her father give their guests a complete tour of the house. They walked through each room as if the manor were a museum, with Megan's father making cursory remarks and apologizing over and over that he didn't know more detailed history.

Mr. Hemmlich remained undeterred. He fired his carefully worded questions at Megan instead. His unending barrage kept her on her toes. She didn't want a repeat of her slip in the parlor.

"If I may ask, what is your interest in Sir Gregory?" She tried not to sound as suspicious as she felt. They were on the first floor, in the regular library, and Mr. Hemmlich had asked about the book collection.

Mr. Hemmlich pulled his glasses off and cleaned them on a handkerchief he produced from his pocket. "Sir Gregory was my mentor. Oh, not in the physical sense," he said in response to Megan's surprised look. "I never had the pleasure of meeting him, but his work…" He replaced his glasses and stuffed the handkerchief back into his breast pocket. "Let's just say, it inspires me."

Megan gave him her best I'm-a-stupid-teenager-I-don't-know-anything expression while her brain whirred with unanswered questions.

And the way he had practically invited himself here still nagged at her.

"Oh, I see. Then being here must be very special for you."

Mr. Hemmlich smiled quite genuine. "Jawohl."

# CHAPTER 4

*The Walls Have Ears. And Eyes. And Maybe Also a Cute Button Nose and Curly Auburn Hair.*

MEGAN WIPED THE SLEEP FROM HER EYES, LOOKED AT HER CLOCK, AND cursed. It was late, or at least later than she had planned on getting up. She threw the comforter off, jumped out of bed, and stifled a yawn. On her way to the bathroom she stretched her arms overhead.

*I guess this makes up for getting up early yesterday. Besides, it's not my fault I slept in.*

Dinner had turned into a late night. Megan thought again about Mr. Hemmlich's many questions as she stood in front of the bathroom mirror and pulled her hair into a ponytail.

*What does he really want to know?* It was the question she couldn't answer, no matter how many times she asked herself. She didn't know why she thought there was more to Diedrich's father's visit, but she had the distinct feeling there was something else he wanted to know. She turned on the hot water tap, and while she waited for it to heat up, she replayed the rest of the evening in her head.

Once the tour was over, Megan's father and Mr. Hemmlich had settled in the lounge for drinks and to talk about business. Megan had shown Diedrich into the family room and let him pick a movie from her impressive collection of DVDs.

A faint enigmatic smile crept onto Megan's face. While they watched *To Catch a Thief*, she and Diedrich had talked. He was polite—he didn't even blink when she told him about her fascination with the goddesses of the silver screen. Megan loved old movies, especially starring women like Katharine or Audrey Hepburn, Ava Gardner or Grace Kelly. Her mother had often taken her to showings at the revival houses in New York and watched DVDs with her. The movies always reminded Megan of those special days with her mother. Plus, the movies were very romantic and the clothes beautiful.

Megan found Diedrich charming and easy to talk to. Despite her unrelenting giddiness, she'd managed to converse with him without sounding too stupid. At ten o'clock, he'd excused himself and gone to bed.

She'd gone to her own room but was too wound up to sleep. When she looked at her phone, there were a dozen messages from Rachel, of course. She wanted to know *everything* about the people they had heard on the landing. For the next three and a half hours, they texted back and forth about the Hemmlichs. But mostly about Diedrich, Megan mused as she rinsed the soap from her face. She had supplied Rachel with enough details to make her completely abandon finishing her history paper to rush over today.

It took a good fifteen minutes for Megan to make sure her unruly hair looked just right, and another ten to choose what to wear to breakfast. She didn't usually use makeup, certainly not around the house, but applied just a little to bring out her eyes, smeared some gloss on her lips, and looked at the clock again. Whoops, she was more than fashionably late for breakfast. After a few deep breaths, she ran downstairs.

She stopped outside the dining room door to catch her breath so she could make at least an attempt at a dignified, sophisticated, older-than-fourteen-years old entrance. She conjured up an image of Kate Hepburn and put her hand on the dining room door.

The murmur of voices on the other side made her pull her hand back and put her ear to the door instead. She ignored the scolding voice in her head, which sounded exactly like Maggie, telling her it was rude to eavesdrop.

"What are we doing here, Pater?" Diedrich said, loud and clear.

"Kindly keep your voice down," Mr. Hemmlich replied in a tone like brushed steel. "We are here enjoying the hospitality of a man with whom I hope to have a working relationship. That is all."

"That's *not* all. I know you, Father, you never do anything without good reason. You could have conducted this business over the phone, or at his office in London. There was no reason for us to come all the way out here." Suspicion and annoyance edged Diedrich's voice.

Megan's brow furrowed. Apparently, Diedrich had the same ideas as she had about their visit. She pressed her ear tighter against the door.

"My reasons are my own, Diedrich, and I will not stand for this insolent tone. There are many things you do not understand. I could not pass up a chance to visit Archibald's manor. This opportunity may not come again."

"What is here that is so interesting? You aren't still on that kick about Sir Gregory knowing—"

"Do not speak of it here, boy. Sound carries in this house." Wood creaked as someone leaned back in his seat. "Aren't you enjoying yourself, my son? You seem to like the company of that girl well enough."

The chair's feet thudded to the floor. "And that's another thing, plying poor Megan with questions. What could she possibly know?"

"That is what I was trying to ascertain."

"Leave her out of this. She's very nice. I—"

"There you are, Megan. What are you doing?"

Megan jumped, probably to catch her heart, which had leapt three feet straight up out of her chest. She spun around to face her father. "Uh, nothing, Dad. I just came down for breakfast."

"We've been waiting for you. I just had to make a trip to the little boys' room." He glanced at Megan's almost overly neat appearance, gave a cockeyed grin, and pushed the door open for her. She checked herself quickly in the gilt-framed mirror and strode into the room.

"Good morning," she said, a bit too cheerily.

Both Diedrich and his father stood as she entered. Diedrich pulled out a chair for her, and

"S–Sorry to keep you waiting," Megan said with an awkward smile, once again fighting to make her tongue work.

Her father took his seat at the head of the table. "Did you have a good night's sleep?" he asked her. "We were beginning to think you weren't going to join us."

Megan plucked her napkin from the table and laid it across her lap. "I was up late last night. Doing homework."

She groaned inwardly. *Homework? Why did I just say that? Diedrich's going to think I'm a total nerd, staying up late to do homework on vacation.*

"Homework, eh?" her father said, one eyebrow raised in accusatory amusement. He passed her a plate piled high with pancakes and gave her a sarcastic grin. "Still? Didn't Rachel come over yesterday to do homework? I'm impressed."

Megan speared a couple of pancakes and moved them to her own plate. Now that she'd let her mouth rush off without her, she was left to dig her way out.

"I, uh, you know, don't want to leave it to the last minute."

Any other morning, her father's jibes would have caused Megan to fire right back, but today there were more important things to worry about, on top of trying not to look like a total dweeb. The conversation she had overheard rattled around in her head, but she would have to sort it out later. Probably with Rachel.

"You are a very responsible young woman," Mr. Hemmlich said, obviously missing the undertone of the exchange between her and her father. "I often tell Diedrich he should not put his work off. Always I am hearing that he's working late the night before a project is due."

Diedrich's mouth pulled into a tight bow, and the knuckles wrapped around his fork turned white.

"And as I always tell him, I work better under pressure." He passed Megan the small pitcher of warm syrup. "You have no complaints about my grades, do you, Father?"

"No but learning to be organized and to finish projects in a timely manner is a valuable lesson," Mr. Hemmlich said sternly. "In the real world, meeting deadlines is part of how you earn respect, a reputation. How will you be successful in business without a good reputation?"

Diedrich sighed. "I'm not going to be a businessman, or even a scientist. I'm going to be a writer. I can meet my deadlines while I'm doing something I enjoy."

Megan concentrated on her plate, not wanting to embarrass Diedrich. This was obviously an old argument between them.

"I told you, son," Mr. Hemmlich said, gesturing at Diedrich with his fork. "You will not live like a hermit, hunched over a keyboard, trying to scrape out a living on something so… impractical… as writing novels."

Diedrich's gaze flickered toward Megan and her father. He closed his eyes and gave a slow, even sigh. "Let's not do this now, please," he muttered, and focused on his meal. "Not in front of our hosts. It's impolite."

Mr. Hemmlich also looked from Megan to her father. He gave a short nod, and father and son returned to their food. An uncomfortable silence followed, only punctuated by knives and forks scraping against china. Cups were raised and lowered, but no one said a word.

*Well, this is pleasant. And I thought I had problems.* Megan plastered on her widest smile.

"Two of my friends are coming over today. We're going riding down to the stream for a picnic. You're welcome to join us, Diedrich."

*Shoot. Megan, you just don't know when to shut up.* It hadn't been her intention to have a picnic. But once again, her mouth spat things out before she thought about them. Now she would have to run to the kitchen and beg Maggie to whip up a basket of food for four people.

*Great. Batting a thousand, and it's only breakfast.*

Diedrich flashed that crooked smile that made Megan forget her own name, and the look in his eyes said he was grateful for the change of subject.

"I would like that. Thank you."

*Okay, that smile totally makes it worth it. Picnic? I'd put together a four-course banquet for another of those.*

"That's a good idea," Megan's father said. He set down his utensils and leaned back in his chair. "Herr Hemmlich and I have some business to attend to this morning. This afternoon I'm going to take him and Diedrich into town. Show them a real English village. You can come with us, Megums."

Megan wiped her mouth and stood up.

"That sounds great. If you'll excuse me, I have to go and ask Maggie to… add more sandwiches to the picnic basket."

Megan managed to get Maggie to agree to the picnic, which hadn't actually involved that much begging, and ran up to her room to change into riding clothes—jeans and a forest-green chambray that buttoned up the front. She spun in front of the full-length mirror in her room—they flattered her budding teenage figure, and the shirt's color went just right with her hair and green eyes. She hoped Diedrich would notice.

*Who even am I? And who am I kidding?* Diedrich had been friendly with her, but once Rachel was here, his eyes would be on her. Megan had some confidence, she wasn't an ogre by any means, but Rachel had the smooth skin, dark hair, and sapphire eyes boys seemed to fall all over themselves for, even though Rachel didn't pay any of them much attention.

Megan took a deep breath. *It's not worth getting upset over, is it?* She had only met Diedrich yesterday. *If he liked Rachel better, that was okay, too. I guess. Besides, it's not like he's staying, so why am I obsessing?*

Megan bounced down the stairs and waved to Rachel and Claire as Bailey showed them in and silently retreated.

"Where is he?" Rachel whispered.

Megan looked around but there was no one to overhear. "He'll be down in a minute. I think he went to change his clothes."

"Rachel texted me this morning. Is he really as handsome as all that?" Claire said. She pushed her glasses up her nose and tossed her short brown hair.

There was the sound of footsteps on the stairs. "Shh. Here he comes."

The girls watched the lithe, athletic form of Diedrich Hemmlich descend the main staircase. He moved his long limbs with grace and held himself with an air of refined elegance. He was dressed in a pair of well-worn but nicely fitted jeans and a red long-sleeved pullover sweater.

"Good morning." He glided across the marble floor and bowed slightly. "I am Diedrich Hemmlich."

"These are my friends," Megan said, suddenly nervous. "This is Rachel Cuthbert." She pushed Rachel forward.

"It is a pleasure." Diedrich took one of Rachel's hands and kissed it. She giggled and tossed her dark hair. Megan felt a stab of jealousy. *She's totally flirting with him!* She grabbed the back of Rachel's shirt and tugged her away from Diedrich.

"And this is Claire McIlhenny." Megan gave the bespectacled girl a nudge with her elbow.

"It is very nice to meet you, Claire," Diedrich said. Claire turned crimson as he gave her the same treatment he had given Rachel.

"I, uh, oh…" she stumbled, losing all use of the English language

Megan tried not to laugh. Claire was the smartest person she knew, and usually calm and logical. Students and teachers alike respected her, but in that "Claire always knows the answer" kind of way. She wasn't used to people, especially boys, giving her attention that wasn't tied to homework.

Diedrich returned her hand, and Megan's next words pulled his gaze away from Claire's flustered face.

"We just have to make a quick stop in the kitchen, and then we'll be on our way."

With picnic basket in hand, the four young people walked out the back door. They walked beneath a cloudless indigo sky toward the stables.

They followed the crushed-stone path that led from the house across the grounds. The manor was as impressive on the outside as it was inside—three stories of dark-gray stone, topped by a peaked slate roof with a dozen or more gables and too many chimneys to count.

The house was U-shaped, with the main house in front and wings that extended back from either end. In the center of the courtyard was a large rectangular reflecting pool.

"That is an interesting bit of landscaping," Diedrich said. He stopped to look at the pool. "I saw it from the window of my room, but it is much more impressive up close."

The reflecting pool was rather incongruous to the design of the house. Instead of the usual modest English embellishments, it was surrounded by Greek statues, columns, and benches of white marble.

"Yes," Claire said. Her scholarly tone said she had finally recovered from Diedrich's greeting. "It's a perfect replica of a pool found in the Acropolis."

"Really?" Diedrich asked.

Claire nodded. "We saw one exactly like it when we were—"

Megan bumped Claire with her shoulder, hard, almost knocking her into the water. She turned around, angry, then seemed to realize what she had been about to say and looked properly horrified.

"Come on, the stable is this way." Megan grabbed Diedrich by the elbow and steered him away from the pool, glancing over her shoulder to give Claire an angry glare.

Claire, cringing in embarrassment, mouthed *I'm sorry* to Megan.

The path divided the courtyard in half and skirted around the pool. Megan led Diedrich, with Rachel and Claire following, into the estate's formal English gardens. The flowers dripped with the remnants of the morning's dew; some had opened to the bright sunshine, while others were closed tight, waiting for warmer weather.

The path came to an abrupt stop at the far end of the gardens. Beyond was a lush emerald lawn, just right for croquet, bocce ball, or a game of cricket. The four young people left footprints in the wet grass as they cut across the manicured lawn and headed toward an outcropping of buildings tucked into the far corner. The garage, the stable, and an old carriage house—now a workshop—were all made of the same round gray stone held together with a thick mortar that might once have been white but was now yellow.

Stephan, the stable manager, leaned against the stable's door frame. A thin, well-built man in his fifties with weathered skin, Stephan was a good man. When Megan and her father had first arrived, he had tried to make the transition from New York to The Parthenon easier for Megan by giving her riding lessons, always having a smile and something cheerful to say. Megan, who had thought horses were terrible, smelly things that she never wanted to come anywhere near, was grateful for his efforts.

He gave the group a cheery wave. "Good morning, folks. Mother Nature's smiling on you today. It's a dilly of a day for riding."

Megan nodded. "Are the horses ready?"

"They surely are." Stephan beckoned them inside. "I think they're as anxious to get out as you are, after being stuck inside all winter."

Four horses, saddled and bridled, stood tethered to a ring attached to the stable wall. Megan undid the reins to Thunder, her big storm-gray gelding, and Annabelle, the chestnut mare Rachel liked to ride whenever she visited. Stephan untied the other two horses — Buttercup, a docile golden mare, and Midnight, the high-spirited but obedient black gelding.

Megan tied the picnic basket to Annabelle's saddle, then handed the reins over to Rachel and guided Thunder out into the stable yard. He stood perfectly still as she climbed up and settled herself into the saddle.

Diedrich swung onto Midnight's back with a dancer's grace. A pleasant shiver crept up Megan's back. She could almost hear the music from one of her favorite movies. Diedrich could have been Cary Grant or Clark Gable.

She shook herself mentally. *Get your head out of the clouds, idiot. This is not a movie.*

"Ready?" she asked, still staring at Diedrich.

"Just a minute." Claire wasn't as proficient a rider as the others, and it took her a little longer to get comfortable. Stephan gave her a boost into the saddle, and soon she was settled.

"Okay." Rachel took Annabelle's reins in her hands. "Let's go."

Megan gave them a mischievous grin. "Race you."

She kicked Thunder's sides hard and urged him to a gallop. The gelding whinnied with excitement as he shot out of the yard and took off across the open wild field beyond the lawn. Rachel and Annabelle fell behind quickly.

The rumble of hooves disturbed the quiet of the countryside as Thunder ran through the tall grass. Megan's heart raced. It felt so good to be out in the open with the wind in her face, running free.

At the end of the meadow, she rounded a copse of oak trees, startling a murder of crows that had taken up residence in the branches. Megan laughed as the birds took off in a black cloud cawing raucously.

She sensed someone next to her and looked to her right. Diedrich raced alongside her. He had Midnight in a full gallop, the horse's body stretched to the limit. He gave Megan a roguish smile, and urged the horse on, pulling ahead of Thunder by a head, then a neck.

Not one to be beaten, Megan leaned forward against Thunder's neck and urged him to go faster. Thunder obliged, the beat of his hooves speeding up. They would have to stop before they reached the woods ahead, or risk being knocked off their mounts by the trees' low branches or one of the horses breaking a leg tripping on the roots. But for now, meadow stretched before them, tempting her, and Thunder led by a nose.

"I'll beat you to the woods," she yelled over the noise of the horses' feet.

Diedrich shook his head.

The trees raced to meet them, and Megan pulled back on Thunder's reins. The horse slid to a stop, three feet before the trees — and two feet in front of Diedrich and Midnight.

"Good race," Diedrich said. "You ride very well."

Megan had to catch her breath — she felt energized, from both the race and the unexpected compliment. "Thank you. So do you."

Rachel and Claire trotted up behind them. Claire bounced terribly in Buttercup's saddle, and she looked a bit sick.

"You could have given us some warning, you know," Claire said. "There was no way we were going to keep up with you."

"Show-offs," Rachel added with a playful sniff. "Bad form."

Megan laughed. "Sorry. I couldn't help it. I've wanted to do that for months." She wheeled Thunder toward the path that cut through the woods. "Let's go, and I promise no more running."

# CHAPTER 5



THEY MOVED AT A SEDATE PACE ALONG THE PATH, TWO BY TWO. DIEDRICH rode next to Megan, in front of Rachel and Claire. Most of the trees were in bud, a few had leaves. The bareness of the forest, but the mostly bare limbs made the wildlife more visible.

Diedrich pointed to a cloud of black-and-brown birds swirling above their heads.

"Starlings."

A tiny gray bird landed on a tree branch jutting out over the path. Diedrich leaned over and whispered to Megan, "And that's a meadowlark."

Megan watched the pretty bird. She smiled as the lark watched them back, and cocked his head, as if he were inspecting them.

"How do you know so much about birds?"

She looked at Diedrich, admiring the way he sat so easily in the saddle. Her stomach wiggled as if the small birds that fluttered across the sky had decided to move into her stomach.

"Bird watching is a hobby of mine. One of the few I have that my father approves of. When I am not in school, he and I travel, and it's something that I can do anywhere. I have some books back at the house I can show you."

"Oh." Megan sighed, and tried to look interested. "That would be nice." She didn't really want to look at books about birds, but jumped at the chance to spend more time alone with Diedrich. She reined in her imagination, which was breaking out of the gate. He was probably just being nice.

The path led to a grassy clearing beside a wide stream, which was swollen and quick-moving from the winter thaw. They stopped and tied up the horses. The place was one of Megan's favorites, so quiet and peaceful. She, Rachel, Claire and Harriet had spent an afternoon here last fall, trying to decipher the poem they'd found in Megan's room that led them to the Library's entrance.

Megan retrieved the picnic while Rachel spread a worn and faded blanket on the grass. Maggie had packed them a veritable feast of ham sandwiches, macaroni salad, deviled eggs and fresh fruit. Diedrich helped Megan unload the food, utensils and four cans of soda, and Claire arranged it everything on the blanket.

"Tuck in," Claire said.

After they were full and the basket repacked, the four of them sat side-by-side on the banks of the stream and dangled their bare feet in the cold, clear water.

"You used to live in New York City?" Diedrich asked Megan. He kicked a foot in her direction and sent a small wave of water up and over her ankle.

Megan splashed him back. "Yes. I lived there all my life, until last September."

"Do you miss it?"

Megan watched a squirrel bounding along the far bank for a moment. "I used to. I loved the busyness of it. The crowded streets, the people, and all the great shops and restaurants. There was always something to do. They had great revival movie theaters." She looked around her and smiled. "But this is nice too. It's grown on me."

"You had to leave your home, and all your friends," Diedrich said. "It must have been hard."

Megan shrugged and then nodded. "It was. When my dad said we had to move, I didn't want to come. I pouted, threw a tantrum, almost threatened to run away. I thought it was the end of my life."

"Aw, Megan, I'm hurt," Rachel teased.

Megan stuck out her tongue and wagged her head at Rachel. "Let me finish. Once I got here, I… didn't love it at first. Everything was so different. But look at that house. Who wouldn't want to live there? The place is a palace. And London is a train ride away. I get the best of both worlds."

"And her new friends are brilliant, you know," Claire chimed in with a grin.

"It is hard to leave a whole life behind." Diedrich studied the water rushing by. "You are very brave."

"Well, I don't know about that," Megan said.

"I do." He held her gaze for a moment before turning his head away, leaving Megan completely speechless.

"So, Diedrich," Rachel burst in, breaking the strange silence. "Megan tells me your father is an archaeologist. That must be terribly exciting. What kinds of things does he do?"

"He's the curator of the Egyptian wing of the Berlin-Dahlem Museum."

Claire gasped. "The Berlin-Dahlem? They have more artifacts from ancient Egypt than even the British Museum."

Diedrich's laugh was short and humorless. "Yes, they do, and my father spends the majority of his time making sure they're all very well cared for."

Megan heard the hurt hiding behind his words, saw it in his eyes. She knew what having a workaholic father was like. She was glad her relationship with her father was better than Diedrich's was with his, and reminded herself to hug her dad later.

"I would love to talk to him," Claire said, starry-eyed. She was top in their year at St. Agatha's, and she loved all things educational.

"I'm sure he would be glad to talk to you about his work." Diedrich skipped a stone across the stream, the corners of his mouth creased with a slight frown. "He enjoys nothing more than hearing the sound of his own voice."

The conversation Megan had overheard in the dining room replayed in her memory. She decided to pry, just a little.

"So, what does he want with my father's firm?"

The boy shrugged. "I don't know. He only said that we were coming here to talk with your father about some business. He does have a lot of money, but he already has an investment agent."

Megan wondered if Diedrich thought his father had any ulterior motives for coming here, but since he didn't offer, she didn't ask.

"Perhaps he wants the firm to sponsor an expedition to Egypt?" Rachel suggested. "Like they did for Sir Gregory."

Diedrich's brows knitted in question "Your father's firm did that?"

Megan pulled her knees to her chest and wrapped her arms around them. "Years and years ago. Sir Gregory dealt in art and antiques, too, remember. He had a little money of his own, and he was friends with the firm's founder, Mr. Baird. Mr. Baird invested in Sir Gregory's work for quite a while. My dad says he made the firm loads of money."

Diedrich tossed another stone in the stream, his expression pensive. "Perhaps that is what my father wants. He's been to Egypt a number of times, on expeditions sponsored by the museum. I know it's a dream of his to lead another one to the Valley of the Kings." He opened his mouth, as if there was something else he wanted to say, but closed it again, his gaze far-off.

"Great," Rachel said cheerfully. "Perhaps your father can help me with my school project?"

"Rachel," Megan scolded. "I'm sure he has better things to do while he's here than to help you with your schoolwork."

Diedrich laughed again, and it was full of glee. "Like I said, my father loves to talk about his work. It's getting him to stop that's the problem."

Megan stood and brushed the dust and grass from her pants. "We'd better be getting back. Dad is probably waiting to take us into town."

She let Claire and Diedrich ride in front on the journey back to the stable while she stayed behind with Rachel. Claire prattled the entire ride, pumping the boy for information—mostly about his father's work. Megan held Thunder back, gradually putting some distance between her and her friends.

Rachel looked over her shoulder. "Come on, Megan."

Megan put a finger to her lips and beckoned Rachel to her. Rachel slowed Annabelle down until she rode beside Megan.

"What's up?"

Megan leaned across the space between the horses. "Don't you think it's strange?" she murmured into Rachel's ear.

Rachel leaned toward her until their heads touched. "What's strange? Diedrich's perfectly charming. If you ask me, he fancies you a bit. What's strange about that?"

Megan gave Diedrich and Claire a sideways glance. Claire still chatted away, and neither rider noticed Megan and Rachel were no longer right behind them. He was charming, and handsome, and he did seem to like her.

*Focus, Megan.* Daydreaming about Diedrich wasn't the point, and it didn't soothe the little itch at the back of her brain.

She looked back at Rachel. "It's not Diedrich that's strange. It's his father, and this whole situation. When Dad told me we were having company, I asked him why. He told me it was Mr. Hemmlich's idea. Don't you think that's odd?"

Rachel sat up straight. "Meg, come on. He's an Egyptologist, and Sir Gregory was a renowned archaeologist. Maybe he's a little starstruck, and he really just wanted to see the house where Archibald lived. And your father's firm has a history of working with people like him. It's not that big a stretch."

"Maybe." Megan straightened in the saddle. "But listen to this." She relayed the conversation she'd overheard in the dining room between Diedrich and his father.

"So, I'm wondering how much he *really* knows about Sir Gregory and his house." She gave Rachel a meaningful look. "Know what I mean?"

Rachel flapped a hand at her. "You're mad. How could he know anything about *that*? Let it go, Meg. Enjoy the fact, for just a moment, that someone like Diedrich has taken an interest in you. You're not just the Librarian, you're also a teenager, for cripes' sake. Act like it, will you?"

She kicked Annabelle into a trot to catch up with the others.

Megan chewed on a thumbnail. She wasn't sure how Diedrich's apparent attention made her feel. It was easier to worry about something she was more able to control.

"Just the same, Rach, I think I'll keep an eye on him," she muttered, though her friend was no longer close enough to hear.

Their trip into town was one of the best afternoons of her life. Megan and Diedrich split from the adults not long after her father parked the car in the small lot near the train station. The two of them spent an hour wandering among the ancient tombstones in the cemetery behind the medieval church that sat in the center of town. Megan showed him several from the fifteenth century, the names and dates almost worn away by time.

"People didn't live very long back then, did they?" he commented.

Megan shook her head. "Plagues, pox, bad dental hygiene. Makes for a short life."

Diedrich threw his head back and laughed. "I guess so."

At the very back of the cemetery, beneath the branches of a large tree, stood a small mausoleum. Diedrich peered at the name on the door.

"I didn't know Sir Gregory was buried here."

Megan leaned over and looked closer at the name engraved on the stone. "I didn't know either. I never, like, looked for his grave or anything." She ran a palm over the words. "Huh, look at that."

"What's that engraved at the bottom—a tree?" Diedrich knelt in front of the door. "It looks like an olive tree. Odd thing to have on your tombstone, isn't it?"

Megan took a step back and looked at the tree. She had seen it before—the same symbol was engraved in the wall above the Special Collection room.

"Yeah, it's weird," she replied quietly. "Come on, let's go. Come and see the rest of town."

Megan took him for a walk along the cobbled streets of the small downtown area of the little village, with its mixture of Tudor, Medieval, and Victorian shops. It was like stepping back in time. They passed the butcher, sides of pork hanging in the front window and a pack of dogs hanging around the door. Next was the small grocery, where the owner, Mr. Watkins, swept the sidewalk. The pub was full of afternoon patrons and late lunchers. Mrs. Steiner, the plump and jolly proprietor of the bakery, gave them each a freshly baked cinnamon scone.

Next they crossed the street to the tiny, cramped used bookshop, where Diedrich languished over the dusty volumes crammed onto the shelves. He purchased two books, both rare according to him, about England's native birds.

Rachel and Claire met them at the coffeehouse at four o'clock, just in time for afternoon tea. Diedrich entertained all three girls with a repertoire of bad jokes over steaming mugs of hot chocolate and biscuits

The sun touched the horizon as Megan and Diedrich left her schoolmates at the shop and headed toward the car. On the way, Diedrich slipped his hand over hers. Megan didn't know what to do. She tried to keep her breathing under control, and couldn't look anywhere but straight ahead. She didn't pull her hand away, though, and Diedrich gave her a shy smile and a wink. Not a word passed between them on the ride home, but Megan could not stop smiling.

She floated through dinner, only vaguely aware there were other people at the table. She kept her gaze glued to her bowl, watching the patterns swirl in her soup. She was afraid that if she looked at Diedrich she would fall into a bout of uncontrollable giggling.

"Josef." Her father's voice penetrated the fog that had overtaken Megan's brain. "I'm sure Megan would be interested to hear the plans for your expedition into Egypt."

It took Megan a second to register what her father had said. Her head snapped up.

"What?" As if it had only been waiting, that itch in the back of her brain roared back. She looked at Mr. Hemmlich, suddenly extremely focused. She tried to appear interested rather than suspicious. "Oh, yes, Mr. Hemmlich, I would like to hear about it very much."

Mr. Hemmlich set his spoon aside, adjusted his tie, and cleared his throat. "Uh… yes, yes. I'm taking a group of graduate students from the University of Berlin into the Valley of the Kings. We hope to locate the tomb of a little-known pharaoh. It is said to contain many lost treasures." He cast a furtive glance at Megan. "The museum doesn't have the funding for the kind of trip I am planning, so I am hoping your father's firm is willing to sponsor us."

Her father sipped his wine. "Your proposal was very intriguing. My employer thinks so too. Herr Hemmlich has done his homework. It's a good investment."

Megan nodded politely, smiled, and went back to her soup. But her thoughts were on Mr. Hemmlich's words. Sir Gregory had once called all of the artifacts he wrote into his enchanted books "treasures". Coincidence? Probably. Treasure could mean anything.

Still, she couldn't help but ask,

"What kind of things do you hope to find?"

Mr. Hemmlich pushed his lower lip out. "Oh, nothing most people would find terribly exciting, I'm afraid. Mummies, sarcophagi, ancient scrolls and writings, and pottery — that sort of thing. To me, and the rest of the archaeological community, they are priceless treasures. Of course, there is the hope of finding the intrinsically valuable pieces these types of tombs usually hold as well — jewelry, gold statues, and the like. That is, of course, assuming a tomb robber hasn't beaten us to it."

"Writings? Like the *Book of the Dead*?" Megan asked, now genuinely interested. She was thinking of the copy she and Rachel had found in the Library of Athena.

Mr. Hemmlich lifted his brows, his forehead crinkled in surprise. "I am impressed." He folded his napkin and placed it on the table. "Not many young people take an interest in the ancient world." He gave Diedrich a pointed look, which Diedrich ignored.

What is a 'Book of the Dead'?" Megan's father asked, then slurped up the last of his soup.

Mr. Hemmlich leaned forward and tented his fingers over his empty bowl with a very self-satisfied look on his face. He was clearly happy to oblige the request for information.

"*The Book of the Dead* is a series of spells. A copy was placed in every pharaoh's tomb, to be used as a guide through the afterlife. During the Old Kingdom, the spells were actually written on the walls of the tomb. Later, in the Middle Kingdom, the spells were carved directly into the outer coffin. Those are called coffin texts."

*I'll have to tell Rachel she doesn't have to worry about waking up any mummies.* Megan suppressed a giggle. "Mr. Hemmlich, were the spells ever, you know, written on paper, bound in a book?"

Mr. Hemmlich looked surprised, as if that were the last thing he'd have expected Megan to ask.

"I've heard of such a thing, but never found or even seen one. If they were written, most were scribed onto scrolls. But it is rumored that what you speak of were used by the priests of Anubis, the god of mummification, because they contained the exact procedure for it—prayers, herbs, the proper removal of organs. The museum doesn't even have one."

*Interesting, but not surprising.* Most of the books in the library were super rare. The itch in Megan's brain lessened just a little bit. Could she have misjudged Josef Hemmlich? His story about the expedition made sense—Diedrich had told her how much his father wanted to go. It still didn't explain why he had come all the way to the manor. *Is he really just Sir Gregory's number-one fan or whatever?*

Bailey entered, followed by two of the staff. Each had a covered dish in their hands. They set the food on the table, and Bailey lifted the cloche to reveal a standing rib roast. The rich, savory scent was almost enough to distract her. Almost.

"So, why do you think there's a tomb that hasn't already been found?" Megan asked as Bailey filled her plate with a slice of roast and modest servings of cranberry sauce, mashed potatoes, and her favorite, green beans almondine. "Haven't people been digging around the valley for decades?"

Mr. Hemmlich's face paled, then flushed, and he suddenly became very concerned about the placement of his silverware. He cleared his throat before he spoke.

"I have spent many years poring over the writings of the New Kingdom."

Megan could swear his voice wavered, but she might have imagined it.

"In several of the lesser-known scrolls, there is mention of a king, one that history has forgotten, and whose tomb has not been accounted for—an unnamed pharaoh."

Megan took a moment to eat a bite of mashed potato. "Certainly he has a name. All of the pharaohs had names, right?"

Mr. Hemmlich nodded while he chewed his roast beef. "I'm sure he did, but it has since been lost to history, the way Tutankhamen's was almost lost when Horemheb erased the boy king's name from nearly everything in Egypt."

"Why would he do that?" Megan said.

"It's not known for certain, but most agree it was a difference of religious opinion. Tut removed the monotheistic worship of the god Aten and reinstated the polytheistic one of the Old Kingdom, under the sun god Amun. When Horemheb came to power, he destroyed everything from every pharaoh between himself and Ahmenotep the Third."

*Wow, it's like he's speaking a different language. I understood about half of that. I'll have to ask Claire what it means.*

"This king I am searching for," Mr. Hemmlich went on, "no real record of him exists. I've only ever seen him called 'The Everlasting One'. The title is often used to refer to the god Osiris, and at first, I thought whom these writings were about. Further study has led me to believe that they, in fact, refer to a person.

"In all of the tombs that have been excavated, none ever call their occupant by this name. I am certain there is a tomb in the valley that has been overlooked, perhaps purposefully hidden."

Megan found the idea unsettling.

"Well, that does sound exciting," Megan's father said. "A mysterious king, a lost tomb. Quite an adventure, I would say." He lifted his glass in a quick toast and drained it. "I almost wish I were going along."

"A fool's errand," Diedrich muttered. "The Everlasting King doesn't exist. It's an Egyptian folktale."

Mr. Hemmlich gave his son a hard stare, but nodded. "Many say so, but I believe, as do the others signed on for the expedition, that he is out there, beneath the sand. And I intend to find him."

Diedrich glared back at his father, but spoke to Megan and her father. "My father fancies himself the next Howard Carter."

Mr. Hemmlich's eyes narrowed, but he said nothing.

After the meal, Megan excused herself and ran to her room. Her phone was on her dresser, and as expected, it had blown up with a group text from Rachel and Claire, dying to know what had happened after they had left the coffeehouse.

She sent back a quick and teasing reply that it was none of their business. Then she sent a separate text to Rachel about the dinner conversation with Mr. Hemmlich. No sense in worrying Claire just yet.

*Diedrich was right — his father wants to go to Egypt to look for some missing pharaoh. Still think he wants something from Sir G, but not sure what it is yet. Probably something NOT related to you-know-what. Oh yeah, Book of Dead will not bring mummies back to life. Thought you'd want to know.*

A second after she hit the SEND button, here was a knock at the door.

"Yes?" She pulled the door open. Diedrich jumped, as if her word was fire.

"Oh, sorry. Am I interrupting?"

"Uh, um, no." Megan smiled, the soundtrack to a black-and-white movie suddenly playing in her head. She straightened up to her full height, and tried to project a confidence she sure as heck didn't have.

"Sorry, I, uh... Do you need something?" *Not bad. At least I didn't sound like a babbling idiot.*

Diedrich scratched the back of his neck. "You, uh, ran off so fast after dinner." He leaned against the door frame. "I thought perhaps you weren't feeling well?"

Megan shook her head. "No, it's not that. I just wanted to come up here and... clear my head. Rest. It was such a long day."

"Oh." He smiled, and Megan's stomach flip-flopped. "I'm glad it's nothing serious."

Silence. Megan looked at the floor, scuffed a slipper-clad foot along the carpet. Things were falling apart fast. She wished she could remember how this went in the movies, but her mind remained blank. She tried, at least, to keep her cool.

"Is there anything else?"

Diedrich stood up straight. "Actually, yes. I wonder if you might like to take a walk with me."

# CHAPTER 6



FIVE MINUTES LATER THEY WALKED OUT THE BACK DOOR AND INTO THE courtyard. It was a lovely evening. The stars shone like tiny jewels in the clear sky, but small puffs of white drifted from their mouths as they walked along the path from the door to the reflecting pool.

The still water reflected an unbroken sheet of light from the nearly full moon, setting the marble statues and columns aglow. They walked past the magical tableau, their hands in their pockets.

Megan didn't know what to say, but wanted to break the tension growing around them. "You know all about me now," she finally decided on, "but I hardly know anything about you. So, tell me about your family. Do you have any brothers or sisters?"

Diedrich shook his head, his lips briefly dipping in a faint frown. "No, I am an only child, like you. My parents, they divorced when I was very young. My mother lives in Switzerland. She studies diseases, searches for cures. I have not seen her in a long time."

Megan winced. *Way to go, me. How horrible to willfully be left alone by both your parents.* She knew a little about how that felt. Even though she'd had no choice about losing her mother, for a while after her death she'd felt her mother had abandoned her. She had been angry. And although her father worked a lot, she could always count on him when she really needed him.

She was ruining the mood. *I'm totally blowing it!* What would Kate Hepburn say? She took a deep mental breath and tried again.

"You said this morning you wanted to be a writer. What kind of things do you like to write?"

Diedrich looked up at the round, blank face of the moon. "Thank you, Megan."

"For what?"

"No one ever asks me about my writing. I usually keep it to myself. Most of my friends do not even know about it. So far, I have only written a few short stories. My professor says I show a lot of promise."

"That's great."

Diedrich gave her a genuine, grateful smile. "Thank you again. I wish my father thought so. I like writing short stories—they are fun—but there is really no living to be made with them. What I would really like to write are books. Stories about things that could have happened long ago but did not, of places and beasts you have only dreamed about."

He shifted his eyes to look at her. "I love folktales and mythology. The way the stories stand for so many things. The ideology of a whole culture wrapped up in stories. I have a hundred books at home, most of them about mythology. It is another of those things my father encourages. I suppose he is still holding out some hope I might choose archaeology as a career."

Megan tried to hide her amusement. *Diedrich might be surprised how much he has in common with one particular archaeologist.*

Diedrich kicked at the crushed stone beneath their feet. A few pebbles scurried across the path and plunked into the reflecting pool, spreading soft rings in the smooth surface. "You probably think I am crazy. It is a hard life, being a writer with no guarantee of a future, even with books."

Megan didn't know what to say, but wanted to be encouraging. He saw her expression and laughed. "I'm sorry. I did not ask you out here to listen to me ramble about myself."

Megan closed her mouth. "No, no, I think it's great you've found something you… love so much. I wish I felt that way about… something." In a bold move that surprised her, she grasped his hand and laced her fingers through his.

"I am having such a good time here," Diedrich said into her ear. His voice was like velvet. "I must admit that when Father first told me we were coming, I did not want to."

"Why not?"

They walked into the gardens and sat on one of the carved stone benches between the flowerbeds.

"Some of my school friends are traveling to the Swiss Alps for the holiday." Diedrich sighed. "I wanted to go with them. But now I am glad I did not."

Megan's heart raced, her hands started to sweat. She fought the urge to pull away from him and wipe her palm on her jeans.

The elegant gardens, so vivid during the day, were now gilded with silver moonlight. To her eyes, they seemed enchanted.

"I'm glad, too," she said softly. The violins of the movie soundtrack playing in her head swelled.

"Yes, I have seen plenty of birds to add to my bird watching book. And I've learned so much about England and English ways. It has been a most enjoyable trip."

Megan's face dropped, and the soundtrack went silent. She would not cry, or let him see her disappointment. It was her own fault, allowing herself to get swept up by her imagination. Too many old movies.

Diedrich squeezed her hand. She swallowed, blinked back the tears, and forced herself to look at him. He was smiling, which almost made her feel worse. He put on that crooked grin that had made her melt earlier. "Can't you take a joke?"

Megan jumped up from the bench and turned to face him, hands on hips. "Y-You... That's not funny."

She thrust her hands toward his chest, meaning to give him a playful shove. He caught and held both of them.

"Of course, I am glad I came because I have met you."

Despite the feeling that her skin burned, Megan shivered. Diedrich put an arm around her shoulders. "Are you cold?"

"Uh... a little," she said, her voice hoarse. She leaned against him, and the smell of his soap filled her nose and made her head swim.

"Maybe we should go back inside and warm up." With his arm still around her, they walked back toward the house. Megan was glad he held onto her — she was sure her sneakers weren't touching the ground.

As they walked around the pool, something caught Megan's eye. A small strip of light peeked out from between the curtains in one of the rooms on the first floor of the south wing. *Dad must be working late.*

But when she looked again, she knew the light didn't come from her father's study. It was in the library. The heavy drapes had been pulled shut, but the light shone around them in a thin yellow outline.

Who would be in there at this hour? Bailey had surely gone to his own rooms, and her father hardly ever went into the library. He would either be talking with Mr. Hemmlich or in bed. That suspicious itch in her brain came back with a vengeance.

Before she had a chance to ponder further, Diedrich guided her toward the back door and held it open for her.

"You know, it's not all that late," he said as they entered the kitchen. "Would you like to watch a movie? Say, *Philadelphia Story* or *Guess Who's Coming to Dinner?*"

Megan barely registered that Diedrich had offered to watch two of her favorite Katharine Hepburn movies. What she really wanted was to check out that light in the library. But not with Diedrich in tow. She would have to get him out of the way for just a few minutes.

"A movie — that would be nice. You go on into the family room and get it set up. I'll make us some popcorn and hot chocolate."

Diedrich kissed her cheek. "I will see you there."

Megan, head swimming, nearly forgot why she needed him to go. She waited until his footsteps faded before putting her ear to the door of the kitchen. When she heard the television room door close, she tiptoed down the empty north-wing hallway, and up to the library door.

Light spilled from the fraction of an inch where the door had been left open. She pushed it open a little wider with her finger and peered through the crack. All she could see was the wall of bookshelves on the right-hand side of the room, but someone was definitely inside. She heard shuffling sounds — books being taken from the shelf, flipped through, and shoved back. Whoever it was also grumbled in a low tone. Megan put her ear to the opening.

"It has to be here," the gruff voice muttered.

Next came the low clatter of the rolling ladder as it was pushed along the shelves on the other side of the room, out of her line of sight. Then footsteps climbing up. More shuffling, more muttering.

A book flew across the room and hit the floor with a thump.

"It's not here!" the voice said. The intruder clunked down the ladder. "Where else could it be? They said it would be here."

Megan put her eye to the door again. The book that had been thrown lay next to of one of the three reading tables. A man walked over and bent to pick it up. He straightened and turned around, and Megan watched Josef Hemmlich return the book to the other side of the library.

She jumped back from the door, her hands clapped over her mouth. She'd known he was up to something! *What is he looking for?*

The room was filled with Sir Gregory's reference books on art, antiques, folktales and mythology, plus some archaeological journals. It was a formidable collection, to be sure, but there was nothing that would warrant a late-night raid. Megan and her friends had searched it thoroughly when she first discovered Sir Gregory's diary and the poem that eventually led them to the Library of Athena.

If Megan thought about it, any book that a man like Hemmlich could want but wouldn't already have or be able to get would be in the...

The thought made her stomach drop. *No, Rachel's right – how could he know about the Library of Athena? He's looking for something, though. I just have to find out what it is.*

Josef continued to pull books from the shelves, ranting like a lunatic about whatever it was he couldn't find and the price he would pay for failure.

"I'm running out of time," he hissed as another book hit the floor. "They will not be happy if..."

Megan didn't hear the rest, because she crept back from the door. She couldn't confront him until she was certain what he was after, and she especially did not want to face him alone. She went back to the kitchen as quietly and as quickly as she could, filled the teakettle with water, set it on the stove to boil before sitting at the counter to organize her chaotic thoughts.

Perhaps she was looking at this the wrong way. After all, she wasn't an expert. Maybe there was something in the library, a book that only Mr. Hemmlich or someone in his profession would find valuable? But how would he know Sir Gregory had it?

It didn't matter. Either way, he had no business sneaking around in there.

She put a bag of popcorn in the microwave and hit the *Popcorn* button. Still contemplating where she should go from here, she made two mugs of steaming hot chocolate, put them and the bowl of popcorn on a tray, and headed to the television room.

"Are you sure?" Rachel's voice was groggy but full of concern. "Maybe he couldn't sleep and was looking for something to read. I know most of the books in that room would put me to sleep in a heartbeat."

Megan moved the phone closer to her face. "Positive. He was looking for something specific." It was too early to be calling her friend, not yet seven o'clock, but she needed to hear someone else's opinion.

She had tossed and turned all night, too wired to sleep, head full of thoughts of what Josef Hemmlich's late-night library visit might mean.

Her imagination had run from the sublime to the ridiculous — at one point she'd considered perhaps he was part of an international ring of evil archaeologists seeking to raise some Egyptian God.

At three a.m., she'd finally given up trying to sleep. She'd sat on her bed, read the book she had started before Diedrich came to the door, and waited for this barely reasonable time to text Rachel. After half an hour with no reply, she dialed her number. Rachel was, understandably a bit put out.

"What was he searching for, do you think?" Rachel yawned loudly in Megan's ear.

"A book, obviously. If I knew which one, I wouldn't have called you at the butt-crack of dawn, now, would I?" Megan sniped. She pinched the bridge of her nose and squeezed her eyes shut. "I'm sorry. I'm exhausted. I've been thinking about it all night, and I don't know what to do. I can't very well go accusing Dad's guest and client of something as… silly… as pilfering the library."

"It's probably nothing," Rachel said. "Just some rare, out-of-print book he wants or something. Probably something no one else even cares about."

"There is some moldy old Egyptian king he says he's looking for." Megan stared at the canopy above her bed. "That's why he's here, to get money for some field trip to find the guy, buried out in the desert." She didn't mention Josef's unbalanced behavior. It kind of scared her, and she didn't want Rachel to freak out.

"There's your answer," Rachel said. "The book he wants is probably about that king or whatever. That wasn't so hard, was it? Can I go back to sleep now, while you get a life? Maybe think more about that absolute snack Diedrich instead?"

Megan wasn't satisfied. "Why the sneaking around? If it's a book he wants, why didn't he just ask for it? Why come all the way here to look? He could have made a phone call, and Dad could have shipped it to him. Or he could have asked to look around the library. It's not like the object of his trip is a secret."

Rachel cleared her throat. "Fine, I guess I'm not going back to sleep. Maybe it's really valuable, and he plans to steal it."

"And if I tell my dad that I caught him last night?"

"He could just say he happened upon it while looking for something to read, and that it's not worth anything. He could avoid having to haggle over the price."

"You know my dad. He'd probably give it to him if Mr. Hemmlich asked for it, especially if it meant getting his business." Megan stifled a yawn. "Those books in the library don't mean anything to Dad or me, they're just — books. On the other hand, they're not ours to give away." She rolled her eyes. "Ugh, back to square one."

"So, what do you want to do about it?" On the other end of the line was the sound of running water, then of teeth being scrubbed.

"What do you mean?" Megan heard Rachel spit.

"It's obvious you aren't going to let this go. So, I'll help you. What do you want to do?"

Megan thought about it for a moment. "I'm not sure. Why don't you come over, and we'll figure something out."

"Okay. Give me an hour. I'll grab Claire on my way. You know she'll have some very strong and definitive opinions."

Megan chuckled. "Absolutely. I'll see you soon."

She splashed some cold water on her face, brushed her teeth, then threw on some clothes and a bit of makeup to cover the dark circles under her eyes.

She plodded downstairs. No one seemed to be up except the staff. She shuffled into the kitchen and almost got run over by Maggie, who bustled by her without a second glance.

"Morning, Maggie." Megan backed up and hovered by the door. The cook looked disheveled — there was flour on her nose, and her usually neat red hair straggled out of its bun.

She shoved a muffin into Megan's hand.

"I'm sorry, miss," she said, out of breath. "Your da has requested a big breakfast this morning. Probably wants to close the deal today. No time to chat with ye right now." She spun on her heel and shuffled off toward the pantry.

Megan grabbed some orange juice from the refrigerator and wandered into the north wing. She pulled the door to the library open and peered inside. It looked as it always did, not a book out of place. The curtains were open and tied back as always, but the sun hadn't yet come around to this side of the house, so the light was muted and gray.

Megan set her food on one of the tables and crossed to the left side of the room. All the ladders were at the very end of the shelves, near the window, except for one. It was against the section that had all the books on Egypt — no surprise there. Mr. Hemmlich had used the ladder last night; she had heard it roll and him climb. What were the odds he hadn't moved the ladder after she'd left?

She took a chance. It was a place to start, anyway. How many steps had she heard him take? She closed her eyes and thought back to last night. *Step, step, step, step.* She climbed up four rungs and looked at the shelf in front of her. She pulled out a book that looked about the size of the one she had seen on the floor.

"A Guide to the Valley of the Kings." At least she was on the right track. But she had gotten a glimpse of the cover of the book Mr. Hemmlich had thrown. That one was dark, while this one was yellow and red. She put the book back and looked at the spine of the one next to it. Queen Nefertari, Wife of the Gods was the title. She pulled it from the shelf and looked at the cover. Jackpot. She tucked it under one arm and jumped down from the ladder.

She settled into a chair and laid the book on the table. Taking a sip of orange juice, and a bite of muffin, she flipped back the cover. On the first page was a drawing of a beautiful Egyptian woman. Creamy brown skin, full lips, dark almond-shaped eyes heavily lined in kohl, and a long, thin nose were framed by dark straight hair. She reminded Megan of Miranda—a younger Miranda. She read the caption beneath the picture.

*Queen Nefertari, also known as Ahmose-Nefertari, one of the most powerful queens of the Old Kingdom. This is an artist's rendition based on the death mask found on the sarcophagus in her tomb.*

Megan turned the page. There was another color plate, this one a photo of a painted wall. Egyptian figures walked across it in a straight line, surrounded by columns of hieroglyphics. Beneath this picture, she read:

*A wall in the queen's temple at Abu Simbel, dedicated to Nefertari by her husband, Ramses II. This much care in the tomb of a queen is highly unusual, and for this reason it is thought that Ramses loved her above all others. This scene depicts Nefertari as the Wife of Amon, or the God's wife. Nefertari was also known as the King's Daughter and King's Sister.*

*Boring.* She rubbed her eyes and stifled a yawn. *Just another ancient Egyptian who's been dead a thousand years. I don't get the fascination some people have with this stuff, even if it is exciting in the movies.*

She took another bite of muffin and paged through the rest of the book. When she came to the middle, she stopped. Another photograph of a wall painting was spread across both pages. Only one figure was in the painting—Nefertari. She sat on a throne of gold, looking regal wearing a gold circlet on her head with the figure of a cobra, poised to strike, on the front. Her arms were crossed over her chest. In one hand she held a rod, painted in alternating blue and gold stripes; three strands of blue and gold beads dangled from one end. In the other hand was what looked like a gold cross, except that the top was looped.

Megan looked at it carefully. The weird cross wasn't just painted yellow—it was shiny, as if it were painted with gold leaf. Lines drawn in red and gold radiated from it like sun's rays. She turned the page and found the caption that went with the picture.

*This image of Queen Nefertari, holding the fabled Ankh of Isis, is on the wall of her burial chamber. The Ankh is a symbol of life after death.*

Megan frowned. Where had she heard of the Ankh of Isis? It sounded familiar. She was certain Mr. Hemmlich hadn't mentioned it. Or was she? Her head was fuzzy—she was too tired to think. She rested her elbow on the table, chin in her hand and stared at the picture. Her eyes grew heavy.

"Find something?" a voice said from the door. Megan jumped and turned in her chair to see Rachel and Claire enter.

"I'm not sure." Megan ran her fingers over the gold ankh and closed the book. "This is the book Mr. Hemmlich threw across the room last night. I've paged through it, but I don't know if it means anything. It obviously wasn't what he was looking for, or he wouldn't have tossed it."

"I've been mulling it over since your call," Rachel said. Pulling out the chair across from Megan, Rachel nicked a piece of her muffin.

"Yes?" Megan said.

Rachel swallowed. "What we need to do is have a peek at old Herr Hemmlich's things."

Megan yawned. "We can't. It's rude. What if he caught us?"

Rachel rolled her eyes. "I know it's rude. It's also rude to invite yourself somewhere and then go skulking about in one's host's house at night. I don't see any other way to put these worries of yours to rest."

Megan sighed. She laid her head on the table. "I assume you have some sort of plan? We can't all just parade in there. Someone should keep an eye on him, my father, and Diedrich to make sure they don't walk in on whoever is doing the searching."

Rachel smiled. "Of course I have a plan."

Claire gave her a hard look.

"Actually, it's Claire's plan."

Megan turned her head to the side, her auburn curls hanging across her face.

"Okay, Claire. What's the plan?"

"It's very simple." Claire adjusted her glasses and leaned in close to her friends. "While we distract everyone, Rachel will go and search his room."

"*That's* your plan?" Megan said. She raised her head slightly. "I could have thought of that. I did think of that."

Rachel chuckled. "She said it was simple. Now come on, let's get to work."

"First, we should go to breakfast." Megan picked the book up from the table and took it back to the shelf. "If I don't show up, it will look strange."

"And how are you going to explain me and Claire being here?" Rachel broke off another piece of muffin.

Megan cocked her head. "Are you kidding? You guys practically live here." She laughed. "Dad won't bat an eye."

# CHAPTER 7



*Some Get to Snoop Through a Stranger's Things.*
*Others Get to Listen to A Mind-numbing Lecture.*

CLAIRE HAD COME UP WITH THE PERFECT DISTRACTION. RIGHT AFTER breakfast, she asked Mr. Hemmlich about his job. Diedrich had been right—the man launched into a long, meandering lecture about ancient Egyptian life, mummification rituals, and the many artifacts within the Berlin-Dahlem Museum. Megan's eyes glazed over after the first three minutes.

"I have a paper due in world history," Claire said. "A project, actually, and ancient Egypt is the topic. I would be terribly grateful if you could give me some help."

"I thought it was Rachel doing the paper on Egypt," Diedrich said.

"She is as well, but my paper deals specifically with mummification rituals."

Megan admired Claire's quick thinking. Claire's history project was actually about the destruction of the Aztec civilization by the Spanish, but it had been decided that Rachel should be the one to look through Mr. Hemmlich's room. Megan would have been missed, and Claire was so meticulous she would take too long to search through Mr. Hemmlich's belongings. Rachel, on the other hand, was much more devious. She knew how to search and do it quickly.

"He'll never even know I was there, Megan," Rachel said when Megan voiced concern over her friend's less-than-orderly way of doing things. "I promise."

Megan had still been a bit hesitant, but they didn't have anything better.

She implemented the second part of the plan. "There are some books in the library here," she suggested in her most innocent voice. "Perhaps you can look through them and tell Claire which ones are the best to use?" That had been her idea. It served two purposes—to get him to the other end of the house, and to see if he did or said anything peculiar about any of the books.

Mr. Hemmlich's eyes narrowed just a bit, but enough for Megan to wonder. *Guilty conscience? Or suspicion that I'm on to him?*

He gave Claire an indulgent smile. "How could I refuse? Never let it be said I don't encourage the scholarly endeavors of the young."

Rachel stood and launched into her prepared excuse. "I'm sorry, but I can't go with you. I need to use Megan's computer to do some internet research. Mine crashed this morning, and the service tech won't be able to look at it until tomorrow. Please excuse me."

The two adults and Diedrich nodded politely and stood as Rachel left the room. Megan said a silent prayer, but for what she didn't know. She wasn't sure anymore whether or not she wanted to know what Mr. Hemmlich was up to, if he was up to anything at all. She really just wanted her life back, and to worry about something normal, like what to do about Diedrich.

She hoped Rachel wouldn't get caught.

Her father and Mr. Hemmlich led the group toward the library. Diedrich walked behind and between them, listening to their conversation.

"How much time do you think Rachel will need?" Claire whispered into Megan's ear.

Megan shrugged. Diedrich turned his head and smiled at her. She gave him a little wave and a smile in return.

"I hope not long," she muttered. "I don't know how much longer I can listen to this man's voice."

"He's one of the top in his field, you know."

"Yes, but he's also very boring."

Megan's father and their two guests had gotten ahead. The girls hurried to catch up right next to Diedrich.

At the library door, Megan's father left them, saying he needed to retreat to his study and make some calls. She wondered if he thought Mr. Hemmlich was as boring as well.

Inside, the girls and Diedrich sat and listened to Mr. Hemmlich ramble on some more. After fifteen minutes, Megan's eyes began to cross. She blinked a few times, trying to clear her thoughts and focus. She needed to pay attention if she hoped to figure out why Mr. Hemmlich had been in the library last night.

"The Egyptians were obsessed with the afterlife," he said. Claire, Diedrich and Megan were sitting at one of the reading tables. Mr. Hemmlich paced before them, one hand behind his back, the other held in front of him and used to accent his words. It looked like a very comfortable and well-used posture.

"Most of their lives were spent preparing their souls for their death. It is why every pharaoh's tomb contains things like boats, chariots, gold, and food, and is the reason for their complex mummification rituals."

Megan tried not to appear to pay close attention as he pulled a book from the shelf. He laid it on the table in front of Claire.

"This is an excellent reference for the layperson. All you need to know about the basics of Egyptian life you'll find inside." He flipped to the table of contents. "Read the folktale about Se-Osiris's visit to the land of the dead. It's very revealing."

Claire took the book and looked up at Mr. Hemmlich. "Are there any other books here that I should look at?"

*Subtle, but effective. At least it doesn't look suspicious if she asks. She's brilliant.*

He gave the shelf a perfunctory glance. "Most of Sir Gregory's collection contains books that would be too detailed for a school project. You wouldn't be able to comprehend much of what they say."

Claire pulled her mouth into a tight little bow and bristled—she wasn't used to being called anything but brilliant, even by adults. Talking down was something you did not do to Claire McIlhenny.

"Thank you, Herr Hemmlich, for all your help," she said with forced politeness.

Megan looked at her watch. Two hours had passed since Rachel had left the dining room table. She hoped it was long enough, because Diedrich's father started toward the door.

He rubbed his right temple. "If you'll excuse me. I have developed a mild headache, and I wish to lie down for a while."

He reached for the knob, but before his fingers touched it, the door flew open and Rachel bounded in. She jumped. "Oh, sorry. You surprised me. I'd hoped you were still here."

Megan lifted her eyebrows. "You did?"

Rachel nodded. "Yes. I've finished what I needed to do, and I was wondering if you were up for a walk. I could use some fresh air." She gave a tiny wink Megan hoped no one else saw.

"Uh, oh, all right, Rach." Megan tried to think of some excuse to go outside. "We can go out to the stables. It's time for Thunder's grooming."

Mr. Hemmlich left, and the four children were alone in the library. Claire glanced at Diedrich, then at Megan. Megan got the message.

"Diedrich, would you please go to the kitchen and ask Maggie for a few carrot sticks for the horses?" she said in her sweetest voice. "And see if you can charm a few chocolate chip cookies out of her, too? We'll meet you outside."

He smiled. "Of course. See you in a few minutes."

Once he disappeared, the girls bolted down the hall. Megan peeked into the study. It was empty—her father must have finished his calls. They ran across the room and out the French doors that opened onto the courtyard.

"Come on." Rachel grabbed Megan's hand and ran down the garden path, leaving Claire to catch up. She kept going, through the flowerbeds, across the lawn, and into the copse of trees beyond the horse paddock. Finally, she let go of Megan's hand. Megan stumbled and nearly fell.

Rachel covered her mouth with both hands. "Oops, sorry."

"I thought we were going to the stables," Claire said between gulps of air. High on her cheeks, bright red blotches bloomed. She wasn't as athletic as her hockey-player friends.

"We will," Rachel said. "After we talk. If we go right to the stables, Diedrich could walk in on us. I don't want him to hear."

"What did you find?" Megan held out hope that the answer was nothing. Based on Rachel's actions, she didn't think that was the case.

"For what it's worth, I'm sorry I doubted you." Rachel looked around to make sure no one could overhear. "It's looking less and less like it was idle curiosity that brought Josef Hemmlich to The Parthenon." She pulled her cellphone from beneath her shirt. "Look at this."

Megan took the phone and flicked through the images. They were filled with choppy, heavy-handed writing. Much of it was in German, interspersed with lines of hieroglyphics.

"What am I supposed to do with this?" Megan said. "I can't read it."

"Look here," Rachel took the cell phone and stopped at one of the images. She handed it to Megan and pointed at something halfway down. It was a drawing of the same strange looped cross she had seen in the book about Queen Nefertari.

Claire looked over Megan's shoulder. "It's an ankh," she said with a shrug. "The Egyptian symbol for life. Pretty common hieroglyph."

"Look at what he wrote under it." Rachel pointed to the passage; this part was in English.

"Sir Gregory's name, and something about The Everlasting One," Claire said. She looked at Megan. "Mean anything?"

"That's the lost tomb Hemmlich is going to Egypt to look for," Megan said. She read farther down the screen. Her eyes grew wide. She grabbed Rachel's arm and squeezed it.

"Here's something about the Ankh of Isis being in that whatever-his-name's tomb." She looked at the next image, and the next. "All this is about the Ankh of Isis, from what I can make of it. Looks like that's what he's really looking for."

Rachel scrolled through the other images. "Here it is again." She handed the phone to Claire, who took it and pursed her lips as she read.

"I've never heard of anything called the Ankh of Isis. I know what an ankh is, like I said before, and Isis is an Egyptian goddess." She gave the phone back to Rachel. "I wonder what it is, and why he's looking for it."

Megan leaned against a tree. She tipped her head back and shut her eyes against the sun that filtered through the branches.

"The Ankh of Isis again. I know I've heard of it before. I mean, before I saw it in that book this morning." She shook her head. "I wish I could remember where."

"Think," Rachel said. "Think very hard. Where would you have heard of it? On television? On the internet? In a book?"

Megan threw up her hands. "I don't know."

"Maybe Sir Gregory's journal?" Claire suggested. "After all, we did read quite a bit of it before Bailey took it."

Megan bowed her head. "That's a good possibility. We'll have to find out."

"You'd better do it later," Rachel said. "Right now, we should get to the stables before Diedrich comes looking for us."

Megan ran into her room and shut the door. Rachel and Claire were sitting sat on the bed.

"Did you get it?" Rachel asked.

Megan pulled a small leather-bound book from under her arm and held it out. Rachel smiled.

"How did you convince Bailey to give it to you?" Claire asked.

Megan flopped onto the bed next to her friends. "I just told him what we were looking for. He remembered an item by that name, but wasn't certain Sir Gregory ever found it."

"And he gave you the journal, just like that?" Rachel said.

Megan tilted her head. "Of course—I am the Librarian, remember? Anything having to do with it, including and especially the artifacts, is my responsibility." She set the journal on the bedspread and opened it. "I had to swear to give this back to him when we're finished, though. He's got some secret, safe hiding place for it. Says it's for my own good." She scanned pages as she flipped through them.

"He didn't ask why you wanted to know about the ankh?" Rachel said.

Megan scrunched up her nose. "I, uh, didn't exactly tell him. I made up some story that Mr. Hemmlich mentioned it during his lecture, and I wanted to know if it was a magical artifact or not."

Rachel raised an eyebrow. "You did, did you?"

Megan gave her a guilty look. "It wasn't exactly a lie."

"No, I suppose not," Rachel said. "You know for certain Sir Gregory actually visited Egypt? If he didn't, then this whole search is moot."

"I know he visited, and more than once," Megan said. "The very first journal entry talks about his taking an expedition there." She stopped turning pages. "Here's where he found the door beneath the Parthenon."

She pointed to a paragraph halfway down the page. The passage described a door of rock, inscribed in Greek. Behind it, he had discovered the Crown of Zeus. The girls had seen a copy of that very door, recreated by Sir Gregory, in his enchanted book. It had been guarded by a Sphinx.

She turned the page and skimmed the next entry. "Here it is. 'The search is on for the Ankh of Isis'," she read aloud. "'Many say that it is a myth, a mere fiction, but I have strong reason to believe that it is real. Writings on the wall of Seti's tomb mention it, as do the scrolls I discovered in the temple at Abu Simbel. I am almost positive that I know where it is buried. I will search until I find it. Something that precious and powerful must be kept safe.'"

"That's all?" Rachel squeaked as Megan skimmed the next few pages. "Nothing about what it actually does, or if he ever found it?"

Megan shook her head. "Nothing."

Claire spun the book around and silently reread the entry. "I can't believe he didn't at least write down if he found the bloody thing or not. What a way to leave us hanging. It's just not right."

Rachel took the book from Claire and thumbed through it. "Not even a map to help us," she muttered. She tossed the book to Megan and flung herself back onto the bed. "So, now what do we do? It's obvious Hemmlich thinks Sir Gregory either found or knew where to find the Ankh."

"Thankfully, he doesn't know about the Library." Megan chewed the inside of her cheek. "I wonder…" she said, staring into space.

"Yes?" Rachel said. "You wonder what?"

Megan tapped her thumbnail on her teeth. "I guess we'll have to go and find out if Sir Gregory found it."

"Then let's go," Rachel said. She got off the bed and took a step toward the door.

"We can't go right now, someone might see us." A playful smile crept over Megan's face. "Can you two stay over tonight?"

# CHAPTER 8

*It's Totally Normal to Sneak Around Your Own House at Night. Really.*

THE GRANDFATHER CLOCK HAD JUST FINISHED ITS TWO A.M. CHIME. Megan, Rachel, and Claire stood huddled on the landing in front of the statue of Athena. Megan flipped the owl over. In the dark and quiet, the click of the secret door's mechanism sounded much louder than it had the other day. Megan cast a furtive glance up to the second floor.

"What's the matter?" Rachel whispered.

"Just making sure no one heard that, or followed us."

The shadows lay thick around them — the night outside was cloudy, so no moonlight shone in the windows to chase them away. Megan clicked on her flashlight and shone it into the dark corners. They were alone.

She led her friends down the winding staircase, through the temple and to the Library door. She unlocked it and stepped inside. Before the lights came up fully, Megan turned off the flashlight, dashed down the long center aisle, and turned left. Rachel and Claire ran to catch up.

"Where are we going?" Claire asked.

Megan continued down the side aisle.

"Is she going where I think she's going?" Claire asked Rachel as they followed Megan.

"Yes, I am," Megan called over her shoulder.

When she reached the back of the library, she turned left again and walked along the stone wall. Not far ahead was a small open arch. Carved into the stone above it was a familiar olive tree and the simple title *Special Collection*.

There was no light — Bailey had told Megan the books were better preserved in the dark. Hanging on a hook next to the door was an oil lantern and matches. Megan lit the lantern and stepped into a long, narrow room.

A bookshelf ran along the left-hand side from the door all the way to the far wall. Like the ones in the main library, it was filled with books.

Unlike in the main library, every book was the same size and shape. Their only distinguishing characteristics were their covers — each was of a different color cloth. A rainbow on wooden shelving.

These were Sir Gregory Archibald's enchanted books. Magical volumes that contained stories he had written himself to hide mystical and powerful mythological artifacts.

Megan shone the light across the books and looked at each title, stamped in gold along the spine. Not far along the top shelf, she stopped, reached up, and pulled down a book with a red-gold cover. Blowing across the top, she sent a small shower of dust into Rachel's face.

"Ugh, thanks a lot," Rachel said, and sneezed. "How long has it been since Bailey dusted in here? Excuse me, would you, I need some air."

The room was too narrow for her to get by Claire, so both girls left the room. Megan stood in the doorway, her gaze on the book's cover.

"Here it is. *The Ankh of Isis.*" She wiped a smudge of dust from the cover and smiled. "So, girls, now that we know what happened to it, what do we do about it?"

There was no answer.

Megan looked up. "Rachel? Claire?" She carried the book to the doorway, where she found her friends. They stood to her right, and both had lost all color in their faces. She gave them a quizzical look.

"Uh, hello? Earth to Claire and Rachel. What should we do with this?"

"I will be happy to take it," said a deep, guttural voice from Megan's left. She turned her head slowly. Josef Hemmlich stood there, a look of smug satisfaction on his face.

"How did you...?" Megan's hands were clammy, her heart raced.

Mr. Hemmlich shrugged. "I followed you, of course. Actually, I waited for you in the lounge. I knew you would check the stairs. You didn't bother to shine the light behind you, or you might have seen me. Children are so predictable."

*Crap, what have I done?* Megan thought, misery like a stone in her belly. She had failed at the fundamental job of Librarian — someone else had discovered it.

"But how did you know we would even be out tonight?" Rachel said. "How did you know to wait?"

"You are not as clever a thief as you might think," Mr. Hemmlich said with a self-important shake of his head. "I knew you had been in my room immediately after I returned this morning. I realized you had looked through my notes."

"How?" Rachel said. "I put them back exactly where I found them."

"Yes, my dear, but they were in the wrong order."

Rachel grimaced. "Oh." She gave Megan a sheepish, deeply apologetic look, and Megan returned it with one that said it was okay. *Everyone makes mistakes, right? Look at the huge, stupid one I just made.*

"I was alarmed you had discovered the true purpose for my trip to this house. I was also puzzled at your curiosity—after all, what could children know of what it is I seek?—but I decided it would be prudent to keep watch."

He took a step toward the girls, and Megan saw why her friends hadn't warned her about his presence earlier. In one hand, he held a small pistol. He pointed it at them.

"Now, if you please, give me that book."

Megan backed away from him, the book clutched to her chest. "You can't have it. You don't know what—"

"Do not presume to tell me anything about the Ankh of Isis, girl," Hemmlich said. His upper lip curled into a snarl. "I have spent half my life searching for it. And that book will tell me where it is.

"I have long known Sir Gregory Archibald knew the location of the Ankh. I have searched through every single thing he donated to the British Museum, every scrap he ever published."

Hemmlich paced, but kept the gun trained on the girls. "I realized he wouldn't put information so precious out in the open. I deduced that his notes regarding the Ankh, including its location, must be here, in his house. But for years, it was inaccessible—gate locked, the house guarded by the staff, especially that wretchedly watchful butler."

"Mr. Hemmlich, you don't understand," Megan pleaded. "This book, well, it's not what you think." There was no way she could let him have the book, and she prayed he was reasonable enough not to use the gun in his hand. It made her very nervous, the way he waved it around.

He stopped mid-pace. "I repeat, child. Do not think to tell me anything." He ran his free hand through his thick black hair, making it stand up on end at wild angles. "I've waited for years to have access to Sir Gregory's private library." He touched the books on the shelf next to him, caressed the leather bindings. "I had thought the book I sought was upstairs, hidden among the mundane texts. I thought everything else was simply wild tales. I never truly believed…"

"Why do you want the Ankh anyway?" Claire asked. She shot a nervous glance at Megan. From the corner of her mouth came the silent words *buying some time.* "What is it?"

Josef gave a maniacal laugh. He reminded Megan less of the calm scholar and more like the man she had seen in the library the other night. He went on.

"My reasons are none of your business. It is something more powerful than you could ever understand. It is… life."

"So, all that crap about searching for a missing pharaoh was just bull?" Megan said.

Josef scowled. "Not entirely. The legend of The Everlasting One is real enough. Whether or not I'm looking for his tomb or another depends on what I find inside that book."

"You can't have it," Megan said. "I won't give it to you."

"What are you doing?" Rachel muttered. "Give him the bloody thing. Let him open it."

"Quiet." Mr. Hemmlich emphasized his point by extending the hand that held the gun. He pointed it at Megan. "You can't get away, so don't bother trying. I will have that book."

Before Megan knew what had happened, he reached out and grabbed Rachel by the arm. Pulling her toward him, he pushed the gun into her side.

"Let her go!" Claire said.

"Or what? What will you do? The book, if you please, Miss Montgomery. *Now.*"

Megan looked from Mr. Hemmlich's face to Rachel's. She saw her friend give the slightest nod. She knew what Rachel meant—she wanted Hemmlich to open the book. He would become trapped in its pages. It wasn't a perfect solution, but it would do for now, before he could hurt Rachel.

Still, Megan wanted some answers before she gave it to him. She tapped the book's cover. "What do you expect to find in here, Mr. Hemmlich?"

"None of your business."

"You think the location of the Ankh is in there, don't you," Claire said. "What makes you think he didn't already dig it up?"

Mr. Hemmlich snorted a laugh. "If he had, I would be having this conversation with Sir Gregory himself instead of you. And if, for some reason, he chose not to use the Ankh, it would be in a museum, or somewhere else in this room. Either way, it would already be in my possession. No, he did not recover it. Now, give me that book!"

Megan was out of time. She had no choice but to give him what he wanted. If she did not, he would shoot Rachel, then Claire, then her, and still take the book.

"If I give it to you, will you let us go?" She tried to keep her voice steady, but fear shook it like a leaf on the wind.

"Megan, no," Claire said. "Don't do it."

Josef Hemmlich narrowed his eyes. "Perhaps." His voice was oily, slick. "What assurance do I have that you will not run to the authorities?"

"Who would believe us?" Megan said, hoping his ego was as big as she thought it was. "Three kids with a story about a hidden library and some crazy Egyptian thing? Come on. You're an upstanding member of the scientific community. Whose word do you think they would take?"

"You're right, of course," Hemmlich said. He chewed the inside of his cheek. "Agreed. Now, give me the book."

Megan held it out to him.

"Don't move," Hemmlich growled at Rachel. With the gun still in her ribs, he reached out with his other hand and took the book. His face lit up in a maniacal grin.

"At last." His gaze caressed the red-gold cover. "You will wait here," he said to the girls. "Count to three hundred before you attempt to leave this room."

Now it was time to attack. Megan appealed to his greed.

"Don't you want to open it? See if what you want is really inside? It would be a shame if you went through all this and didn't get what you wanted. You won't be able to come back, you know. This is your only chance"

Mr. Hemmlich licked his lips. "Yes, I should. I need to be sure. There is no room for failure." His voice was tinged with both desperation and fear. With the gun still pointed at Rachel, he balanced the book on his arm and wiggled his fingers between the pages. The book fell open.

"Rachel, move!" Megan took a step back, then closed her eyes and covered her ears as light and sound erupted from within the book. A cyclone whipped around them. She reached out to Claire, and felt the warmth of a hand as it clasped hers.

The cacophony lasted only a few seconds. When all was quiet again, Megan opened her eyes. The library was still in perfect order. Claire, still gripping Megan's hand tightly, was not in perfect order. Her glasses sat askew on her nose, and her hair was windblown.

"Wow." Megan touched her own head — most of her curls had escaped their elastic band. "So, that's what it's like from this side."

Claire put her glasses on straight. "And I thought it was bad being the one sucked into the book."

"Where is the book?" Megan looked for it as she quickly adjusted her hair.

It had slid across the polished wooden floor and come to rest a few feet away, against the back wall of the library. She picked it up.

"So, now Mr. Hemmlich's in the book. Think we can keep him in there? At least we've got some time to think about it."

"Megan," Claire said. "We've got a problem."

Megan turned the book on its side and looked at the gilded edges of the pages.

"If we tear one of the pages out, I'll bet he'd be stuck inside. Problem is, so would the Ankh. What do you think?"

"Megan!" Claire shouted.

"What?"

"Rachel's gone."

Megan looked around. "What do you mean, she's gone? Where did she go?"

Claire stared at the book in Megan's hands and shook her head slowly. "I don't think she moved fast enough."

Megan's eyes widened. "Oh, no. She's...?" Claire nodded.

"What are we going to do?"

"I don't think we have a choice — we're going to have to go and get her."

"This is not good," Megan said. "The last time we went into a book, we nearly got killed. At least twice. I didn't exactly plan on doing it again."

"We have to," Claire said. "If we don't, Hemmlich will probably kill her. Or worse, leave her in there. Either way, without help she's pretty well scr —"

"I know, I know." Megan, book in hand, went to the reading area. She set the book down on the nearest table and walked into the main part of the library.

"What are you doing? We need to get going."

Megan ignored her and turned left. Halfway down the row, she slowed down, her gaze locked on the books on the shelf next to her shoulder. She mumbled as she read the titles.

Claire ran to catch up with her. "Megan, stop, please. At least tell me where you're going."

Three-quarters of the way down the aisle, Megan stopped.

"Here it is." She plucked a book from the shelf and turned back the way she had come.

Claire jumped out of her way. "Here what is?"

Back in the reading area, Megan dropped the book on the table next to the enchanted text *Ankh of Isis* and plopped into a chair. Claire sat across from her.

"This is the index of all the magical items." Megan turned the heavy parchment pages. Each one was illuminated in bright colors and elegant calligraphy, like a medieval manuscript. She scanned them until she found the one with an illustration of the Ankh. It looked just like the one in the photo of the wall painting in Nefertari's tomb — a golden cross with a looped top. Her lips moved slightly as she read the passage written beneath it.

"Uh-oh."

"What now?" Claire leaned her elbows on the table and put her hands over her face. "How could this possibly get worse?"

Megan spun the book around, and Claire read aloud.

"'The Ankh of Isis. A magical talisman. According to legend, it was given to Queen Nefertari by Isis herself. However, it was not among the possessions in her tomb, nor mentioned in any of the ancient texts after her death. Instead, the Ankh was discovered among the treasures of the tomb of Amenhotep I, the great architect of the New Kingdom, and the first pharaoh of the Eighteenth Dynasty. The Ankh is the mythical symbol of Isis, the great Mother Goddess of Egypt, and the goddess of magic.'"

She looked up at Megan. "I already knew most of that. So what?"

Megan pointed to the bottom of the page. "Keep reading."

"'The power of the Ankh of Isis is that it grants the possessor eternal life.'" Claire gave a long whistle and sat back in her chair. "So, that's why he's so keen to find it. Eternal life, that's big. Who wouldn't want to live...?"

Her gaze drifted from Megan's face to just over Megan's left shoulder. Something behind her made a soft sound, and Megan spun around.

Diedrich stood in the space between the shelves.

"How did you get down here?" Megan said, sharper than she'd intended.

Diedrich jumped as if he'd been slapped. "I, uh... I went to my father's room about an hour ago to say goodnight. I knocked, but he was gone. I looked upstairs, did not find him, so I came down to look for him. I saw him disappear behind that big statue upstairs."

"How long have you been lurking down here?" Claire asked.

"Not long," he said apologetically. "Just long enough to find you two. It took me quite a while to figure out how to open that little door behind the big statue."

He looked around the corners of the bookcases and behind him. "Where is he? Where is my father?"

Megan looked at Claire. Claire shrugged.

"He's gone," Megan said.

"What do you mean, gone?" Diedrich asked. "Where did he go?"

Claire picked up the enchanted book from the end of the table. "In here. He's looking for the Ankh of Isis."

"The Ankh?" Diedrich looked confused, then cursed under his breath. "I knew that was why we were here. That story he told you, about The Everlasting One? He made that up, sort of. He was looking for a lost tomb, but only to find the Ankh. He did not tell anyone, except me, his true purpose in going to Egypt, because he thought his colleagues would laugh at him. The Ankh is a myth, just like that crazy Everlasting One he keeps going on about."

Megan gave a short, harsh laugh. "Not anymore."

Diedrich scratched his head. "You said he was in the book? How could that be?"

"We don't have time to explain," Claire said. "The point is, he's got our friend with him. We have to go and get her."

"This time we're going in prepared." Megan got up and headed for the front of the library.

"Wait, I still do not understand," Diedrich said. "Where is she going?"

Claire grabbed his hand. "Come on."

Megan ran back to the section on ancient Egypt. She picked a single book from the shelf—the wooden-bound *Book of the Dead.*

"We'll take this," she said to Claire and Diedrich as they approached, "because I don't know anything about Egyptian mythology."

"How do you know we'll even be able to take it in with us?" Claire asked. "Our clothes don't even go through. Last time—"

"Last time, we didn't try to take anything from this room with us," Megan interrupted. She raced by the two of them, back toward the tables. "We didn't know any better."

Claire jogged along behind her, and Diedrich followed in their wake. Megan put the book down on the table and drew the red-gold enchanted volume toward her.

"I think this will work. This book is from ancient Egypt, after all. *The Book of the Dead.*"

"I've heard of it," Claire said.

"Mr. Hemmlich told me it was a book of spells—funerary spells. And he also said the ancient Egyptians were obsessed with the afterlife. The book might come in handy, especially since Mr. Hemmlich is an expert in ancient Egyptian folklore. He'll have such an advantage over us, and we need all the help we can get."

"I guess it can't hurt to try," Claire conceded.

Diedrich stood behind the girls; he looked upset. "Can you please explain to me what is going on? What has happened to my father?"

Megan turned around. "It's a very long story. All you need to know is that your father and Rachel are inside this book." She tapped it with her finger. "And if we don't go after them, Rachel is probably going to end up trapped inside, or worse. I don't know if the gun he had with him made it into the book. I hope not. But the Ankh of Isis could wind up in his not-so-mentally-stable hands, and that would be bad. Understand?"

"Uh, I think so." Diedrich's face was pale. "You are all crazy. The Ankh of Isis is a myth, it does not exist, no matter what my father thinks. Where is he? Clearly *not* inside a book."

"Ugh, I don't have time for this," Megan said. *I am so not in the mood. I don't care how cute he is.* "Are you coming with us or not?"

"Meg, are you sure that's wise?" Claire said with a furtive glance at Diedrich. "We don't know if he's working with his father or not."

"Look, whatever my father has done, I had no hand in it." Diedrich's tone was solemn. "I have no idea what is even going on, but if I can help, please let me."

Megan, thinking of the conversation she had overheard in the dining room, gave a short, curt nod. It was unlikely Diedrich was in on the scheme, but just in case…

"If you give me one reason to suspect…" She closed her eyes and shook her head. Her heart and her head pulled her in two different directions. But now was not the time to think about it. She picked up the *Book of the Dead*, tucked it beneath her arm, and grasped Diedrich's hand.

"Are we ready?"

Claire nodded and took Diedrich's other hand. "Whenever you are, Meg."

Diedrich shrugged. "I still think you are crazy, but…"

"Good, let's go. Oh, Diedrich? Don't let go." Megan didn't want him to suddenly decide to bail on them. She situated the enchanted book directly in front of them on the table. With a deep breath, she reached out and pulled the cover open.

Once again, the wind howled as a bright light blazed from the book's pages. This time, Megan felt the odd sensation of being lifted by her shoulders, her friends beside her. Then she was thrust headfirst straight into the book.

The noise grew as they fell. It was all around them, through them. It made Megan's teeth hurt. She opened one eye and saw nothing—no light, no stars and no book pages—just darkness.

Diedrich had a death-grip on her hand; he had pulled himself close to her, and he screamed in her ear. The sound of it, mixed with the rest of the noise, pounded like a drum inside her head.

Everything stopped. Megan thudded to the ground, landing on her left shoulder with a crunch.

Diedrich landed next to her. "Oomph."

"Ugh." Claire landed to his right.

Megan sat up and caught her breath, then pushed herself all the way up and moved her sore shoulder to make sure nothing was broken. She went to Claire and held out her hand.

"Are you okay?"

Claire grasped her hand and got to her feet. "Fine, I think." She moved her arms and legs. "I hate that part."

Diedrich sat on his haunches with a dazed look on his face and a bruise forming on his left cheek. Megan and Claire each took a hand and helped him stand.

His eyes went wide. "Where are we?"

Megan gave a wry smile. "Welcome to ancient Egypt."

# CHAPTER 9



*The Travel Agent is Fired. So is the Costume Mistress.
And the Prop Master.*

THEY STOOD IN A STRETCH OF GOLDEN DESERT. IN THE DISTANCE, BARELY visible, stood a grove of palm trees. The treetops swayed gently in a breeze Megan did not feel. The sun reflected off the sand, nearly blinding them; it beat down with brutal ferocity. Behind them stretched more sand, and along the horizon ran a ragged mountain range. The peaks looked blue-gray in the hazy heat.

Diedrich brushed the sand from his legs. "Excuse me? Ancient Egypt?"

Megan nodded. "Well, Sir Gregory's version of it, anyway. We're inside a story he wrote."

"You people really are nuts. Where is my father?" He looked down at himself and swore loudly. "And what am I wearing?"

Megan giggled. Diedrich was bare chested, with only a short white cloth draped around his waist. A wide collar of lapis lazuli, amethyst, and gold hung around his neck, and a piece of wide-striped cloth, like a veil, sat on his head, secured with a gold circlet.

"Nice headdress," Megan said. Her face twisted as she tried to hold in a laugh. Her own pajamas were gone, and both she and Claire wore simple form-fitting ankle-length white linen dresses with wide shoulder straps. Strands of lapis and amethyst beads hung around their necks, and several gold bangle bracelets circled each wrist. All three had brown thong sandals on their feet.

"Is this a skirt?" Diedrich said. "Why am I wearing a skirt?"

"Because, in the book, we wear the clothes of the civilization we are in," Claire said with a shrug, as if it should be the most obvious thing in the world. "I'm not in charge of costuming."

"In the book?"

Megan rolled her eyes. *Is he really this thick? And why is he still adorable when he's being thick?*

She shook the thought free and focused. "We told you that's where we were going. It's not my fault you didn't believe us."

"But—"

"Look, we don't have time right now. We have to find your father and Rachel. And some shade."

A dark square of wood sat on the ground near where they had landed. Megan picked up the Book of the Dead and shook the sand from it.

"It made it," Claire said. "I'm amazed. I really didn't think it would. You're brilliant." She took the book and looked over the cover. "Megan, you do realize you can't read this, right?"

"I know, it's in hieroglyphics or something," Megan said. "But there's a translation in the back. I saw it there before."

Claire turned the book over and opened the back cover. "Nope, sorry."

She showed it to Megan—the tag Sir Gregory had taped inside the cover and translation were gone.

Diedrich gave her a sidelong glance. "You really cannot read hieroglyphics?"

Megan groaned. "Uh, no, duh. This is great. Now what are we going to do?"

Diedrich took the book from Claire and looked through it. He put his arm around Megan's shoulders and leaned close to her ear.

"You do not think, being the son of an Egyptologist, that I never learned anything?"

Megan raised her eyebrows in an unspoken reply. Diedrich nodded. She threw her arms around his neck, any suspicion she had about him forgotten.

"I am so glad we brought you along."

"Yes, well, I am glad I can be of some use. Look, wherever we really are, and however you managed to get us here, can we get going, perhaps? It is getting hot."

Megan released her grip on him and looked over the landscape. "There's nobody here to tell us which way to go. Remember little Homer?"

Claire nodded.

"Little Homer?" Diedrich asked.

"When we were inside the last book, there was a little boy named Homer who was tending sheep. He told us about a path that led to the first clue," Megan said.

"Clue?" Diedrich said.

"But he wasn't right where we came into the story, either," Claire said. "We had to walk across a field to the village, remember?"

Megan spun, arms outstretched. "With all this sand, everything looks the same. I don't know which way to go." At the moment, she was more worried about Rachel than the Ankh. She didn't really care if they found the guide. They could worry about that later.

"We go that way." Diedrich indicated the grove of palms.

"How could you possibly know that?" Megan said.

He pointed at the ground. Two sets of footprints marched away across the sand and toward the grove.

"Ah. Okay, then," Megan said. "Come on, maybe we can catch them." She took off, Claire and Diedrich on her heels.

She didn't run for long before the heat made her slow down. The air wavered in front of her and made shimmering pools in the distance. Her eyes stung as sweat poured down her face into them. She tried to wipe it out, but the sweat on her hands only made it worse.

"How much farther?" Claire panted. Her face was the color of a ripe tomato.

"I can't tell," Megan said. "Every time I think we're almost there, it seems to get farther away."

"Please, don't let it all be a mirage," Claire begged.

"I need a drink," Diedrich said; his throat made a click when he swallowed. "I hope there's water."

Finally, they came to the oasis. Megan touched the trunk of the nearest tree and patted its rough bark.

"It's real." She leaned against it with a grateful sigh.

Claire stumbled toward her. "Ah, shade." She found a big patch of it and flopped down, cross-legged, in the long, coarse grass that grew beneath the trees.

The oasis was beautiful. The uneven, rough yellow grass that ringed the edge changed to a carpet of lush emerald as it grew toward the center and — the most beautiful sight Megan could imagine at the moment — a pond. A deep pool of clear, sparkling water reflected the sun, winking little diamonds at the three of them. There was the breeze — it was warm, but welcome.

Three camels lay in the shade. They chewed their cuds, looks of disinterest on their long faces. Other than the animals and the three teenagers, no one else was there.

Diedrich staggered to the water's edge. He peeled off the headdress and let it fall to the grass. Dropping to his knees he stuck his entire head in the pond, then threw it back and sent a wave of water behind him.

"Ah—wonderful." The water ran down his back in little streams and pooled around his feet. He wiped his face with his hands and blinked the water from his eyes.

Megan let go of the tree and walked on wobbly, heat-exhausted legs to kneel next to him. Instead of dunking her whole head, she cupped her hands, scooped up some water and splashed it over her face.

"It's fabulous." She sucked the droplets off her upper lip. "The best water I've ever tasted." She dipped her hands again. This time she brought the water to her mouth and drank the whole of it in one gulp.

"Refreshing, too." She burped. "Excuse me."

Diedrich lay back on the bank of the pond. "Can you please tell me what is going on now?"

Megan sighed. "Okay. I guess we can take a short break. Sir Gregory Archibald, the man who built my house, was not only an archaeologist. He was also a wizard."

Diedrich let out a hearty laugh. "You are joking... next you are going to tell me that you have met the tooth fairy, and the Easter Bunny lives in your garden."

Megan gave him a reproachful look. "Let me finish. He was a self-taught wizard."

Diedrich still didn't look convinced. "Really."

"He wasn't always that way—he didn't start studying magic until later in his life."

"What prompted the sudden interest in magic, I wonder?"

Megan shrugged. "I don't know exactly. He never mentions it in his diary."

"His diary?"

"It's another long story. But I'm pretty sure it was not long after someone tried to steal the Crown of Zeus. I'll have to ask Bailey."

"Bailey? Your butler? He knows about all... this? And what is a Crown of Zeus?"

"Yeah, Bailey knows. The Crown of Zeus is another artifact. Sir Gregory went digging around all over the world, and he collected a bunch of things that many people believe don't exist."

"Like the Ankh of Isis," Diedrich said. He sat up and wrapped his arms around his knees.

"Exactly."

"I never believed my father when he said it was real." He picked up a small stone and skipped it across the water. "If I had, maybe all this would not have happened."

"You can't blame yourself," Megan said. "Your father… well, he seemed a little… off-balance when I last saw him." Obsessed was what she really wanted to say, but she thought that would be too harsh. Diedrich had enough to worry about. She had only met him two days ago, and she already cared about him.

"All he wanted was someone to believe him. I was too busy fighting with him about everything else to listen." Diedrich took a deep breath. "So, you were telling me about Sir Gregory and his magic library."

*Avoiding much?* "Yes. He wanted to hide these things, these artifacts, to keep them safe from people who might want to try and use them. Most of them are pretty dangerous. So, he hunted down an old spellbook somewhere."

"From the looks of that library back there, I'd say he hunted down every magic book in the world."

"In this book," Megan went on, giving Diedrich a small glare, "was a spell that would allow him to write a book and actually place the artifacts inside the story. It's called The Art."

"Which is where we are now, right? Inside the story. That is… incredible."

Megan nodded in agreement. "Whenever someone opens one of the special books, they get sucked inside. In order to get out, they have to recover the item the book is hiding."

Diedrich lay back on the grass. "Of course, it won't be easy. It couldn't be easy, or else what would be the point?"

"No, it definitely won't be easy." Claire sat next to Megan and sank her hands into the water. "Sir Gregory will have left us a series of clues, and we have to follow and interpret each one correctly to get to the next one. Assuming we survive, at the end of the story we'll find the Ankh and go home."

"That is, unless, your father gets to it first." Megan shuddered. "I don't want to think about what will happen to us if that happens. First of all, he doesn't know we're here. And no offense, Diedrich, but I don't think he'd wait for us to catch up to him if he did know."

"My father is not a monster," Diedrich said. "He may be driven, but he would not hurt people on purpose."

*Yeah, tell that to the gun he had pointed at us.* Megan stood—she didn't want to waste time with an argument.

"Let's get started."

"Where?" Diedrich asked.

Megan looked around. She was a little worried because they were still alone. "I don't know why there isn't a guide. Unless he only hangs around when the first people enter the book. Or maybe it's just so obvious where you're supposed to go when you get here Sir Gregory didn't write one in." She pointed across the pond. "There."

Beneath the tallest palm tree stood a wooden podium. Atop the single square leg, a carved owl served as the top of the lectern. The bird's body was in the center; its outstretched wings formed the wide, flat plinth. A book sat on top.

"Ah, here we are," Megan said.

The book had a familiar red-gold cloth cover, with an ankh stamped in gold on the front. There was no title. She opened to the first page.

"'Greetings, traveler,'" she read. "'And welcome to the Ancient Egypt of My Mind. The book you opened in the Library has transported you inside its pages. You are now in pursuit of the Ankh of Isis…'"

Claire bobbed her head back and forth, flapping her hand open and shut like a duck's beak.

"Blah, blah, blah. Can we skip to the first clue?"

"Okay, fine. I just wanted Diedrich to get the full experience, so sue me. The first clue in the Crown book was carved into a rock. Look around for something with writing on it," Megan said. "It should be right near the book."

The three of them searched the oasis. They turned over every rock, looked up every tree, even into the packs the camels wore on their backs.

"Nothing," Megan said. "What if the clue disappeared after Diedrich's dad read it? Or if it was written on something small, something he could carry, and he took it with him? We won't know where to start."

Claire looked pensive. "The first clue last time didn't disappear. At least, I don't think it did. It could have, after we left the hilltop. Or maybe Mr. Hemmlich just destroyed it, so no one could follow him."

Diedrich stood in front of the podium and turned to the next page of the greeting book.

"Uh, girls? Did you ever think it was right here?"

"What do you mean?" Megan said. She ran around and leaned in front of Diedrich to scan the page he was looking at.

"This is all Ancient Egyptian," she said. "In the other book the pages were all Greek. Don't know what it says, or why. I can't read it. The clue should be here somewhere in English."

"'From brothers who were bitter rivals, the God's box will ensure your survival.'" Diedrich ran a finger down the columns of tiny pictures as he read. He drummed the fingers of his other hand on the book. "Set and Osiris."

Megan stared at him, mouth agape. "You really can read that? That's what it really says?"

"I told you I could."

"I wonder why the clue is in the book," Claire said.

"Right now, I don't care," Megan replied. She turned her attention to Diedrich. "What do you mean, 'Set and Osiris'?"

"Set and Osiris were brothers. The sons of Geb and Nut, who, according to Egyptian legend, created the world. Set was the God of Chaos and Evil, and jealous of his brother, because Osiris was more important."

"And Osiris is…?" Megan asked.

"The God of the Dead."

Megan wrinkled her nose. "Creepy."

"He didn't start out that way. Originally, he was the prince of all the gods, and heir to his father's throne. Set wanted to kill his brother and take his place as his father's favorite, so he set a trap. He built a box made from cedar, inlaid with ebony, gold, and silver. No one had ever seen or built its equal, it was so beautiful. And it was made to Osiris' exact measurements.

"Set held a great feast. The only guests were his seventy-two conspirators and his brother. At the end of the meal, Set brought out the box and said that whoever fit inside the box could have it. Of course no one fit except Osiris. When he lay down in it, Set and his friends slammed the lid and nailed it shut."

"That was stupid," Megan said. "You would think a god would see something like that coming."

"Set threw the box into the Nile, and it floated away, into the ocean. It came up onto the shore of Byblos, where it grew into the trunk of a cypress tree. The King of Byblos admired the tree, and had it cut down and turned into one of the pillars that held up his palace."

"So, the God's box must mean we have to find the coffin of Osiris?" Claire said.

"And finding the coffin means finding either the tree or the pillar?" Megan said.

Diedrich nodded. "Just like Isis did. Finding the tree would be tough — the legend does not say where along the coast the tree grew. If I had to choose, I would look for the pillar first. I know where the palace is supposed to be."

"And where is this Byblos place?" Megan said.

It was Claire who answered. "In the Mediterranean, in what is now called Lebanon. But here I suppose it's still Phoenicia."

Megan clucked her tongue and shook her head. "You're such a history geek." She slung her arm around Claire's neck. "And I'm so glad."

"How do we get there?" Diedrich said. "I do not know where we are, but Byblos is probably a long walk."

"That must be why they're here." Megan pointed to the camels, which still lay in the shade, contentedly chewing.

"Have you ever ridden a camel?" Claire asked. "Because I have not, and frankly it seems terrifying."

"Oh, come on," Megan said. "It can't be much different than riding a horse." She glanced at the animals. "Except for the hump."

Claire gave the camels a nervous look. "Yeah, and we all know what a brilliant horseman I am."

They raced across the desert. Megan clutched the reins of her camel for dear life. The camel's gait wasn't anywhere as smooth as a horse's, and there wasn't anywhere for her to hold on with her legs. She bounced in the cloth saddle strapped to the top of the camel's hump and prayed she wouldn't fly off.

The *Book of the Dead* hung safely tucked away in the tooled leather bag attached to the back of the saddle. Like a neon sign showing them the way, a single track of camel prints tracked through the sand, telling them where Josef Hemmlich and Rachel had gone. Megan wondered if they were riding on the same camel or on two camels traveling single file. If it were the latter, how was Mr. Hemmlich able to keep Rachel with him? Megan thought there was a good chance he no longer had the gun, since the English translation of the book hadn't come through, or their regular clothes. But what if it had changed into something else? Perhaps his gun had turned into something of a similar nature when they came into the book, like a sword or some other type of weapon.

*I hope she's all right. It should have been me that got sucked in with Hemmlich, not her.*

Megan squashed her guilt and urged her camel on.

Diedrich pulled his mount to a stop. Megan and Claire rode up next to him.

"What's up?" Megan asked.

Diedrich looked at the sky. "Do you think Sir Gregory created this Egypt to be exactly like the real one?"

Megan nodded. "Almost positive."

"Then we are heading in the right direction."

"How do you know which way we should be going?" Megan said. "I thought we were just following your father's tracks. That's the only direction I care about right now. We have to get to Rachel."

"Assuming my father read that clue and solved it, which he should have, he would know the right way. I wanted to double-check." Diedrich looked at the horizon, then the ground, and then the sky again. "We are in the desert to the west of the Fertile Crescent."

He pointed to the mountains off to the right. "On the other side is the valley of the Nile. The sun is to the left of us, and it is descending. So, we are all headed north, straight toward Lower Egypt."

"Lower Egypt?" Megan asked. "Wouldn't that be south?" Diedrich shook his head. "The Nile flows south to north, into the Delta and the Mediterranean Sea. Upriver is actually south, called Upper Egypt."

"And the North is Lower, because it's downriver," Megan finished, impatient. "I get it. No more dawdling, keep moving, before they get farther ahead than they already are."

They pushed the camels into a gallop across the blistering sand. Megan's throat was parched, her tongue felt like sandpaper. The sun beat down on them, merciless. What she wouldn't give for another oasis! How long can a person live without water?

"How far ahead do you think they are?" she called to Diedrich, her voice creaking like a rusty door hinge.

He shook his head. "I do not know. I cannot see them up ahead, but they could be between dunes, in a valley. The camels cannot keep this speed up much longer, though. We are going to have to slow down."

"I hope we catch them soon, or come to a shelter," Claire said, her knuckles white as she clutched her camel's reins. She bounced roughly in the saddle. Twice already Megan had thought Claire would be thrown, but she'd managed to stay atop the animal.

"Why?" Megan asked.

"Because once the sun goes down, it's going to get cold."

"In the desert? How can it get cold in the desert?"

"Sand doesn't hold heat like regular soil. When the sun sets, the temperature drops, fast. Without wood to make a fire, or shelter, or warm clothes, we could conceivably freeze out here. Assuming that conditions in the story are the same as in the real world. Which I do, based on our previous experience."

Megan's heart sank at the same time her shoulders did. "Great, just freaking great." She spurred her camel on.

The desert seemed endless. Miles and miles more the three of them traveled, still following the tracks of their quarry. Their shadows stretched out beside them; the sun painted the sand in stripes of pink, orange, and red. Still nothing—not a building, a tree or people.

*This stupid desert goes on forever, I just know it.* Megan watched a snake, mottled brown to match the sand, wind up and over a dune sideways, while a scorpion scuttled across her path. Vultures circled above them.

*Hope they're not waiting for us.* Megan's arm broke out in goose bumps, and she shivered. And not only at the thought of vultures eating her carcass; the air had grown chilly. It felt like sunburn, hot and cold at the same time.

Next to her, Claire gripped her camel's reins with one hand and held the other crossed over her chest. She rubbed her upper arm briskly.

"This is crazy," Megan said, and her upper lip cracked and bled. "We're either going to die of dehydration or frostbite."

"Neither," Diedrich said. He and his camel were stopped at the crest of a high dune. "Come and see."

Megan and Claire rode up beside him and gasped. The desert sloped away into a line of scraggly grass. Beyond the grass was more sand, but it glistened with moisture in the dying sunlight. A beach. And then the sea, sparkling like a polished aquamarine as it stretched away to meet the horizon, which was quickly becoming bathed in twilight. Palms and flowering plants waved to them along the shore, and the scent of jasmine tickled Megan's nose. If she hadn't known better, she would think she was looking at the travel brochure from some tropical paradise.

The trail cut a straight line toward the water. Megan shaded her eyes with her hands and squinted. It was hard to see after being blinded by the sun for so long. Spots danced across her vision. She scanned the shoreline. "I don't see them."

"One camel moves faster than three trying to stay together," Claire said.

"Not if two people ride on it," Diedrich said. "They couldn't have gotten that far ahead."

"Assuming they're both on one camel," Megan said. "Regardless, we should keep following the trail," Claire said. "I'll bet those tracks go right to the water. They must have been as hot as we are."

Megan swallowed, but she had no saliva, so it made a thick *click* sound in her throat. "And as thirsty."

Claire gave her a guarded look. "Meg, uh, I wouldn't..."

Megan kicked her camel hard. With a disgruntled cry, it raced down the dune toward the sea. She jumped from the saddle almost before the camel stopped, and ran to the shore. She scooped up a handful of water and —

"Ugh, gross." She spat the water back out. "Salt water."

"I tried to warn you," Claire said. Her camel sauntered over next to where Megan was trying to get the taste out of her mouth and nudged her.

"I didn't even think about it," Megan sputtered. "I was just so thirsty. I guess this is supposed to be the Mediterranean?"

Diedrich dismounted and walked to the girls. His body shook with laughter. "Did that taste good?"

Megan kicked water at him. She looked up and down the shore. "I don't see any footprints. Where did they go once they left here?"

"If they were headed to Byblos, they have to go that way." Diedrich pointed up the shore to the right. "If they stayed near the water, the sea has washed away the footprints by now."

"What, do you have a map in your pocket?" Claire said. She looked at the wrap around his waist and grinned. "Oh, no pockets. Sorry."

Diedrich smirked. "Ha-ha. No, I do not, obviously, but I have been looking at maps of Egypt my whole life." He shook his head. "The real Egypt, I mean. It's still hard to wrap my head around being inside a book. Byblos should be northeast of here, on the other side of the Delta."

"It'll be dark soon," Megan said. "We should get going, and find somewhere to camp." She shook the remaining droplets from her hands. The sea breeze, which should have been refreshing, only added to her gooseflesh. "It's really getting cold. And we need some fresh water."

# CHAPTER 10



*A Brief Stop at a Lovely Seaside Resort. Just the Place for a Ghost Story.*

THEY PICKED UP THE TRAIL AGAIN, IN THE DAMP SAND JUST OUT OF THE sea's reach. It was now obvious they were chasing one camel. Megan kept an eye out around them, in case Hemmlich had ditched Rachel somewhere so he could go on alone. Darkness crept in and made it difficult to see, but before the veil of night lowered completely they came across what looked like an abandoned fishing village.

There were five small huts, all made from off-white bricks of dried mud. The roof of each, which might originally been made from palm fronds, had long since decayed, leaving the huts open to the sky.

With the camels secured to a tree, the three young people had explored the place in only a few moments.

"Hey, look what I found." Claire came out of one hut carrying a pile of rough woven blankets. "They were piled in a corner."

Megan held up one and looked at Claire through the eye-sized hole in the middle. "I guess it's better than nothing."

Inside another hut, Diedrich found a well. Miraculously, it still held clear, fresh water. Each of them gratefully drank their fill directly from the bucket that came with the well, which was surrounded by a short wall.

"What are these?" Megan lifted up one of a series of gourds that hung from the wall. Each had a corked hole in the top.

"Canteens, I would imagine," Claire said, water running down the front of her dress. "The fishermen needed fresh water while out on the boats."

They decided to settle in the largest hut. It was warmer inside, but not much. At least they were out of the breeze, which had built into a steady wind that hummed outside and threatened to chill them all to the bone. They built a fire in the middle of the floor. The fallen roofing was dry—perfect for burning. Megan had been impressed by

Diedrich's ability to spark the fire by banging a couple of rocks—pieces of a crumbling wall—together.

Still hungry, but feeling much better, Megan picked up the *Book of the Dead* and flipped through it. She scanned the rows of hieroglyphs and pictures and wished again that the translation had made it through to this side. It was a long book, and she hated the thought of Diedrich being their only way of reading it if they needed it. She trusted him—not sure why she hadn't in the first place—but if something happened to him, and they needed this book, they'd be stuck. It wasn't just that, of course. She didn't want anything to happen to any of them, her friends or her...whatever Diedrich was. The danger here went beyond monsters and magic.

The biggest monster here might just be human.

"Don't read from the book," Diedrich muttered into her ear.

"Huh?"

"The *Book of the Dead*. Isn't that what they say in all the movies? You'll raise the mummy or some nonsense?"

Megan tilted her head to one side. "It's a book of spells, isn't it?"

"Yeah, but not spells like you think. More like prayers for the dead, meant to guide the soul into the underworld." Diedrich sat next to her and took the book. "It is really a story, a guide for the soul's trip to the Fields of Peace. Some call it The Book of Going Forth by Day. Spirits could come out of their tombs and walk among the living by day, but had to be back before sunset."

Claire wrapped her blanket around her and sat across from the other two. "Sounds intriguing," she said. "Quite the opposite of what most people believe now—ghosts only come out at night and all."

Diedrich laid the book across his lap and turned to the second page.

"Not really. Most ghost stories are about restless spirits. An Egyptian who couldn't enter the underworld was doomed to walk the earth for eternity. So, his soul would wander at night. So, it's kind of the same thing."

"How do you know all this?" Megan asked.

"I told you, I love mythology. My father and I agree on one thing—Egyptian mythology is one of the most fascinating." He flipped to another page and pointed to a line of writing. "This part of the book is all about the mummification process. It tells how many days the body should lay out, and what mixtures of herbs to use, blah, blah, blah. Boring."

"Did they really pull all the organs out of a body?" Megan asked. Her nose wrinkled in disgust at the thought. "I heard that somewhere."

Diedrich nodded. "They took out the liver, stomach, intestines and brain and put them all in jars, called canopic jars. Most of the ones I've seen are very beautiful, and expensive. Painted in gold and encrusted with jewels."

"I don't want to know how they took out your brain," Megan said.

Diedrich leaned in close and gave her a wicked grin. "They pulled it out in big chunks through the nose."

Megan groaned and clutched her stomach.

"I would have thought they would remove the heart as well," Claire said. "It's a big organ."

"No, that they left in, and there's a very important reason for it." Diedrich turned a few pages, and showed Megan one with pictures of a man with a dog's head, and another with a bird's head. "Here it is. Once the body was properly mummified, the soul—they called it the ka—would travel by boat through the land of the dead and into the Hall of Judgment. All the gods were gathered in the Hall, with Osiris presiding over the proceedings. See, that's Osiris, the one with the two staffs that looks like a mummy."

"Who's the dog-faced man?" Megan asked.

"Anubis, God of Mummification."

"Ick."

"No, he was one of the most important gods," Diedrich said. "Right up there with Osiris."

"It all sounds very formal," Claire said. "How do you judge a soul?"

Diedrich stood the book up on its edge and showed it to them, as if he were reading a story to children.

"See that?" He pointed to a small set of scales next to a man with a tall crown. "The ka's heart is put on one side of the scales, and the feather of Ma'at is placed on the other."

"Who's Ma'at?" Megan asked.

"The Goddess of Justice and Balance. If the heart is heavier than the feather, the soul is not allowed to pass through to the afterlife."

"That's doesn't sound too bad," Megan said.

"Oh, but it was the most horrible fate an Egyptian could suffer. To the ancient Egyptians, moving to the afterlife was everything," Diedrich said. "The basis of their whole civilization."

"It's all perfectly morbid, I think," Claire remarked. She took the book and looked at the picture more closely. "What would happen to those who didn't pass the test?"

Diedrich leaned in close to the fire. The flames threw his face into sharp relief; he looked very spooky.

"Their hearts were fed to Ammut, a vicious demon, and the ka would be lost, doomed to roam the earthly plane forever."

Megan gave a nervous laugh. "Nothing like a good ghost story before bed." She lay down on the floor and pulled her own blanket up over her. "Now I'll have nightmares. Thanks, Diedrich."

"Sorry. You did ask."

Diedrich and Claire had also lain down, and soon all of them dropped off, lulled to sleep by the white noise of the sea.

Megan threw back her blanket, got up and went to the window. Something—a sound?—had jolted her from her slumber. She hadn't been sleeping well anyway. She turned and studied her two friends, still sleeping deeply, and wondered how long she had slept. The fire was cold, and the moon had slipped low in the sky. She grabbed the blanket and pulled it around her shoulders before returning to the window.

The remainder of the moonlight painted the ground with deep purple shadows. The sound that had woken her was a shuffling noise, like feet sliding through the sand. The air was much colder than when she had gone to sleep, so she doubted any of the desert animals, like snakes or scorpions or lizards, were out and about. Still, she kept her ears open.

Her stomach growled. They hadn't found any food in the huts, and at the time she had been more than willing to settle for water and warmth. Now she wished she had something to eat—even a hard piece of bread would be welcome.

*I'm probably not the only hungry one out here. Do jackals or wolves live in the desert?*

She swallowed hard. Cautiously she stuck her head out of the window and looked around, but saw nothing.

*I probably imagined it. That story Diedrich told about souls being doomed to walk the earth or whatever. Now I'm hearing things. Mummies come to life, come to eat our brains. Rachel would say something like that.*

Rachel. Megan looked at the watchful moon and said a silent prayer that her friend was all right. *We'll find you soon, Rach. I promise.*

There it was again, that shuffling sound. Megan still couldn't tell if it was a four-legged animal or something else. She scanned the compound again and froze

One of the shadows had moved. A large shadow. It lurched between the well and another of the huts.

Megan wanted to wake Diedrich and Claire, but hesitated. What if she woke them and it was nothing but her imagination, or a stray dog, or something else harmless. She would watch for a while, and go and check it out herself if she thought it necessary.

Picking up a piece of leftover firewood, she stood to one side of the open doorway. Trying to remain still, she took short, shallow breaths. The shadow hung near the door to the well, curled into a ball. Then, whatever it was stood, and Megan held back a gasp.

The shadow had the shape of a person about her height.

Whoever it was stumbled inside the well building. She glanced at her friends — there wasn't time to wake them. She needed to move if she wanted the element of surprise. She tightened her grip on the wood and crept across the compound.

The smell of enclosed dampness and minerals hit her nose as she approached the door of the well. She stopped just outside and listened.

Silence.

*Ready or not, here I come.*

She pressed her back against the door frame and turned her head to look across the room to the far corner. No one was there.

*I knew it, I imagined the whole thing.*

To be sure, she turned around and leaned inside to see the front corner. Something grabbed her elbow from behind and pulled her into the hut. Someone pressed their body against hers.

"Please help me."

Megan screamed. The wood dropped to the floor and bounced away. The person who had gripped her elbow spun her around and pushed her outside, backward. She took three steps before she fell hard onto the sand. The shadowy figure loomed over her, ready to pounce. Megan, still screaming, pulled her legs back and got set to kick out as hard as she could.

"Megan? Megan! It's me, stop screaming. And don't you dare kick me."

The person stepped into the light and dropped down next to her. She wore a white dress and beaded collar like Megan's. Megan looked up and focused on a familiar face. Long, dark hair with beads woven into it in, violet eyes, freckles that stood out on skin made pale by the moonlight.

"Rachel?" Megan hugged her friend and cried for joy. "Oh, Rachel, you're all right."

Rachel returned the hug, but it was weak. She pulled away and looked at Megan. Tears glinted in the corners of her eyes.

"How? When?"

"Oh, come on, like we weren't going to come after you." Megan wiped her own eyes. "How did you get away from Hemmlich?"

"What is going on out here?" Diedrich ran out of the shelter. Claire, rubbing her eyes, was right behind him. He looked at Megan, still on the ground. "We heard you scream."

"All the mummies in Egypt heard you scream," Claire said, and yawned. "Are you all right?"

"I'm fantastic," Megan said. "Come here and see."

Claire's face lit up when she saw Rachel. The two girls hugged.

"You look awful," Claire said. She brushed Rachel's hair away from her face, revealing a bruise over one eye and several scratches along her cheeks, matched by more on her arms. Her wrists bore red marks, like burns.

"I've been running all night." She looked at Diedrich, and her mouth twisted into a sneer. "Your father is mad, you know that?"

Diedrich's face was in shadow, so Megan couldn't read it.

"So I am learning," he said. "Sorry. I really had no idea."

"Yeah, well..." Rachel said, not sounding like she believed him. She turned her attention to Megan and Claire. "He wants the Ankh of Isis."

"Yeah, we figured," Megan said. "Where is he?"

Rachel gave a wistful look over her shoulder toward the well.

"Can I get a drink first?"

"When we first got here, Mr. Hemmlich was very confused," Rachel said.

Diedrich had remade the fire while Claire and Megan helped Rachel get a drink and clean her wounds. The four of them now sat around the fire and listened to Rachel tell her tale.

"He had no idea where we were, or how we got here."

"Duh," Megan said. She remembered how confused she and her friends had been when they fell onto a grassy plain in ancient Greece.

Rachel pulled her blanket closer around her. "I wasn't about to tell him. He got angry and dragged me to the oasis. He's not quite right in the head, that one."

"Why didn't you try to get away then?" Diedrich asked.

"Where was I going to go?" Rachel said with a contemptuous glance at the boy. "We were in the middle of the desert."

Megan patted her friend on the back. She understood Rachel's attitude—she had every reason not to trust Diedrich right now. Megan squeezed her friend's shoulder.

"It's okay, Rach. Does he still have his gun?"

"My father had a gun?" Diedrich said. A dark look passed over his face, angry and confused.

"Yeah, he did. And he pointed it at us," Rachel shot back. She shook her head, her face grim. "He doesn't anymore, though. It changed when we fell in here."

"What do you mean?" Claire asked.

"Now it's a nice sharp saber, good for running people through."

Megan sighed, but said nothing about being right about the gun. *This sucks. Big time.*

Rachel went on. "Once we got to the oasis, he read the book, and he figured it all out—he's horribly bright. He found the first clue, and we were off. He didn't know that if he just went on ahead and found the Ankh I would be stuck in here. I wasn't about to tell him."

Claire said. "Good thing, too."

"Right. I let him think his threatening me was the worst that could happen, and I went with him. I decided I'd try and get away later, maybe find the Ankh myself."

"Way to go," Megan said.

"We rode for hours, through the desert to the sea, then along the shore. Right past here, actually. Finally, he stopped at another fishing village about, oh, I don't know how far from here. Walking distance, that's for sure. Unlike this one, it has people. He talked to someone—a man at one of the homes. He speaks the native tongue, by the way."

"Of course he does," Diedrich said. "He is fluent."

Rachel ignored him. "He got a family to put us host us for the night. He tied me up." She imitated Josef Hemmlich's voice, "'I don't want you running off on me.' I tried the whole lost-little-girl act, told him I wouldn't dare run away, but he didn't buy it. Not only is he a loony, he's also a bit paranoid."

"Well, you did run off, didn't you?" Megan said. "It's not paranoia if it's true."

Rachel gave a cheerless laugh. "I guess so. Won't he be surprised when he wakes up."

Megan gave Rachel another squeeze and a broad smile. "Come on, Rach, lighten up. You're safe now, and we're all together."

Rachel returned the smile, but it was pained. She stared into the fire.

"It took me almost all night, but I managed to pull out of the ropes. I just took off, didn't pay much attention to which way I was going, and I recognized this place. Lucky for me, you were here." She put her chin on her knees. "He's headed toward someplace called—"

"Byblos," Diedrich finished. "Yeah, we know."

"What he's looking for once he gets there I don't know." Rachel tipped over and lay down next to the fire with a gigantic yawn. "Something about some moldy old god named…"

She was asleep. Megan adjusted the blanket to make sure Rachel was covered.

"We should stand watch for the rest of the night. No telling who else is out there, or if Hemmlich will come to look for Rachel."

"I will do it," Diedrich said. "You girls go to sleep, but do not get too comfortable. If we leave before dawn, maybe we will be able to catch my father." He looked at his feet. "I'm sorry for what he did to your friend. Really. And when we find him I am going to tell him just what I think of him. Meg, you do trust me, right?"

Megan looked into his eyes. The last rays of moonlight that glinted through the window made them an even paler blue.

"It's not your fault, I know that. Yes, I do trust you. Give Rachel some time, and she'll come around." Megan curled up next to her friends and listened to the fire crackle. Her eyelids were heavy, she was warm and…

"Megan, wake up."

She pulled the blanket up over her nose. "Uh-uh. Just five more minutes." She felt hot breath in her ear.

"No, come on, we have to go," Diedrich whispered. "I let you sleep as long as possible."

Megan sat up. The fire had long since gone out, and the air still held a chill. The sky above her was a still, deep blue, but the stars had dimmed, almost gone. Morning would be here soon.

"Is there anything to eat?" she asked hopefully.

She knew there wasn't, but it never hurt to ask, especially when her stomach felt like it was collapsing in on itself.

"Sorry, no," Diedrich replied. "But we'll find something soon. The next village, maybe."

Megan walked out into the compound, behind the well building, and into the smallest of the sandy-colored structures. Inside was a privy. Three deep, wood-capped holes were cut into a waist-high bench made of the same material as the walls. It looked very much like a modern-day portable toilet. She flipped up the lip over the one in the center and got ready to hold her breath. To her surprise, the hole smelled sweet, like lavender. She did her business and joined her friends.

The camels were ready. Diedrich and Claire had filled some of the gourd canteens and tied them to the saddles.

"Rach, wanna ride with me?" Megan said.

"Uh, I don't know," Rachel teased, apparently in a much better mood. "Last time I rode with you we wound up forty feet in the air. Fighting a sea monster."

Megan laughed, a little relieved for Rachel's joke, more like her old self. "I don't think that's going to be a problem this time, unless this camel has wings hidden somewhere."

Safely secured in the saddle behind Megan, Rachel guided them along the route she and Josef Hemmlich had taken the previous day. They followed the sea toward the rim of coral and pink that highlighted the horizon as the sun rose.

Soon, Rachel directed them away from the water and onto a wide, hard-packed road. On their right, the desert turned to wheat and bean fields. A cool breeze blew over them from the sea as the sun peeked up from the hills and put its heat into the day.

They were only a few miles from the abandoned huts when they arrived at the outskirts of a village. Megan looked up and down the street. The little town was still asleep — not a single fisherman was out, not a baby cried.

*Creepy. I guess these people weren't written as early risers.*

The three camels stood abreast of each other. They nearly blocked the road.

"Which house did you and my father stay in?" Diedrich asked Rachel.

She pointed to the largest house on the street. Or rather, it was a small complex more than just a house. The house was two stories tall, made of stone blocks covered in white stucco. The stucco had chipped in places, showing the block-and-mortar beneath. A long roof separate from the house — perhaps a barn or stable — was just visible over the top of the eight-foot-high wall that surrounded the property.

They rode toward the wooden front gate.

"Should we knock?" Claire said.

Diedrich shook his head. "I do not want to alert my father to our presence. If he woke up early and found Rachel gone, we may already be too late."

"But he doesn't know that you, Claire, and I are here in the book," Megan said.

"Still, I do not want to take a chance." Diedrich pulled his camel alongside the wall. "My father is not stupid. I think he would expect Rachel's friends to at least try and come after her."

He handed the reins to Megan, stood up in the saddle, and leaned over the top of the wall to look inside. "Coast is clear. Wait here." With one swift move, he vaulted over and disappeared.

Megan sighed. *Better than a movie hero.* What was she thinking? *Ugh, come on, Megan, focus. We have to get through this in one piece first.* In this world, distraction could end up being very costly.

A moment later, the scraping sound of a bolt being slid back broke the quiet, and Diedrich appeared from between the gate's doors. He beckoned the girls inside.

The large, open yard was home to several animals — more camels, plus sheep, cows and horses. Ducks huddled on the ground, still asleep, their beaks tucked beneath their wings. There were also several well-tended gardens in block-walled beds. Desert flowers bloomed, yucca and flowering cactus, along with sandalwood and jasmine.

"We're not just going to walk in the front door, are we?" Claire said. "It's terribly rude."

Megan left her friends in the yard and walked toward the back of the house. She followed her nose — something smelled delicious. Her stomach agreed.

"Come on, this way," she whispered.

She found the source of the scent—it floated from a back window. She peeked inside. Two women, both with dark straight hair and bronze skin, stood in a room filled with food. Herbs hung from the ceiling, fruit was piled in baskets and bronze bowls. One of the women cut up vegetables and put them into a pot that sat over a fire pit in the center of the room, while the other kneaded dough into round flat loaves. She took several of the unbaked rounds and carried them toward the door.

Megan, her mouth watering, shuffled backward toward her friends. "Someone's coming."

# CHAPTER 11

*Paper Boats Make for Lovely Cruises.*

THE FOUR OF THEM PRESSED INTO THE SHADOWS AGAINST THE WALL OF the house. The woman with the unbaked bread walked right past them and straight to a clay oven that sat at the other end of the yard. She laid the loaves on a flat wooden paddle, like the ones used to slide pizza in and out of an oven. The woman slid the bread inside and turned back to the house.

She caught sight of Megan and her friends and jumped. "Oh!" She put a hand to her mouth, and her eyes grew wide. "Who are you?"

Megan's mind raced as she tried to think of something to tell the woman before she alerted the rest of the house.

Claire stepped forward. "We are friends of the man you took in last night. We are supposed to meet him this morning. Is he still here?"

"Good thinking," Rachel muttered.

*Thank goodness for Claire,* Megan thought.

The woman nodded. Recognition flicked across her face as her gaze fell on Rachel.

"He is still asleep. I will show you." She walked through the door and into the kitchen.

"It is a good thing she does not speak Ancient Egyptian or Hieratic," Diedrich said. "Or we would be in trouble."

"You read that clue okay," Megan said.

"Yeah, I can read it, but I can't speak it."

"Sir Gregory wrote the stories in English," Claire said. "Just like in *The Crown of Zeus,* everyone in here speaks English as well as their native tongue. I guess Josef didn't figure that part out."

"Or he just wanted to show off," Rachel muttered.

They crossed the kitchen, and Megan reached out and snatched an apple from one of the tables. It was better than nothing.

The woman led them down a dark, narrow hall that emptied into a large room furnished with backless wooden chairs, large pillows, and brightly colored woven rugs. She stopped at the bottom of a flight of rough wooden stairs; they looked more like a ladder set on an angle.

"Upstairs." She pointed up to the second floor. "Your friend is in the last room on the left."

"Thank you," Megan said, the stolen apple behind her back. The woman gave a small bow and retreated to the kitchen.

"I'll go first, keep him off his guard," Rachel said. "If he hasn't woken up, he won't know I ever left."

"And if he did?" Megan asked.

Rachel shrugged. "I suppose he'll be surprised I came back, but it won't be as much a surprise as if you all just pop in on him."

"Are you sure you want to go up there by yourself?" Megan said. "He's dangerous."

Rachel thrust out her chin and put on a smile that was almost brave. "It's the best way. You guys stay here. I'll let you know when to come up."

Megan hugged her best friend. "You be careful."

Rachel took a deep breath and carefully climbed the stairs.

"Do you think she'll be all right?" Claire asked.

Megan bit her lower lip. "I hope so."

Her insides twisted into a knot. Rachel was tough, but she had been through quite a bit already. She didn't have a bottomless capacity to deal with stress.

*I shouldn't worry. She knows to expect the unexpected in here. She'll be all right. She'll be all right...*

Rachel had barely disappeared down the upper hallway.

"Megan, Claire, get up here. Now!"

All three of them bolted up the stairs, Megan in the lead. Rachel stood in the room at the end of the hall. There was a crude wooden bed with a straw-filled mattress in one corner, and a small wooden table with an oil lamp. That was all.

"Where is he?" Diedrich said. Rachel shook her head. "He's gone."

Megan crossed the room to the one and only window. Directly below was the flat roof of the first floor. She looked across and down into the yard behind the house. Someone, tall, and with dark hair, ran around the corner, just out of her vision.

"He's down there. He must have heard us and jumped out the window."

They ran downstairs and out the front door just in time to see Josef Hemmlich mount his camel and race through the front gate. He looked over his shoulder—his face registered surprise, and then his mouth curled into a wicked sneer.

"Fools! You shouldn't have followed me. The Ankh is mine!"

"Come on, we've got to catch him," Megan said.

She went to her camel and hoisted herself into the saddle. Claire and Rachel were right behind her, but Diedrich didn't move.

"What's the matter? Why aren't you coming?" Megan said, impatient. "We have to go now, or he'll get to the next clue before us."

"He wants his dad to get away," Rachel said. "I told you."

Megan looked from Diedrich to Rachel. "Don't be dumb, he doesn't want to get stuck in here." She turned to the boy, her heart in her mouth. "Do you, Diedrich?"

Diedrich still made no attempt to follow his father.

"Of course not. But maybe there is a better way." He turned on his heel and walked back into the house.

The boat rocked gently as it cruised on the water. Megan watched an ibis swoop and dive until he finally came up with a large fish in his beak and flew away. She hugged the soft cloth bag that held the *Book of the Dead* closer to her chest.

Diedrich's idea was brilliant. Back in the courtyard of the house, to the girls' amazement, he had left the gate behind and knocked on the door. The same woman who had shown them upstairs answered. Diedrich spoke with her briefly, and she fetched the lady of the house.

The mistress, a beautiful Egyptian woman, showed the four of them into the front room. She returned a few moments later with her husband, who took one look at Diedrich, then at the girls, and beamed.

At the man's word, the house became a flurry of activity—food and drinks were brought and placed before the visitors, who were seated on the finest of the floor cushions. Diedrich was given what was certainly the master's own carved chair. Megan wondered why they were being so well cared for—after all, they were strangers. But she didn't argue as she inhaled the huge breakfast of bread, hummus, dried fish, and fruit the servants set in front of them.

"You honor me with your hospitality," Diedrich said. He took a sip of the strong tea the servants had poured into beautifully painted clay cups.

The man, named Hepu, sat in the only other chair. His wife, Meryet, sat at his feet on another floor cushion, watching them with a curious gaze.

"You honor me and my house with your presence," Hepu said. "How can I be of help?"

Diedrich nodded. "I am looking for passage to Byblos by boat. We have an appointment there, and I am afraid we are terribly behind schedule. A boat ride would ensure we do not miss it."

Hepu wiped his mouth on a piece of cloth. "Certainly. I have several boats that can take you this very morning."

Diedrich studied the man. "Of course, we would compensate you for your trouble."

The man looked uncomfortable. "I would not ask you for anything. An esteemed man such as you is welcome to all that I have."

Megan considered the man curiously. *What did he mean? Why did he think Diedrich was a man of "esteem"?*

Diedrich was right, though, they should at least try to pay their way. She pulled two of the gold bangle bracelets from her arm and handed them to the man.

"Please, take them. It's only fair that we give you something besides camels."

Hepu looked at the bracelets, then at Diedrich, who gave a slight nod. Hepu took them with a small bow and a thin smile.

Diedrich folded his hands in his lap. "As she has already mentioned, the three camels we came on are also yours. For your hospitality."

Hepu bowed his head again. "Most generous. May the gods grant many blessings to you on your journey."

Diedrich finished his meal and stood, his gaze turning to the girls. "We had better go now if we want to, uh, keep our appointment."

They followed their host through the village and down toward the river, and into the strangest boat Megan had ever seen. It was long, low to the water, and crescent-shaped, with a single mast and one rhomboid-shaped sail in the center. It also had four oars, each manned by a dark-skinned, bare-chested Egyptian. The vessel was made of nothing but bundled reeds.

"It is papyrus," Diedrich told her when she asked. "Reeds of papyrus bound together and stacked on top of each other. My father has several miniature replicas in his study, and I think there is a full-size one in the museum."

"It won't sink?" Rachel asked as they boarded. "Isn't papyrus what they made paper from?"

Diedrich shrugged. "It worked for the Egyptians for thousands of years, so I will take a chance and say no, it won't sink."

The little boat proved sturdy and quick, and now Megan watched as the shore sped by. With favorable winds and weather, they would get to Byblos an entire day ahead of Josef.

Palm trees grew on the riverbank. Beyond them, fields stretched away into the distance. Men and women hunched over large woven baskets tucked between the rows, picking beans and tending the fields. Little naked brown-skinned children ran between the rows, playing a game that looked like tag. It was a perfect scene of day-to-day life in ancient Egypt.

Megan smiled. It all seemed so… normal. It was hard to believe that a race for life and death was going on at this very moment.

*None of them are even real,* she reminded herself. It was so easy to believe everything here was part of the real world. Sir Gregory could weave an impressive spell, that's for sure.

The beauty of the land was spellbinding, the delta so green and full of life, a far cry from the image that usually came to mind when she thought of Egypt—dry deserts, unending heat, pyramids, and mummies.

"There is the mouth of the Nile." Diedrich pointed at a break in the terrain where the wide river flowed into the sea. Boats moved down and across it, piled high with goods or filled with people or animals.

"Where are the pyramids?" Rachel had reiterated her distrust in Diedrich when he'd allowed his father to escape but started to warm up to him over breakfast. And when he had suggested the boat ride, Megan was sure she had almost apologized.

Claire answered Rachel's question. "Giza. On the western shore of the Nile, farther than we can see from here."

Rachel sighed. "I would have liked to. I mean, I know this is all Sir Gregory's imagination, but this may be as close as I ever get to the real thing."

"Cheer up, Rach, we might make it there yet," Megan said. "You never know where the next clue will lead."

The wind picked up, the sail billowed, and the Nile slipped behind them as they entered the Mediterranean. Megan noticed a gradual shift in their surroundings. The coastline changed from white sand to rocky, less-inviting shore. Villages sprawled closer to the water until they stood right along its edge. The buildings were built not from sand and mud or even from block, but from uncut rock held together with thick white mortar and wood. Instead of dirt, flat stones paved the roads that cut between the structures, and on them walked more horses than camels.

It was early afternoon when one of the oarsmen called out to Diedrich. He had a brief talk with the man, and then came to sit with the girls.

"We are almost there. Another hour, maybe two. I asked about the tree. The king has already cut it down. We are definitely looking for the pillar."

"What do we do once we arrive in Byblos?" Rachel said.

Megan had been thinking about that for most of the journey. "Head straight for the palace." She had been thinking about it for most of the journey. "Then we find the box, get the next clue, and move on before Diedrich's father can find us."

Rachel crossed her arms, staring at the shore. "You hope. Or else we're well and truly sunk."

When they reached the harbor of Byblos, one of the oarsmen threw a rope to a man on the dock. The boat was tied up, and Diedrich and the girls disembarked. As they thanked the oarsmen, Diedrich tipped the harbor master with one of Claire's rings, and then the four of them walked into the city. Cargo ships lined the docks, and slaves loaded and unloaded their lumber and cloth under the watchful eyes of their masters.

"Traders," Claire said. "The Phoenicians were traders. I remember reading about them. They exported cedar to Egypt and ran trade routes all over the Middle East and into Western Europe. Dyed cloth was one of their most sought-after exports."

"Thank you, Wikipedia," Rachel said. "Where's the palace?"

Megan studied the buildings, packed together tightly along cobbled streets. The street in front of them was lined with booths, covered in brightly colored striped cloth, and people were selling things out of the booths. A market.

*Probably called a bazaar or something here, though. If we were in Greece it would be an Agora.* Funny, the things she remembered about Ancient Greece. She had almost had a panic attack in the middle of the crowded Agora. *Trauma burns things into one's brain, I guess?*

"We should just ask for directions." She took a few steps toward the bazaar. "It'll save time."

*Uh oh. What did I do?* Several of the vendors and many of the shoppers were giving her odd glances. One child being pulled along by his mother openly stared.

She grabbed Diedrich's arm and whispered in his ear, "People are looking at me weird."

"We do sort of stand out." Claire gave Megan a sidelong glance. "I don't think they've ever seen hair quite that color before."

Megan touched her auburn locks. "Oh, I guess not." *Either that, or they're wondering where I left my hairbrush.*

Diedrich scratched his cheek, which had grown the smallest bit of stubble.

"I don't think that's quite the issue. We have to be careful here. Outside of ancient Egypt, many cultures did not see women as equals."

Megan remembered well heir walk through ancient Athens. The four girls had had to be accompanied across the city by a male guide because young, unmarried women were not allowed to walk the streets alone.

"You girls stay close to me." Diedrich gave a short, barking laugh. "They are looking at me as much as you, Meg. They are probably wondering who I am, to be able to afford three wives."

"Wives?" Megan said. "You can't be serious. I'm fourteen years old!"

Diedrich shrugged. "I didn't make up the rules. Most people married young. Rich men and kings were able to afford more than one wife. I am new in town, these people are traders, and we are in the bazaar. It's possible they believe they are looking at a rich man, and are curious to see what I am in the market for."

Megan realized it was probably the same reason Hepu had treated them so well and offered them the use of his boat.

Rachel snorted. "Women aren't equal? What rubbish is that?"

"It's their culture, Rachel," Claire said quietly. "We should respect it."

"But we're in a bloody book," Rachel complained a little too loudly. "This place isn't real, just made to look like it, right?"

At the sound of Rachel's raised voice, more people stopped and turned to look. Diedrich nodded and leaned in close to Rachel, a sympathetic expression on his face.

"And you know, better than I, that Sir Gregory wrote this book to be accurate to the land and people. Who knows what would happen if we were to ignore the local customs. It would be best if we tried to blend in."

Rachel's jaw clenched, then relaxed. Megan could tell that she still didn't trust Diedrich. But she wasn't stupid.

"Oh, all right, fine. I'll play along if it will get us out of here."

He stood straight and glanced up and down the street. "Wait here. I will get directions to the palace." He crossed the street to the nearest vendor, a dark heavyset man selling bronze pots from a wooden cart pulled by a donkey. Diedrich gave a cheery greeting and a short wave. Megan couldn't hear what they said after that, but she assumed Diedrich was inquiring which way they should go.

The man pointed down the street and gestured with his hands to the right and left. He held up three fingers.

Diedrich nodded his head and stuck his hand out for a handshake. The man stared at it as if it would bite him. Diedrich's face turned red, and he pulled his hand back and gave a quick bow instead.

"I guess they don't shake hands here, either?" Megan said as he rejoined them.

"No, and I completely forgot that," Diedrich said. "It is not far. He said we should walk three blocks, and then turn left—we can't miss it."

# CHAPTER 12

*Phoenician Hospitality Doesn't Suck, But May Include Insects.*

The palace sat in the center of a huge square in the middle of the city. They saw it as soon as they turned the corner—an enormous building that gleamed in the sun. It was topped with a golden dome, flanked on either side by smaller domes, also of gold. A hundred turrets surrounded the central building, with elegant, colorful spires that reached for the sky like needles. The dozens of windows were shaped like mushrooms with pointed tips.

The whole thing was surrounded by a tall, white stucco wall, at least twelve feet high. It must have been several yards thick as well, because guards walked along the top, spears in hand.

"It's amazing," Rachel said.

Megan agreed. "I've never seen anything like it. Sort of reminds me of one of those big ice cream sundaes."

They started toward it.

"Makes you wonder if this is what it really looked like," Claire said.

"What do you mean?" Rachel asked.

"Well, I can't imagine the real palace of Byblos still exists, except as ruins. The Crusades in the thirteenth century saw to that, and every war to rage across Lebanon ever since. So, is this what it really looked like, or just how Sir Gregory's imagined it?"

"It's still beautiful, either way," Rachel said. "But how are we going to get inside?"

The large front gate was of thick wood, bound in iron, guarded by four equally thick, men, also bound in iron. "I don't think we'll just be able to walk up and ring the bell."

"How did Isis get inside?" Megan asked Diedrich. "Since we seem to be on her journey, maybe that's the key."

"If I remember correctly, she disguised herself as a hairdresser." Diedrich stroked his chin. "She taught the queen's maids how to braid their hair, and make perfume. But that would not work."

"Why not?" Rachel tossed her own expertly plaited hair, which was tied off at the end with a strip of leather she had bartered from one of the servants at Hepu's house. "I don't have any perfume, but I'm brilliant with braids."

"Because after Isis was inside, the queen took a liking to her, and asked her to take care of her child, the little prince. Isis loved the baby so much she wanted to make him immortal. She put him inside a magic fire to burn off his humanity. Then she turned herself into a swallow and flew above him and around the pillar. Once the queen realized who Isis was, she gave her whatever she wanted, which of course was the box inside the pillar, Osiris's coffin."

Rachel's face fell. "Oh. I guess we can't do that. Besides, if I went in, there would be no way for you three to follow. Sorry, Meg, but you're all thumbs when it comes to plaiting."

"What if we posed as musicians?" Claire suggested. "We could get in to see the king that way."

Megan wrinkled her nose and shook her head. "Uh, Claire, have you ever listened to me play in music class? I can't carry a tune if you put it in a jar. I'm sure they would figure out we were faking, and then they'd probably throw us in jail. Or worse. Not a good plan."

Claire grimaced. "Oops, didn't think of that. Sorry."

Megan turned to Diedrich. "Do you really think the people here believe you're an important man?"

Diedrich nodded.

"Good, then we'll go with that. We'll just ask for a place to stay. Being important, we're allowed to do that, right?"

Diedrich nodded again.

"Think of a name for yourself," she said. "An Egyptian name."

Diedrich pursed his lips, his brows knit together. "Tutankhamen?" He shrugged. "I know that won't work, will it."

Claire rolled her eyes. "Why don't you just call yourself Osiris and get it over with?"

"Yeah, pick something a little less conspicuous?" Rachel said. She looked around nervously. "And hurry it up. We don't know how long until your father gets here."

Diedrich scratched his head. "The only names I can remember are pharaoh's names. How about Ay? He was the pharaoh after Tut. Of course, scholars do suspect him of killing Tut to assume the throne."

"Never heard of him," Megan said. "It's cool with me. Claire, what do you think?"

Claire nodded. "That'll do."

Diedrich walked up to the gate and approached one of the guards. Not making the same mistake twice, he raised his right hand in a kind of salute.

"Hail. I seek an audience with the king."

The man looked Diedrich over, then at the girls. Megan cast her gaze down, as she had seen Meryet do when around her husband, although she hated herself a little for doing it.

"What business do you have with King Malcander?"

Diedrich didn't skip a beat. "I am Ay, from Thebes. I am traveling through Byblos on my way home from the west, and I seek the king's hospitality for my household this evening."

The guard narrowed his eyes, and glanced at the visitors. Megan's stomach quivered with nerves, and she crossed her fingers. The story was simple enough to be believable. She hoped the guard bought it.

"Where is your caravan? Camels, tents, and servants?"

*Oops, I didn't think about that.* Megan bit the inside of her cheek. *Please, Diedrich, think of something good.*

"We arrived by boat. Our barge is in the harbor, being looked over by my servants." Diedrich gave Megan a quick wink in response to her astonished look. "We have also stopped here to trade with your people for Byblos's excellent cedar and beautiful cloth. I am buying for the pharaoh's house, of course."

At the mention of the Egyptian king, the guard straightened up and looked alert.

"Wait here." He gave a quick bow and slipped inside the gate.

Megan pulled Diedrich's ear toward her mouth. "Are you nuts? What will they do when they find out we're not here to trade, and that the pharaoh didn't send us?"

"Relax. We did arrive by boat, that is true enough. And what are they going to do, ring up the King of Egypt and ask for references? Shoot him a text? By the time they get suspicious, if they even do, we will be long gone."

Megan pulled her face away, so that their eyes met. She lifted her eyebrows and smiled. "That's genius."

"Thanks. Just play your part and follow my lead. Once we're inside, keep your eyes open for that pillar."

The guard returned. He bowed deeply to Diedrich. "King Malcander and Queen Astarte are most honored to have you, and invite you into their home." He moved aside and pushed the gate open.

Diedrich grasped Megan's hand as they walked through. A path, paved with finely crushed white stones, guided them across the wide lawn of lush, green grass. A garden of exotic flowers grew to the right of the path, their fragrance wafting on the warm breeze. A circular stone fountain stood to their left, the *splish-splash* of the water laying a calming melody over the courtyard. Peacocks and peahens wandered about, their startling cries echoing off of the walls.

Rachel gasped. "It's like something from a fairy tale."

"We are in a fairy tale of sorts, aren't we?" Megan replied. *A fairy-tale ending would be great, too. Would beat being trapped in the storybook. She glanced at Diedrich. Even if I wound up being trapped with Prince Charming.*

"Yeah, if you mean a Grimm's fairy tale, where people routinely are chopped to bits and blinded by birds," Claire said.

"You just had to spoil it, didn't you?" Rachel said with a sigh.

The path branched into three different directions—one toward the flowers, another toward the fountain and the third straight ahead to the palace doors.

The double doors were intricately carved from wood and ivory. When they were closed, they formed one of those mushroom shapes like the windows. They were set into a doorway of brightly painted wood inlaid with gold. Another guard stood beside the doors. He opened them, bowing as the guests passed.

A floor of black marble greeted them. Huge pillars, each more than four feet in diameter and painted much like the doorway, stood along either side of a center aisle. At the far end was a platform. Atop the platform a man and a woman waited, each seated in a gold chair. As the four teenagers approached, the man and woman stood, the man opening his arms wide.

"Welcome," he said. "Esteemed guests, please come. Our home is your home."

Diedrich tugged Megan's hand, urging her forward. They walked toward the king and queen, and Megan glanced at the pillars. The one they were looking for was probably in this room. But which one was it? They all looked the same. She would have to talk to the girls and Diedrich later, and work out a plan to come in here when they could look without drawing attention to themselves.

The queen was gorgeous. What had the guard said her name was? Megan couldn't remember. Tall and slender, with olive skin and deep-brown almond-shaped eyes lined with kohl. A wide, well-formed nose above full red lips. Her hair was hidden beneath a sheer purple veil, and gold earrings dangled from her ears. She wore something that resembled an Indian sari—a length of deep-purple fabric draped around her body over a shift of purple-patterned fabric. Her arms clanged with gold and silver bracelets, and two large, jeweled rings sparkled from her long, elegant fingers. When she shifted her feet, tiny bells jingled on gold anklets.

The four of them stopped in front of the king and queen. Diedrich bowed deeply, his hand to his chest. The girls each dropped a curtsy, which the king and queen regarded with strange looks, so Megan quickly bowed her head.

"Greetings, Your Majesties," Diedrich said. "Thank you for so graciously taking us into your home."

"It is our pleasure," the king said. "Our neighbor Pharaoh and his emissaries are always welcome."

"I am Ay." Diedrich extended his hand toward Megan. "And this is my first wife, uh—"

The large color panel from the book in the manor's library flashed into Megan's head. "Nefertari."

Diedrich tried to hide his look of surprise. He turned to Claire. "And this is, uh…"

"Nehesput," Claire said.

Diedrich nodded.

"And finally…" Rachel smiled. "Cleopatra."

Megan nearly choked holding back her laugh. She looked at Rachel, who just gave her a small shrug.

The queen—*Astarte, that was her name*—looked the three girls over. Her gaze lingered on Megan's auburn hair and pale skin.

"You must be tired and hungry after your long journey," she said, her voice soft yet commanding. She clapped her hands, and three women dressed the same as she was but in plainer fabrics appeared through a doorway to the left. The women knelt on the floor in a straight line before their queen.

"Please take our guest's wives to the baths, then to a comfortable room and see that they are well fed," Astarte said. "They are friends of the pharaoh, and we are honored to have them in our house."

The women touched their heads to the floor before they stood. One bowed to Megan and led her toward the door from which the three servants had come. Megan looked over her shoulder and motioned with her head for Claire and Rachel to follow. Diedrich stayed behind. Megan felt uncomfortable leaving him, but it didn't appear they had much choice.

The girls were taken to a room with mosaic tile and a large pool in the center. It reminded Megan of the bath they'd used in the Acropolis of Athens, but more colorful and exotic. She, Rachel and Claire were bathed in warm, fragrant water and dressed in clean dresses. Megan adored the soft green fabric the women deftly tucked and draped around her without using a single pin.

"It brings out your eyes." The woman slid a pair of slippers made of the softest leather on Megan's feet.

The girls were then taken to a large airy pavilion that looked out on a walled courtyard and more gardens. A lotus bush bloomed, white flowers with pointed petals and a beautiful fragrance. Megan took a deep breath, and the scent of jasmine and patchouli mixed with the lotus to fill her nostrils.

Three different servant women came in and placed several large jewel-colored cushions on the floor. The girls sat, and more serving women arrived, carrying bowls of food and pitchers of fruit juice.

One of the girls gave Megan a bashful smile.

"This recipe comes from India," she said as she set a bowl in front of Megan. Inside was a thick red paste. Megan picked up a piece of bread and scooped some up, then popped it into her mouth without a second thought.

Her mouth was on fire. She grabbed the carved wooden cup in front of her and drank down every drop of the pomegranate juice. It helped, but not much. Her eyes watered, and tears streamed down her face.

Flapping her hands over her mouth in an effort to cool her tongue, Megan looked to Rachel for help.

"Eat the bread, that will take the burn out," Rachel said, practically rolling on the floor in laughter.

Megan stuffed a piece of plain bread into her mouth. Immediately, the burning receded. She gulped down another cup of juice and it was almost gone.

"What was that?"

Rachel giggled. "I think it's a spicy curry." She took a smaller helping of the paste and ate it. "Yep, curry in a bean paste. It's rather good if you don't eat a whole bowl in one bite."

Megan stuck her tongue, which felt back to normal, out at Rachel. "Thanks for the tip."

"Don't mention it. My dad loves Indian food—he actually took a class so he could cook it himself. We have it at least once a week."

Diedrich came in. He was also dressed in new clothes, and his hair was still wet from his bath. He plopped down cross-legged onto the cushion next to Megan. Reaching over, he reached over and picked up a piece of bread and some dried fish. He put some of the curry paste on the bread, put the fish in the paste, wrapped the bread around it like a sandwich and took a big bite.

"Don't!" Megan said. "That stuff is hot."

Diedrich looked at her, no alarm on his face. He chewed and swallowed.

"This? I have had hotter. I am used to spicy Middle Eastern food."

Megan felt left out, like someone had told a joke she didn't get. She wished she had visited more Indian restaurants in New York—apparently it was all the rage with Europeans. She made a mental note to ask Maggie if she knew how to make any.

Diedrich picked up a small bowl holding some yellow-tinted grain.

"Here, try this, it is saffron and rice. You will like it." Megan took a small taste. It was delicious, rich and mellow.

"Mmmm."

"Where did they take you?" Claire said.

"To a bath a bath, the same as you. It was the one for men. They gave me—I mean us—a suite down the hall to sleep. I'll show you when we're done eating."

Rachel glanced sidelong at the servants, who stood in a line along the one solid wall, their eyes straight ahead. She leaned in close to her friends.

"What are we going to do about the you-know-what?" she whispered. "We need to find it, fast."

Megan swallowed. "We'll have to wait until night, I guess. Get into that throne room when no one is looking. The pillar we're looking for is in there, right?"

"According to the legend," Diedrich said.

"Do you think we have time?" Claire said. "Before Mr. Hemmlich gets here, I mean."

"My father will not be a problem," Diedrich said. "When you girls left I told the king there is someone who might come and try to gain entrance. That he may claim to be my father or some other representative of the pharaoh. I told the king not to believe him, that he was a fraud, and not to let him in."

"Good thinking," Rachel said dryly. "I'm almost impressed."

Megan sighed. *I thought we were past this.* She hated that her best friend couldn't get along with her… whatever he was. Something else to figure out later.

"That might not be enough," Diedrich said. "My father is a clever man. And he is determined. If I know him, he will find a way in here. We have to be quick. And prepared."

Megan grabbed a handful of small black, crunchy things from another bowl. She munched on them.

"Mmm, these are good. Wonder what they are?"

Rachel looked in the bowl and laughed. "I think they're roasted ants."

# CHAPTER 13

*When Searching for a God's Box, Look for the Disco Bird.*

THE SUITE THE KING AND QUEEN HAD SUPPLIED WAS LUXURIOUS, TO SAY the least. Everything was inlaid with ivory and gold, the furniture elegantly carved, the pillows covered with exquisite fabrics. Like much of the palace, everything was painted or made using deep, rich colors—ruby, sapphire, emerald.

Diedrich dismissed the servants, who were never more than three steps behind Megan and her friends, and closed the double doors. Three other rooms led from the main room, but none had actual doors, just archways.

"I'm exhausted," Rachel said.

"We should try and get some rest." Claire lay on one of the large cushions in the suite's main room. "We might have a long night ahead."

"Yes, once we find the box, we will have to get out of here quickly." Diedrich sat on a cushion next to Claire. "I am afraid we will also have to steal some sort of transportation. Camels or horses."

"We don't know where the next clue will lead," Megan said. "Maybe we should figure out where we have to go next before we plan an escape. If we can find it quick enough, we can be back in here before morning, and leave tomorrow."

She lay on her own soft cushion and closed her eyes. "Who's going to wake us up when it's time?"

She got nothing but soft snores in answer.

"Ow!"

Someone had kicked something—a chair? Megan kept still, her eyes closed, and listened.

"Be quiet, we don't want to wake the whole house."

That was Claire. Megan opened one eye. Diedrich stood next to her, a torch in one hand.

"Is it time already? I don't want to get up." She rolled away from him.

"Get up, you great lazy thing," Rachel said. "Quit your lolly-gagging."

Megan threw a small pillow at her.

"All right, all right, I'm up. But when we get out of here, no one had better wake me up for two days, okay?"

"Shh," Claire said. The torchlight flickered across the lenses of her glasses, making her look like a giant bug. "Keep it down."

Megan collected herself, and the four of them tiptoed out of the suite. The servants lay on the floor outside the door, in case any of their charges needed anything during the night. One of the women let out a grunt and rolled over. Her arm brushed Megan's ankle; Megan froze. *Come on, come on, go back to sleep.* The woman's hand slid over Megan's foot and onto the floor. Megan let out a small sigh and continued on.

Diedrich held the torch high and led them back to the throne room. In the dark, the room looked like a cave. A single ray of moonlight shone in through an open skylight in the ceiling and formed a circle of light on the floor. The smallest sounds echoed, and Megan wondered how long it would be before someone heard them. What would happen if they were caught?

*I hope this pillar and box are easy to find.*

"We won't have much time," Megan said, as quietly as she could. "Let's spread out."

"How will we know when we've found the right pillar?" Rachel whispered.

"The legend does not say," Diedrich replied. "But there are only ten pillars here. Maybe there will be an identifying mark, or maybe it is painted with a different pattern than the others. It is a special pillar, after all."

"I can hardly see anything over here," Claire said, standing in the shadows. "Is there another torch?"

Diedrich pulled one of the unlit torches from a bracket on the wall and used the flame from the one in his hand to light the new one, then handed it to her.

"You two go look on that side." He clasped Megan's hand and pulled her toward the pillar closest to them.

The pillars were painted with beautiful designs of birds and animals. Megan wrapped her arms around one; they didn't even reach halfway.

There were five on each side of the room, lined up one beside the other. The first two she and Diedrich looked at were exactly the same. Diedrich rapped on them with his knuckles, but nothing happened.

"Anything yet?" Claire's whisper floated across the room.

"No," Megan whispered back. She circled the third pillar, squinting in the flickering light from the torch. It was the same as the other two.

*Wait a sec…?*

"Diedrich, bring that light closer."

He came around and stood next to her. "What did you find?"

"Look here." She traced her fingers over three small squares carved into the wood. Inside each square was a relief of a different animal-like creature.

"These weren't on the other pillars."

"Wait here a minute." Diedrich ran to the other end of the room and checked the remaining two pillars. He came back to Megan.

"Nope, not on either one. This must be it."

"Rachel, Claire, over here."

The girls padded across the room and stood beside Megan.

"What do we do now?" Rachel said.

"We have to get the box out of the pillar, maybe?" Megan said. "Does the pillar open up somehow?" She tried to grip one of the squares around the edges with her fingers and pull it out, but she couldn't get a grip on it. "Guess not. What do you think those animals mean? I mean, they're obviously important."

Claire tilted her head. "They look like hieroglyphs." She touched the first one, a snake. "What do they symbolize?"

"Set," Diedrich said. "In the New Kingdom, he became the God of Evil, the treacherous snake who betrayed his brother."

"Why is the snake always the bad guy?" Rachel said to no one in particular.

Diedrich pointed to the second. "A jackal. That's Anubis. Remember, Megan, I told you about him—Set's son, and the god of mummification. He taught the process of embalming to the Egyptians and led Osiris into the underworld."

"I remember. And this one?" Megan pointed to the last one. It looked like some kind of bizarre bird. It was purple and had a pair of curved horns on its head. "The God of Disco Birds?"

"No, that is the Benu. An Egyptian phoenix of sorts. It is usually symbolic of Ra, the sun god. If it had a disc on its head I would say it was Ra, but..."

"But what?"

"I remember my father telling me the Benu is also associated with Osiris, because of the eternal renewal thing. God of the underworld and all that. When it is painted with the headdress like this..." He touched the horns. "It is Osiris. The Benu flies to the Heliopolis, the city of the sun, and burns every evening. In the morning it is reborn from the ashes."

"So, we have Set, Anubis, and Osiris," Claire said, touching the squares in order.

Diedrich shook his head. "Egyptian, like Hebrew and Japanese, is read right to left. So it is 'Osiris, Anubis, and Set'."

"This is all quite fascinating," Rachel said. "But how does that help us? I don't see a hole or a knob. Or even a sign that says 'open me here'."

Megan, for some reason, was reminded of standing in front of the elevator in her old New York apartment building.

"Don't laugh at me, all right?" She pushed the square with the bird. It sank into the wood, but nothing else happened. Megan tilted her head. "Um, where's the box? I figured if I pushed the one I wanted, it would give me what I wanted."

"It's not a vending machine. Maybe you have to push them all." Claire pushed the snake and the jackal. There was a click, and all three buttons popped up, and resetting themselves.

Diedrich rubbed his chin. "Pushing them all might be right, but the order is wrong." He reached out and pushed the snake, then the bird, then the jackal. A panel in the pillar, a little shorter than Megan but wide enough to walk through, slid open.

"How did you figure that out?" Megan said.

Diedrich shrugged. "I followed the story of Osiris. Set killed Osiris and put him in the box. Then Anubis took him to the underworld. Just made sense."

"Bring the torch a little closer, would you?" Rachel said.

"I can't see a thing." She ducked down and stepped into the black space.

"What do you see?" Megan said. "I would think a coffin, or a sarcophagus, whatever you call it, would be a pretty big thing. Like, you-can't-miss-it kind of big."

"I don't think it would fit in there lying down," Claire said. "Is it standing on end, Rachel?"

"Uh, guys, you'd better come here."

Megan stepped through the opening, and promptly bumped into Rachel.

"Oops, sorry."

Diedrich and Claire were framed in the entrance, their faces lit by the torches.

"Hmm," Diedrich said. "The coffin should be right here, according to the story."

"Yeah, but myths are always subject to interpretation," Megan said. "This is really Sir Gregory's story, isn't it? And inside the pillar doesn't necessarily mean at the bottom. Claire, hand me that torch, would you?"

She held it above her head, lighting up the smooth, circular interior of the pillar. A tightly wound spiral staircase curved upward, connected to the pillar's wall.

"Where does it go?" Rachel said.

"Duh, it goes up," Megan said. "I can't see much more than that. So, I guess we go up." Pictures were painted on the curved walls, spiraling up alongside the stairs. "What do these mean?"

"It is hard to say, but it looks like the story of Osiris. Here is where he gets into the box, and Set traps him." Diedrich climbed a few more steps. "And this looks like Isis searching for him, and finding the pillar." He continued to follow the paintings. "See here. Set was so angry that Isis had found Osiris, he ripped Osiris's body into thirteen pieces and scattered them throughout Egypt."

"How is it you know this story so well?" Rachel said. "You didn't seem like you were interested in your father's work."

Diedrich chuckled. "As I explained to Megan and Claire, I love mythology, and while you were listening to stories of Cinderella and Sleeping Beauty, I was being told the story of Isis and Osiris and the journey to the Land of the Dead."

The stairs ended in front of a plain black door with a brass ring in the center. Diedrich stopped and moved to the right. Megan stopped in front of the door, and was shoved forward. Her head banged against the wood.

"Hey, cut it out."

"Sorry, my fault," Claire said from below. "Why did you stop?"

"There's a door here."

"What are you waiting for? Open it," Rachel said.

Megan inspected the door. It didn't make sense for it to open outward. When it swung open it would knock her down the stairs. So, why the pull ring? She put her hands on the door and pushed. It didn't budge.

She shrugged. Okay, pull it is.

"Rachel, Claire? Take a step back, please," Megan said. "Diedrich, catch me if I fall, okay?"

Diedrich nodded.

She gripped the ring with both hands and pulled. Nothing. She pulled as hard as she could, even put a foot on the door for leverage, but the door didn't move.

"What the heck?" Megan let go of the ring and took a small step back. "How do we open the door?"

"Maybe the ring isn't for opening the door." Rachel mused. "It kind of looks like a knocker."

"Huh. Good idea, Rach." Megan lifted the ring and banged it against the wood three times.

The door swung inward.

"I'm going in," she called over her shoulder.

"Be careful," Claire called back.

Megan stepped into a long, dark, narrow room with a high ceiling. Unlike the palace downstairs, this place was plain. Spiders had clearly been hired to decorate; the walls and ceiling were covered in thick sheets of webs that flowed like drapes in the breeze that blew when Megan opened the door.

*If these are the webs, I don't want to see the spiders.* Something crunched under her feet. She lowered the torch and saw an array of dead scarabs, scorpions, and other creepy-crawly things. Their sharp edges poked her feet through the thin slippers.

"Ick."

"What was that?" Rachel said.

"Nothing..." *...you want to know about...*

On the floor at the far end of the room was a long rectangular box. *Looks like a coffin to me. This must be it.* Megan pushed through the webs, some of them going up in brief, bright flame as the torch touched them, and stood in front of it.

"Don't touch it," Rachel said from right behind her.

Megan jumped. "Don't sneak up on me like that!"

Rachel, Claire, and Diedrich stood a few feet behind her.

"Sorry," Rachel said with a shrug. "But you shouldn't touch it, it could be booby-trapped."

"I don't doubt it." Megan wiped the dust from the lid. Gold, silver, and ebony designs were inlaid into the smooth, polished dark wood. It glittered in the flickering torchlight.

"I don't see anything written on the box," Claire said. "So, where is the clue?"

"It must be inside." Megan took a deep breath and immediately regretted it. She coughed up the lungful of dust and spider webs. "We'll have to open it."

"Ugh." Rachel wrinkled her nose. "I don't really want to look at some dried-up old mummy, thank you."

"It won't bite you or anything." Megan smirked and decided to keep the comment that sprang to mind about the mummy coming back to life to herself. "Fine. You stand back, we'll open it." She put her fingertips beneath the lid and pulled. "It's stuck."

"I don't see how it could be," Rachel said. "There's no latch or lock. I would think when Set put Osiris in, he could just lift the lid and hop on out."

"Set sealed it with hot lead." Diedrich squatted beside the coffin and looked closely at the seam where the lid and box came together. "Yes, there is something in there. We need to pry it out."

"Well, I'll just jog on down to the local hardware and grab a crowbar," Rachel quipped.

"I think we already have something that will work." He took the lapis collar from his neck, thrust an edge into the seam and wiggled it back and forth.

"That's not long enough," Claire said. "You won't get enough leverage."

"I am not looking for leverage." Diedrich pulled the collar out and looked at the seam. "Lead is a fairly soft metal. Gold is, too, but if I can make a dent, maybe I can get a finger in there and pull the lead out."

"That's going to take forever," Rachel said. "We're on the clock, remember?"

"Relax, my dad cannot get in the palace."

"No, but sooner or later someone downstairs is going to notice we're not in our rooms and come looking," Megan said, and glanced over her shoulder to make sure they were still alone. "I'm sure they have guards that make rounds during the night or some such thing. They'll see the open pillar and—"

"Got it." Diedrich pulled out a long, thin strip of metal. It broke off at the corner. "Quick, Megan you take that corner and I'll work on this end."

The rest of the lead came out easily. Diedrich put his fingers under the lip of the lid.

"Here we go." He lifted up. His muscles strained, and the lid raised a quarter of an inch. He dropped it, and it made a huge *bang* that Megan was sure the entire palace heard.

Diedrich leaned his forearms on the box, looking a bit out of breath. "That is a lot heavier than it looks."

"I'll help." Megan handed her torch to Claire. "Rachel, relight the other torch and go watch the door. Claire, hold that light steady."

"This time let's lift just a bit, then shove," Diedrich said. "Slide the lid across. On three. Ready?"

"I guess?" Megan gripped the edge of the lid.

"One, two, three."

Megan lifted with all her strength, then pushed. The lid shifted sideways.

"Turn it, or it will drop inside when we let go," Diedrich said. They shifted it so it lay at a forty-five-degree angle.

"What's inside?" Claire's voice sounded both afraid and excited.

*She probably loves all this.* Megan hadn't actually thought about it before, but it was almost as good as being on an archaeological dig. Except for almost being killed all the time, and the magic stuff, of course.

Megan looked inside the box and lifted out a large carved wooden beetle. "It's a big bug."

"It is a scarab," Diedrich said. "To the Egyptians they were powerful amulets. This one could have been a heart scarab."

"And just what the heck does that mean?" Megan turned the scarab around so the others could see it.

"It was placed over the heart of a mummy. There was usually something written on the back, a spell to protect the dead, so that Osiris would allow the deceased into the underworld."

*And Diedrich is the docent in this crazy museum.* Megan smiled at the thought and flipped the scarab over.

"There is something written here, but I can't see what it is. It's small and it's too dark in here."

"Let's figure it out later," Rachel said. "This place totally creeps me out."

"There's nothing else in there, so I guess we can go," Megan said.

"Guys, does it seem like this room is smaller?" Claire said.

Megan dusted off her hands. "It's your imagination. I'm claustrophobic, and I'm feeling fine. I think it's that the ceiling is so high."

"No, I think Claire's right," Rachel said. "The walls are moving." She ran out the door and down the stairs. "Come on, hurry!" She called back.

Just as Megan turned, something moved. She turned back just in time to see Osiris's box sink into the floor. The walls *had* moved, while they had been distracted. They were almost close enough for her to reach out and touch on both sides.

"We have to go now!" Diedrich grabbed her wrist and dragged her across the room, which was now only a corridor. The walls slid toward each other at an alarming rate. Claire leapt the last few feet to the door and onto the stairs with Rachel.

Megan and Diedrich were only a few yards from the door. They took another step, and a piece of the floor in front of them dropped away. The torch slipped from Megan's hand and fell into the hole, lighting a brief path into a bottomless abyss.

"We're not going to make it," Megan said. The walls pressed in on them from both sides. The door looked a thousand miles away.

"Yes, you are." Diedrich scooped her up and threw her across the gap. She landed on the other side with a thud, still inside the shrinking room. Claire and Rachel's hands came through the door and dragged her onto the steps.

Megan looked back, and her heart jumped into her throat. Diedrich took two long steps back, ran to the brink of the gap and launched into the air. His feet touched down on their side, but his balance was off. He teetered on the edge of the hole, the walls ready to close in on him at any second.

"No!" Megan screamed. She stretched her arm as far as possible, but she couldn't reach him.

Diedrich gripped the closing walls with his fingertips and threw himself forward. He belly-flopped onto the steps next to Megan, his top half outside the door. He rolled to his back and pulled his knees to his chest. His feet just missed being crushed by the walls. They came together with a deep, dull clunk.

"Are you all right?" Megan sat beside his head as he lay across the steps, head down.

"Considering the alternative, I am fabulous."

"That was bloody brilliant," Rachel stated. "Like watching an action movie in real time."

Diedrich turned his head and stared at her for a moment, then laughed. "Thank you. I think."

Megan helped him up. "Okay, hero, let's get out of here."

The four of them raced down the stairs, Claire and the remaining torch in the lead. They reached the bottom and tumbled into the silent throne room. The panel slid closed behind them. Its edges disappeared into the curved surface of the pillar, as if it had never been.

Rachel looked around. "No one here, thank goodness. Do we still wait until morning, or do we get out of here now before anyone suspects?"

"I vote for now," Claire said. "We're already awake."

"We have to go back to the room first," Megan said. "I left the book there."

"I will go," Diedrich said. "You stay here." He looked at Megan. "Keep safe, I will be right back." He jogged into the dark.

"While we're waiting, let's have a look at that clue," Claire said.

She and Rachel flanked Megan and looked over her shoulders at the scarab. Megan turned the carved beetle over in her hands.

"We lucked out this time. I can read this one."

"What do you mean?" Rachel said.

"The last one, the one in the book, was in Ancient Egyptian," Claire said. "Didn't you see it?"

Rachel shook her head. "I was too busy trying not to make Hemmlich mad and figure out how to get away. He didn't read it from the book, though. I thought I told you. It was on a scroll he found in the camel's bag, I think. He took it with him."

"So, that's why we couldn't find it," Megan said. "I thought the book would reset it when we came in, but I guess as long as there's someone in here, the first person to get the English clue takes it. Anybody that follows is out of luck."

"We'll worry about bugs in the system later," Claire said. "Read the clue, Megan."

"Yes, by all means," a gruff voice said from the dark. "Read it."

# CHAPTER 14

*Hide-and-Seek Isn't Just for Kids.*

JOSEF HEMMLICH STEPPED INTO THE CIRCLE OF MOONLIGHT. THE BLADE of the long saber he brandished flashed as the sharp, curved edge caught the light.

"I am most anxious to hear what it says."

The girls took three large steps backward, and Hemmlich stepped forward, back into the shadows.

"How did you get in here?" Rachel said. "Diedrich told them not to let you in."

Mr. Hemmlich snorted. "Did you really think they could stop me? Two tired guards by the front gate, and a host of shadows I could use to hide from the wall sentries? I went by them easily. Of course, I needed a little diversion— for insurance."

"What does that mean?" Megan said, suddenly uneasy. "What did you do?"

Something was not right. She glanced across the room and noticed that the front doors of the palace stood open. The scent of smoke wafted into the throne room. Voices, raised in alarm, accompanied the smell.

"You set something on fire?" Claire said.

Josef shrugged. "Just a house."

Megan's heart was in her throat. "With people inside?"

"Hmm. I'm not sure. I think so. I did hear someone scream."

"You're horrible," Claire said.

Josef's face twisted into a malevolent smile. "No, I'm just a man who knows what he wants, what he needs, and is willing to do what it takes to get it. Besides, we all know that these... people... aren't real. Yes, ladies, I've figured it all out. I'm smarter than you are, remember?"

"Run," Megan muttered to her friends.

"What?" Claire whispered.

"I said run. He lost the gun, so he'll have to get close to get the scarab. If we split up, he'll chase me because I've got the clue." She tucked the scarab into her sari, bent her knees slightly and tensed her muscles, as if she were preparing for a race. "Ready, get set—"

"Go!" Rachel yelled.

Claire threw the torch at Mr. Hemmlich and ran left. Megan shot off to the right, into the dark. Out of the corner of her eye, she saw Rachel run toward the back of the room and duck behind the two golden thrones.

Josef cursed. "You're only delaying the inevitable. I'll find you sooner or later."

From her hiding place, in the shadow of a doorway, Megan saw the torch slide across the floor and sputter out. Now the only light came from moonlight that shone from above and through the front doors. The wind blew faint shouts and a woman's screams into the room along with light smoke.

Mr. Hemmlich turned slowly in the light, the saber in front of him. He stopped facing the far end of the room.

Three large steps took him out of the light, but right in front of the thrones. Megan's hands shook, and her heart jumped into her mouth. If he looked over the top, Rachel wouldn't see him until it was too late.

She took a deep breath. "Rachel, watch out!"

Mr. Hemmlich turned his head toward the sound. Megan saw a Rachel-shaped shadow take advantage of his distraction and bolt from behind the chairs and to another part of the room. Josef climbed from the dais; his face twisted in a snarl.

He stalked toward where he had heard Megan yell from. She was already gone, having sprinted to a corner. Rachel met her there.

"Give me the scarab," Rachel said.

"Why?"

"Because he'll think you still have it." She took it and tucked it away. "Now, run. Go find Claire."

Megan shot from the corner, but Hemmlich must have heard her, because he turned in her direction immediately. She barely saw Claire in another corner, behind a huge vase that looked remarkably like the one she always stubbed her toe on in the dining room. Megan crept over to her.

"Where's Rachel?" she whispered.

"She's fine."

There wasn't enough room for both of them behind the vase, so Megan took off, toward the front door. Josef blocked her path.

"Give me that scarab!" He swung the saber, and she felt the wind from the blade as it blew through her hair. She took a step back and dove behind a pillar, catching a glimpse of Rachel tossing the scarab to Claire. Claire dashed back into to the shadows, behind a large potted palm.

"Over here, you wanker," Rachel yelled. "I've got it, come and get it."

When he spun toward Rachel, Megan shot out from behind the plant. She wanted to run out the front door but couldn't abandon her friends. She went right, stumbling through the dark until she came to a wall. There was a door, just a few feet to her right. If she could get Rachel and Claire over here, they could escape.

She pressed her back against the wall and scanned the room for any sign of her friends. They were nowhere to be found. Mr. Hemmlich walked through a patch of light, saber in hand. He turned and looked right at Megan. Her heart pounded and she froze. Josef must not have spotted her in the dark, because he moved on.

Megan's knees buckled. Suddenly, it was hard to breathe. Trembling, she slid down the wall, unable to get up. She tried, but her limbs would not obey.

*I can't stay here. He's going to find me. I have to get up. Megan Montgomery, move your butt!*

The door beside her opened, and a dark figure strode into the room with something large in one hand. Megan finally saw Rachel, crossing the center of the room where Josef had been moments earlier. To Megan's horror, Rachel tripped on her dress and fell, landing in the pale circle of moonlight.

Then Josef was there, standing over her, saber ready to strike. Megan wanted to run, to scream, to do something to help Rachel, but she couldn't. She hoped whoever had come in was able to get to her before it was too late.

Hemmlich sneered at Rachel. "I don't know how you got away from me before, you little witch, but it won't happen a second time. I need that scarab, and I need the Ankh, and none of you will stop me."

Rachel screamed, throwing her arms over her head. The new arrival stepped behind Hemmlich and hit him on the head. The saber clattered to the floor, as Josef fell into an undignified heap.

Diedrich stepped into the light and stood over his father's prostate form, a heavy bronze statue in his hand. Megan recognized it—it had been on a pedestal in the hallway outside their suite. He tossed it away and bent over his father.

Megan was stunned. She knew Diedrich would do the right thing, but how easy was it to knock out your own father, even if you knew he was about to hurt someone else? She couldn't imagine. At all.

Diedrich turned to Rachel. "Are you alright? He did not hurt you, did he?"

Rachel's voice sounded small and far away. "No, I'm okay, I think." She looked up at Diedrich with genuine gratitude. "You saved my life. Thank you."

"Don't worry about it." Diedrich called out, "Megan? Claire? Where are you?"

Megan's limbs finally decided to work again. She ran to him and threw her arms around his neck.

"He wanted the clue. He was going to—"

"I know what he was going to do." Diedrich patted her back gently and stroked her hair. She welled up, tears dripping down her face and nose in what was sure to be a most attractive way.

"It's okay," he whispered. "You are safe now."

"Hey, Diedrich," Rachel said. "I'm really sorry about all that… stuff… I said. And… the stuff I thought that you didn't know about. You were brilliant."

"Forget it. It is all right. If I were you I probably would not have trusted me, either."

Rachel nudged Josef with a toe. "Is he… dead?"

Diedrich knelt beside his father and put two fingers to his neck. Megan's stomach rolled with anxiety. What would happen if Diedrich had…

"No, he is alive. But he is going to have an enormous headache when he wakes up. Not that he doesn't deserve it. I cannot believe my father would even think of doing such a thing."

"Sorry, Diedrich. That couldn't have been easy." Megan slipped her hand into his and squeezed.

Diedrich stared at his father. "I do not even think I know him anymore. I wonder if I ever really did." He looked around. "Where is Claire?"

"I'm here." Claire called from beside the front door. She ran up to them, obviously still shaken.

"Do you have the clue?" Rachel asked.

Claire nodded and held it up. "If we're going to get away, we should do it now. I peeked outside—there's still plenty of confusion from the fire. We can slip away and nobody will see us."

"I have the book." Diedrich held up the cloth bag. "Give me the scarab." Claire handed it to him, and he slipped it into the bag. He clasped Megan's hand. "Let's go."

"We could take him with us." Rachel pointed to the prostate form on the floor.

Diedrich hesitated, but shook his head, anger coloring his features. "No, he is on his own. Father or no, what he has done… There's no excuse. I want to see you girls home safe. He will be along eventually, I am sure."

Out in the courtyard, an orange glow rose from beyond the palace's outer wall. Servants and guards ran in all directions. Men fighting the fire scooped water from the fountain with wooden buckets and ran out the gate. Women rushed in and out of the palace, their arms loaded with bandages, blankets, and pots of burn salve. People lay on pallets on the front yard, some badly burned.

"We should help." Megan looked at one man, his leg red, shiny, and covered in blisters. He moaned in pain. "This is our fault."

"No, it isn't," Rachel said gently. "It's Josef's. These people aren't even real, remember?"

Megan shot her a hurt, accusing look. "How can you say that?"

"Because it's the truth. I know it sounds horrid, but once we're out of the book they'll be right as rain." She pulled on Megan's dress, giving her a sympathetic look. "The best way we can help them is to get out of here as soon as possible."

They ran around the side of the palace and into the long stone building with the thatched roof that was the stable. Camels and horses, spooked by the confusion outside, stomped nervously in their stalls.

"Horses," Rachel said emphatically. "I'm not riding another bloody camel." The camel in the stall nearest her let out a snort. Rachel looked at him and shrugged. "No offense, but all of you stink."

Claire and Rachel collected four saddles and bridles from the rack on the wall, while Diedrich and Megan chose horses. Megan opened one stall and found a golden mare with soft blue eyes.

"Hey, there, beautiful. Want to come with me?"

The horse nuzzled her outstretched hand with a velvet nose.

A few minutes later, they led the horses out an unguarded side gate. Beyond the noise of the palace, the city was dark and deserted—the only sound was the clomping of horses' hooves on the cobbled streets. They walked to the city limits and stopped.

"Before we go any farther," Megan said. "We should take a look at that clue and figure out where we have to go next."

Diedrich reached into the bag, which was tied to his saddle, and pulled out the wooden scarab. He flipped it over and tilted it until the letters engraved into the bottom caught the scant light.

"'Avenging son quells evil's wrath, the Eye of the Raptor shows the path. Wisdom's book is what you seek.'"

Rachel groaned. "It's not a very good poem. More like a haiku. What the bloody hell does it mean?"

"Only so much fits on the bottom of a scarab," Megan reasoned. "And if we knew what it meant it wouldn't be much of a challenge, would it?"

"No, but our lives would be far easier."

Megan smiled. "True. Diedrich, you've led us this far. Any ideas?"

She had learned through experience how to deal with the fact she didn't always understand the clues. Everyone had something they were good at, and she wasn't good at this. Relying on her friends didn't make her weak or stupid.

Diedrich shook his head. "I can guess, but I am not positive. The avenging son might be Horus."

"And just who was he?" Rachel said.

Diedrich looked at the sky, painted with a million stars, as if the answer were written on them.

"He was Osiris's son, but only a baby when his father was killed. I think the story goes that Osiris's spirit visited him while he was a child, and Horus killed Set when he grew up. Cut off his head or something."

"Why must every one of these stories be so gross?" Megan asked.

Diedrich stared at the scarab. "I am trying to remember. There was something about a god who helped Horus."

"Can we move this along?" Rachel said. "Who knows how long your dad is going to be unconscious."

Megan pulled her lips in tight and narrowed her eyes.

Rachel shrugged. "What?"

"Could you chill, for just a minute?"

Rachel's mouth fell open, and Megan could hardly believe she'd spoken to her best friend like that. "Badgering him won't help. It's okay, Diedrich, take your time."

Rachel glared at her, then looked away.

"Yeah, sorry, Miss Librarian. I'm a little on edge. Can't imagine why."

Her attitude stung. "That was mean."

Rachel shrugged, but said nothing. Megan let it go. She'd apologize later, when they had time to talk.

Diedrich leaned against the flank of his horse and smacked himself on the top of his head.

"Think, think."

"Come on, come on," Rachel muttered, with a nervous glance behind them. "Please."

His head popped up. "I know where we have to go. Come on, we have a ride ahead of us."

The sun came up as they rode out of the city and into the fields and farmland that surrounded it. With Byblos miles behind them, Diedrich started talking.

"I remember the whole story now. Once Horus was old enough to avenge his father's death, he sought out Thoth, the god of wisdom. Horus asked to look into Thoth's eyes, for it was said that one could see the future there. Set saw what Horus was about to do, and changed himself into a black boar. The boar distracted Horus, and his eye was burned out."

"Ouch," Rachel said. "So, what's the rest of the story?"

"Thoth put Horus into a dark room and cared for him for three days. His eye, the Eye of Horus, became a symbol of protection to the Egyptians. There is even some mathematical equation that goes along with it. It is all very scientific."

"But the clue said 'the Eye of the Raptor'," Claire said. "Not 'the eye of the son'."

"Ah, but Horus is represented by a falcon-headed man, or sometimes just a falcon," Diedrich said.

"And a falcon is a raptor?" Megan said.

"Yes," Rachel said, with a bit of attitude. "You know, a bird of prey?"

"I'm not the birdwatcher," Megan said. *Why is she still mad at me? I apologized for snapping at her twice already!* Once they had left the city, Megan had offered her heartfelt apology to Rachel. Rachel had seemed to accept, but she was still a bit raw, it seemed.

"Where does all this lead?" Rachel asked. "And what's this book of wisdom that we're supposed to be seeking?"

"I am just guessing here," Diedrich said, "but there is a temple dedicated to Horus at Edfu. It is along the west bank of the Nile, south of Thebes. If we keep a good pace, do not lose our way, and cut cross-country, we should be there by nightfall. We will have to find someone to take us across the river."

He sighed. "As far as the book is concerned, it could be the *Book of Thoth*. It is like the *Book of the Dead*, but made of gold. It is filled with spells used to enchant the heavens and earth, and to learn the language of the birds and beasts."

"What makes you think that's the book we're looking for?" Megan asked.

He shrugged. "Thoth is the god of wisdom, remember? It is the best I could come up with. I am probably not right anyway. The book is a myth—it does not exist."

Megan clucked to her horse and sped up. "Haven't you learned yet? In Sir Gregory's world, Diedrich, nothing is a myth."

Twilight settled over Edfu. Four horses clopped along the streets, which glistened from a short shower that had passed through a while before. It had been a long, hot journey from Byblos. They had reached Thebes at mid-day and stopped to rest the horses and get some food. Thebes was a huge city, crowded, filled with people of all races and from all places; no one bothered them or gave them strange looks like they had in Byblos.

They kept an eye out for Josef Hemmlich, knowing he would follow them if he had even an inkling of where they were headed. But there was no sign of him. If he was following them, he was an expert at hiding.

Rachel traded her necklace to the owner of a pole barge to get them across the Nile.

"It's not like I can take it back with me," she said, just a little wistfully, to Megan as she handed over the lapis-and-turquoise collar. "I won't miss it."

Once across, they rode south. At Diedrich's suggestion, they stayed outside of Edfu proper until nearly dark. Edfu was smaller than Thebes, and they would be more easily seen. They would wait until they could slip inside the temple unnoticed.

The temple loomed high above the city, its two flat-topped, rhomboid-shaped pylons reaching into the velvet twilight sky. The size of it struck Megan with awe. It was easily fifteen stories, the size of a small skyscraper, and sand-colored.

"How did the Egyptians build something so big without any machines," she said.

"Very slowly," Diedrich said. "Although there are about as many theories about the exact method as there are stars in the sky. My father told me most scientists think the Great Pyramid at Giza took over twenty years to complete."

"Twenty bloody years?" Rachel said, aghast. "Talk about job security."

Claire pushed her glasses up her nose. "There was definitely job security, but it was dangerous work. There was also a good chance you could die in the process."

Rachel shuddered. "I'm so very glad I live in the twenty-first century."

Shallow bowls of flaming oil stood on either side of the temple steps to light their way. They dismounted and climbed the stairs to the huge front doors. No one was there.

On the other side of the door was an open-air, colonnaded courtyard, lit only by the stars and moon. At the opposite end was a tall stone statue of a falcon.

"We need to find that book," Megan whispered. Although they were out in the open, and no one else was around, the temple exuded an air of mystery. The shadows seemed to murmur secrets of the ancient world. She didn't want to disturb whatever it was that lived here.

Claire must have been thinking the same thing, because she whispered back, "Remember the treasury in the Parthenon? This temple might also have a place where they keep all their treasures and sacred objects, I should think. We need to look there first."

Holding hands, they crossed the courtyard and found a door at the far end behind the falcon statue. Beyond it was a room supported by smooth, round columns with tops that were carved in the shape of lotus blossoms. It was wider than it was long, and empty.

"This is one of the hypostyle halls," Diedrich said. "I do not remember what it is used for, just the name."

"Fabulous," Rachel snapped. "Let me get you a little flag, and you can lead this tour."

"Sorry," Diedrich said. "I just thought you might be interested."

"The only thing I'm interested in is going home, thanks." Rachel's shoulders drooped, and she closed her eyes. "I am so sorry; I tend to bite people's heads off when I'm nervous. It's a defense mechanism. This place is quite eerie. Makes my skin crawl."

There was a second hypostyle hall beyond the first. Three doors led from the hall—one directly across from the columns, and one on each end. Megan opened the one on the left and found a library.

It wasn't like any library she had been in before. Instead of shelves, hundreds of small cubicles lined the walls. Tightly rolled scrolls filled each one. There were hundreds, if not thousands, of pages. The Library of Athena had cubbyhole shelves just like these, but on a much smaller scale. Bailey had mentioned once the scrolls were from some library in Alexandria.

Megan wondered what was written on these. Carefully, she pulled one out and unrolled it. Rows of tiny pictograms covered the page. She rolled it back up and put it away.

Rachel stuck her head into the room on the other end and reported it was nothing more than a storeroom.

The third door opened into a small room Diedrich said was a vestibule. The walls here were inscribed with the story of Horus and Hathor, Horus's wife and the Egyptian goddess of goodness and love.

"Why couldn't we be looking for something of hers?" Rachel said. "Goodness and love sounds like a lot more fun than this."

They passed through a second vestibule, covered in more hieroglyphs.

"I wonder where all the priests are," Diedrich said. "I did not think they left the temple at night."

"Maybe they sleep somewhere else," Megan said. "Like in a dormitory or something."

The next room was large and square. The sanctuary.

Lit braziers, hung from the ceiling, painted the walls with an eerie pattern of light and shadow. A brass branch of four lit candles, stood inside the door. The right-hand wall, like the vestibule, was covered by a series of drawings.

Set into the back wall, which was made of polished granite instead of sand-colored stone, was an alcove as tall as Megan and three feet wide. The outer edge was decorated with small hieroglyphs carved into the stone. In front of the recess sat another statue of Horus, this one made of gold.

"Okay, no book in here," Rachel said. "Now what?"

"Look," Megan said, pointing. Directly above the alcove, a large, colorful eye was painted on the wall. Megan had seen it before, in textbooks and on websites about Egypt.

"Is that the Eye of Horus?"

Diedrich nodded. "The eye of the Raptor. The clue said it guards the path. We just have to figure out which way it is leading us." He turned from the niche and studied the painted wall. "I think we have a problem."

"That's nothing new." Rachel left the statue and stood next to him. "What kind of problem?"

He pointed to the drawings.

"This says that in order to get the book, we have to defeat the monster that guards it."

"Do you know what the monster is?" Megan asked.

Diedrich shook his head. "I may be wrong, but I have an idea. I've been thinking about the *Book of Thoth* itself."

"I thought it was a myth," Claire said.

"It is. There is an obscure story that surrounds it that says the book is kept in an iron box and guarded by a snake that cannot die." He ran a hand over part of the painting. "According to this, Sir Gregory's taken that story to heart."

Megan put a hand on her hip and ran the other through her hair.

"So, we have to kill a snake that can't die, to get a book that doesn't exist." She slapped herself on the leg, annoyed. "This sucks. Once again, time to try and avoid death. La, la, la. Who thinks this stuff up? Wait, don't answer that, I already know. Fine. We might as well get started."

"First we have to find the path." Diedrich searched the perimeter of the room. He pushed various places on the wall with the hieroglyphs, but it didn't budge. He circled the walls, pushing and pulling on things.

Something tugged at Megan's memory. She pulled the scarab out of the bag and put the bag on the floor.

"The Eye is here." She pointed at it, above the recess. "So, I'm thinking wherever we have to go is here, too."

"Is that not kind of obvious?" Diedrich said.

Megan pursed her lips. "Well, yes, obvious as to where the path is, but not how to get in."

Rachel sighed. "This is unbearable. My brain hurts." In her most dramatic way, she gave another sigh and leaned her arm on Horus's golden beak, her forehead on her arm. There was a click, and the great bird's beak dropped.

Behind it, the back of the granite niche swung inward.

"Brilliant," Claire said.

"Clever girl." Megan mussed Rachel's hair. Rachel swatted the hand away like it was a gnat.

Diedrich stuck his head inside the opening and pulled it back out.

"What's it look like in there, Diedrich?" Megan said.

"Dark."

"Gee, thanks."

Behind the door was a long, narrow hallway of rough-hewn gray stone. Diedrich took the lead, lighting the way with one of the candles from the stand in the sanctuary. Rachel and Claire followed next, and Megan took the rear with another candle.

Her hands shook, and her mouth went dry. She hated small, cramped spaces, but on top of that, she was afraid. She had faced monsters before. A Gorgon who could turn a person to stone, Cetus the sea monster. The Minotaur, who ate people sent as a sacrifice. A Sphinx who had threatened to kill them if they didn't answer her three riddles correctly.

Her friends had known how to beat those, at least in theory, because they knew the monster's stories. But this? A snake that could not die? That was a different thing altogether.

She watched the back of Claire's head bob along ahead of her. Claire was smart, possibly the most book-smart person she knew. Rachel had street-smarts, and she was quick on her feet. And Diedrich was knowledgeable and had turned out to be incredibly brave, much braver than she could be. Megan trusted them, even with her life.

She hoped one of them knew how to defeat this monster, or they all could die.

# CHAPTER 15

*If You're Stealing the Book of Thoth, Bring Breath Mints.*

AT THE END OF THE PASSAGE, THEY WALKED INTO A DARK CHAMBER FORTY feet wide and sixty feet long. Six plain stone columns held up the rough, flat ceiling. The chamber was dark and shadowy, and the air cool and damp. Somewhere nearby, water dripped.

A shiver ran up Megan's spine, but it had nothing to do with the temperature. A few torches burned, and Megan wondered who had come down here to light them.

At the far end of the chamber, on a carved stone pedestal surrounded by tall brass candlesticks, sat a box.

"Well, this certainly has the creepy thing going for it, but I don't see a monster," Megan said. "Maybe it's his day off?" she quipped as she scanned the walls and floors. "I mean, we can hope, can't we?"

"There's the box," Rachel said. "I'll just pop over there and nick it, and we can be off."

"Don't move," Claire's whisper was urgent. "Keep your eyes on the floor. Whatever you do, don't look up."

"Uh, Claire, we sort of need to see where we're going," Rachel said.

"I've been thinking," Claire said, her gaze pinned to the floor ahead of her, "and I think there's a basilisk in here guarding that book."

"A what-a-lisk?" Megan asked. *How does she know all this stuff? I can't even remember what homework is due when, half the time!* She was often in awe of Claire's ability to remember the tiniest details of things they learned in class.

The schoolteacher tone in Claire's voice came through loud and clear. "A basilisk. The basilisk is a creature found in the myths of many ancient cultures. There are many different descriptions of what it actually looks like, but most agree it's a hooded snake of some size. A few scholars believe the basilisk is nothing more than an exaggeration of the Egyptian cobra."

"Sounds pretty stupid to me," Rachel said. "Cobras are real."

"Yes, but the basilisk has many of the same characteristics. It's been described as having a white mark on its head, and a hood, and it's supposed to spit deadly venom, just like a cobra. But a basilisk is only born from a spherical egg laid by a seven-year-old cock during the time when Sirius the Dog Star is in the sky, and hatched by a snake or a toad."

Rachel laughed—it echoed around the chamber, and she put one hand over her mouth until the giggles subsided.

"So, that exhibit at the London Zoo is empty, then?"

"Rachel, I'm serious," Claire retorted. "As I was saying. A basilisk's breath can break rock, and it can kill with just a glance."

"Like Medusa, but with killer breath?" Rachel replied.

"And I thought our English professor was the King of Halitosis." Megan knew their situation was serious, but, like Rachel, she needed something to break the terrific tension she felt growing in the pit of her stomach.

"So, how do we kill it?" Diedrich glanced around the chamber. "If it can sneak up and kill us, how can we kill it?"

Claire continued, "I'm not sure, exactly. As far as I remember, only two things can kill a basilisk—the crowing of a cock, and its own reflection."

"Just like Medusa," Megan said. "That's how we killed her, we showed her her own reflection and she turned herself to stone."

"Almost, yes. If it sees itself, it will scare itself to death. Unlike Medusa, we can't look at the reflection. We won't die, but something bad will happen. I think."

"What do you mean, you think?" Megan said.

"I'm not positive. I don't remember. There are so many different stories. I never thought I would actually have to face one."

"Can I ask where in the world you read about basilisks?" Rachel said.

"I was bored one Saturday, and I did an internet search of mythical creatures. It was after the Crown of Zeus. There are some fascinating beasts. I found a listing of them, and the basilisk was one of the more interesting ones."

"None of you happens to have a rooster in your pocket, do you?" Rachel fumed. "Can't we just once have something be simple?"

From the shadows came the sound of something sliding across stone.

Not sliding.

*Slithering.* Megan felt her heart skip a beat and then speed up. Oh. No.

"Listen," Claire said. The slithering echoed through the room. "It's behind the walls. It might not know we're even here. Let's get the box and be gone before it does."

"There is probably at least one booby trap between here and that box," Diedrich said. "Besides, there has to be a way for it to get out here. The snake could still jump out and bite us, or spit its venom at us."

The slithering noise sounded much closer this time.

Rachel choked back a sob. "We're going to die here."

Megan was inclined to agree. *I can't see how we're going to get out of here. If we leave now, we don't get the book, which probably has the clue. And if we go for the book, we'll probably get killed by the snake. This sucks.*

Claire cleared her throat. "No, we're not. We're going to do the best we can. Everyone just needs to pay attention to what's around them. If you see something moving, look away."

Rachel's voice squeaked—Megan heard the panic and fear behind it. "How can we?"

Megan took a deep breath, and reached for Diedrich's hand. It was strong, warm, and comforting.

"We do it together, and we watch out for each other."

They started toward the far side of the room. Megan kept her eyes to the floor, but the view wasn't pleasant. The shifting firelight revealed bones, large and small, sitting in piles and strewn across the floor. The leftovers of Basilisk's Meals Past. It reminded her of the Minotaur's cave, except it didn't smell half as bad.

"Something's over there," Rachel said. Her head was bowed, but her eyes were shifted to the right.

Megan peeked. She shouldn't have, but she couldn't help it. A glint of something shiny—gold, or perhaps brass—leaning against the wall caught her eye. "What is it, do you think?" she asked.

"Doesn't matter," Claire said. "We need to keep on-task."

Quiet as mice, they continued across the room. The slithering stopped, and the only sound Megan heard was Diedrich's breathing. She kept close to his side.

They reached the other end of the room safely. "So much for booby traps," Rachel said.

"We're not out of the woods yet," Claire warned. "We still have to get out—with the book."

"I'll get the book," Megan said.

"No," Diedrich said. "I will do it."

Megan shook her head. "I'm the Librarian. This is my job, okay? Just… let me. You guys back up, just in case." If she managed to get the book, they'd be a step closer to getting home, and maybe Rachel would stop being mad at her.

"In case of what?" Rachel said. "Oh, wait, never mind. I don't want to know."

Megan's heart thundered in her ears as she reached out and grasped the handles on either side of the box. She tugged, but the box didn't budge.

"It's too heavy, I can't move it." She felt Diedrich's presence beside her.

"I told you not to," she said.

"We are all in this together. The only reason you are in here is because of my father. So… let *me*." He grabbed the handles, and the muscles in his forearms strained. There was a small grunt as he hoisted the box from its place.

"I have it," he whispered. "Let's get out of here."

"Go out the same way we came in," Claire said. "Seems safest."

They hadn't yet turned away from the pedestal when they heard the slithering sound, this time extremely close. Megan couldn't look up. She also couldn't move. Once again, she was paralyzed with fear.

"Where is it?" Rachel whispered.

"Can't tell," Diedrich said. "But this box is very heavy. We cannot stay—"

There was a grinding sound as the pedestal sank into the floor.

"Booby trap," Claire said.

"Thanks for the update," Rachel replied.

A door—a large door—slid open in the rear wall.

"It's coming! Run!" Claire yelled. "Keep your eyes down, and head for the exit."

They had no sooner turned around than one of the columns that supported the roof burst into a thousand pieces.

Megan's body unlocked, and then she was on autopilot. Her legs propelled her across the room. The rustling of the basilisk sounded right behind them. Rachel kept pace with Megan easily—they were in good shape from playing hockey — but Claire was much slower, and Diedrich carried the heavy chest. Both of them fell behind.

"We have to do something." Megan panted to Rachel between breaths. "We have to help them."

"Distract it," Rachel gasped. "Split its concentration." She grabbed Megan's wrist and pulled her to the left. They doubled back, ducking behind broken pieces of rock. The tail of the basilisk slithered past.

*This running-away thing is getting old. If it's not a man with a big knife, it's a giant snake with murderous halitosis.*

"Head down." Rachel jumped out of her hiding place and yelled, "Hey, over here — snake!"

"Rachel," Megan called. "Snakes don't have ears. They feel vibrations." She had no idea why that little factoid had suddenly come to her, but when was the last time she faced a giant snake?

"All right then, I'll just have to get his attention another way."

Megan saw Rachel's feet leave the floor — she jumped up and down on the floor, pounding her feet into the rock.

The slithering stopped.

"It's coming back, Meg," Rachel screamed. "Watch out!" There was a strange, terrible sound, like an angry roar. Megan saw a flash of golden scaly hide. Another column at the front of the room crumbled in a shower of dust and falling rock. Rachel ran back to Megan, and together they went to the very back of the room.

"Make sure you stomp your feet," Rachel said. "I want him to follow us."

They turned left and ran along the back wall. Megan grabbed one of the candlesticks from beside where the pedestal had been and banged it on the floor, making a sound like a bell. The basilisk's golden body made a wide circle as it turned to follow.

Megan dropped the candlestick; it made a racket as it hit the floor. She ran toward the corner then cut it short. Heading again toward the front of the room, she pressed against one of the remaining columns.

"We can't run forever. My legs are starting to feel it. We need to get back to the door."

"Claire, Diedrich, where are you?" Rachel shouted.

Claire's voice sounded far away. "We're okay. Bring him back this way. Hurry."

"What? Are you nuts?"

Diedrich answered. "Just do it."

"You've run farther during a hockey game," Rachel scolded Megan. "Come on."

Megan knew she had to make it, no matter what her legs told her. Rachel darted toward the center of the room. Megan wiped the sweat from her forehead and followed. Up the center aisle, Megan on Rachel's heels, they headed for the door.

Diedrich and Claire were there. They held something large and shiny between them, and their faces were turned toward the wall.

Megan felt the basilisk behind her. It was going to be close. The snake was going to have to come down to her level if it wanted to kill her. She wasn't going to make it easy—he was going to have to just eat her. She refused to turn her head and look at it.

Burning pain shot through Megan's leg. She stumbled and fell. As she clutched her calf, and her first thought was the snake had shot its venom into her leg. She touched it, and found it whole. The muscle quivered and jumped. It was just a cramp.

She had little time to rejoice. The basilisk was almost on her. She stood, but when she put her full weight on the cramping leg, it buckled.

"Megan! Come on, you can make it." Rachel stood next to Claire, but her face was not turned away. She locked eyes with Megan. Megan forced herself forward. The pain seared up her leg, protesting the effort.

She was only three feet away from Rachel's outstretched hand when she slipped again.

"Arghhh!"

A high-pitched screech bounced off the stone and echoed around the room. Face down on the floor, Megan laid her head against the cool stone and waited for the basilisk's strike to come. She covered her ears and tensed her shoulders. Any second now, it would all be over.

She thought about her father. How would he take losing another member of his family? She wished she could say goodbye; and she hoped, if nothing else, the monster would be so busy with her that her friends could get away and figure out how to get home.

*Bailey's going to have to find a new Librarian.*

She heard yelling, and a thump. Then, everything went silent.

"Hey, Megan, you wanna get up off the floor?" Rachel said.

Megan lifted her head. Rachel stood over her, beaming. "Would you like some help?"

She rolled over. Diedrich and Claire stood on either side of her. In their hands, they held a round, shiny, shallow bowl above her body like a shield.

"Where did you find that?" she said, ecstatic to be alive.

"It was the shiny thing against the wall that Claire said didn't matter," Rachel said.

"Would you move, please?" Claire said. "My arms are burning, and I don't think you want me to drop this on you."

Megan scooted out from beneath the bowl, and her friends let it fall to the floor with a resounding crash. She sat up... and screamed.

The basilisk lay on the floor, dead. It was a huge beast, easily twenty feet long and four feet thick in the middle. Its eyes, the same bright-yellow shade as its skin, with black slits for pupils, were frozen open. The beast's mouth gaped, its long fangs dripping with thick, slimy venom.

"It was bizarre," Diedrich said. "That thing saw its own reflection and, well, dropped dead. Just like Claire said it would."

"It can't hurt us now?" Megan's whole body shook violently as the realization of how close she had come to death settled over her. Her stomach churned—if there had been anything in it, she would have thrown it up.

Diedrich sat next to her, put a reassuring arm around her shoulders, and pulled her close.

"No, it cannot hurt us," he said into her hair.

Megan burst into tears, and immediately felt stupid for doing so. She wept like a baby, big choking sobs that wracked her body. *I want to go home.*

Diedrich rocked her, and Claire and Rachel joined the embrace.

"It's all right now, love," Rachel whispered, and just like that, everything between them was okay again.

"You were right. This is all your father's fault," Megan mumbled into Diedrich's chest.

"I will make him pay for it, too. Do not worry."

There was a rumbling above and around them, like an earthquake.

"Great bloody snake took out most of the roof supports," Rachel said. "I think it's going to collapse."

Megan's tears subsided, and they all stood up. She still couldn't walk well, although the cramp had finally relented. Rachel and Claire each took an arm to support her, and helped her to the door. Diedrich collected the box for which they'd risked their lives.

They single-filed back through the narrow corridor that led to the sanctuary. Megan braced herself against the walls, and Rachel kept a hand on her back to steady her. There were more rumblings, each one longer and louder than the last.

"Can we please speed things up?" Rachel said. "Sorry, Meg, but I don't want to be in this tiny space when that room back there crumbles."

They squeezed around the golden statue of Horus and emerged into the still-empty sanctuary. Rachel pushed the falcon's beak straight, and the door swung shut. Not more than three seconds later, there was a mighty crash from behind the wall.

Megan took a grateful breath of fresh air and slumped onto the floor. She rubbed her calf vigorously. The muscle throbbed. She had been through this enough times to know she needed water.

Diedrich set the box in front of her.

"I think you have more than earned the right to open it."

Megan scooted forward. The box was not locked; a simple turnkey stuck out from the front of the lid. She spun it once, and two latches sprung open. With a deep breath, she lifted the lid.

A brilliant golden glimmer washed over her face. Megan reached inside and took the book out of the case. It was three-ring bound, with two hard covers engraved with hieroglyphs like the black *Book of the Dead*. But the covers of this book were heavy, the pages made of polished gold, hammered almost to paper-thinness. This wasn't just a book — it was a work of art.

"It's so beautiful," Rachel said. "Do you think it's the real one?"

Diedrich cocked an eyebrow. "Are you serious? I told you, this does not really exist. Sir Gregory probably wrote it into the story based on the myth."

"Yeah, and Pandora's Box isn't real, either, but I've seen it." Megan ran her hands over the cover. It was cool to the touch, the tiny pictographs like a miniature landscape of hills and valleys. "And like the Pandora's Box I found in the Minotaur's cave, this is probably a copy. The real one might be in the vault back in the Library, or in its own book, for all I know." She pushed her hair back off of her forehead. "What does it say, Diedrich?"

He bit the inside of his cheek and inspected the book's front cover.

"It is a spell to understand the language of animals." He pointed to each hieroglyph as he read the spell aloud in ancient Egyptian.

"That's not much help to us, now, is it," Rachel said. "Where's the bloody clue?"

Megan flipped the book open and paged through the golden leaves. She couldn't read any of it, of course, but something at the back caught her eye.

"Wait a second, this looks promising."

The last page was not gold, but thick, soft papyrus. There were no hieroglyphs, only words written in elegant English script—Sir Gregory's handwriting.

"'In the home of the queen who was called goddess, she who held eternity in her hands—the path of death leads you to life.'"

"Could it be any more vague?" Rachel kicked a small rock, and it skittered and clattered across the floor. "That makes even less sense than the last one."

Megan tilted her head to one side. Something about the clue sounded familiar—it reminded her of something she had seen recently. She closed her eyes and knitted her brows, thinking. What was it?

The answer hit her like a lightning bolt. "I know what this means."

She watched the eyes of her three companions grow wide.

"How?" Claire said.

Megan smiled. Ha! *Claire isn't the only one who remembers what she reads.*

"Because of the book Mr. Hemmlich threw across the floor the night he was skulking around the upstairs library. The one I was looking at when you and Rachel found me the other day. It's Queen Nefertari."

Diedrich smiled. "I think you're right. Father said something about her in relation to the Ankh not long before we left for England. I blew him off, figured he was ranting again."

"There's a painting on the inside of her tomb of her holding the Ankh. That's probably why your father looked at that book in the first place. He might have thought Sir Gregory hid his notes about the Ankh in there or something."

"And she's the queen that was called a goddess?" Claire said.

"She was the wife of Rameses II, and he was totally devoted to her. At some temple, uh, Abu Simple—"

"Abu Simbel," Diedrich corrected.

"Whatever. Anyway, there is a huge statue of Nefertari dressed as Hathor."

"That goodness-and-love girlie?" Rachel asked.

"The book said Nefertari was also called the Wife of the Gods." Megan sat back and smiled, happy to finally feel like she'd contributed.

Rachel's face lit up as she put it all together. "Where is this temple?"

"Abu Simbel," Diedrich said, "is not far upriver. But we have to go the other direction."

Megan's shoulders slumped. *What does he mean?* She was so sure she knew the answer.

"Wait a minute. Why…?"

Diedrich patted her on the shoulder. "You were almost right. The clue says 'the path of death leads you to life.' If we are looking for Nefertari on the path of death, we have to go back to Thebes. To the Valley of the Queens."

"Please don't tell me we have to break into someone's tomb," Rachel said.

Diedrich nodded.

"Figures."

# CHAPTER 16

*Nefertari's Secret Will Bite You On the... Finger.*

"We should not have to actually break in." Diedrich helped Megan to her feet. She slid the golden book inside the bag beside the *Book of the Dead*, then hoisted the bag over her head and across her chest. It was heavy, but not uncomfortable.

She put her arm around Diedrich's waist, and he held her by the shoulders. Her leg felt almost normal, and she was able to keep up with her friends as they left the vacant temple.

"I thought they were sealed," Megan said. "Once the person was, um, put inside."

"It will be closed, probably, but not sealed. The Egyptians were all about being comfortable in the afterlife. A queen as important as Nefertari would have servants to look after her and her tomb—make sure she had fresh food and such."

"Isn't she dead?" Rachel said. "What use could she have for food?"

"As I explained to Claire and Megan before we caught up with you, the Egyptians believed the souls of the dead walked around during the day, and returned to their tombs at night. The soul needed sustenance."

"These people were nuts." Rachel shook her head. "Feeding dead people. Absolutely mad."

Diedrich boosted Megan onto her horse, made sure she was settled, and went to his own mount, who gave a loud whinny. He froze, one foot in the stirrup. A strange look crept over his face.

Megan looked around, thinking perhaps his father had found them again. Diedrich put his foot back down and stood beside his horse's head. He put his ear close to the roan's nose and listened. The horse shook his head and gave another loud whinny.

"Diedrich, what's wrong?" Megan asked. "Is your horse okay?"

The strange look remained. "He is fine, but he is hungry, and he says he could use some water."

Megan wrinkled her nose. "Huh?"

"All the horses need a drink, at least that is what I think he said." Diedrich took a step back and rubbed his face with both hands. Nearby a dog barked. Diedrich's head whipped in the direction of the sound. "No way. It is not possible."

"Diedrich?" Rachel waved her hands to get his attention. "Mind sharing? We can't go until you tell us which way."

"That spell I read, on the cover of the book. It... worked," Diedrich muttered, as if he were talking to himself. "I can understand what the animals are saying. The horses are thirsty, and that dog was telling someone to get away from his house before he bit them."

"You're mental," Claire said, her brow furrowed with concern. "The stress has finally broken him."

Diedrich shook his head. "I thought so, too, but, no. I understand them as clearly as I do you."

"I guess that resolves the question of whether or not the book is real," Rachel said. "Well, then, let's get the horses a drink, plus something for us to eat, and move on."

They rode north, back toward Thebes. The road was filled with carts, horses, and camels. It was early morning when they left Edfu, with everyone sufficiently watered and fed. People were out and about with the rising sun to avoid the heat of the day. The Nile ran swiftly alongside the wide, hard-packed dirt road. Papyrus reeds grew tall along the shore, swaying in the current. Turtles sunned themselves on rocks. It was really quite beautiful—if you ignored the bugs. Megan slapped at a large mosquito that landed on her upper arm. Silently she cursed Sir Gregory Archibald. You would think he would have left the insects out of the story. She watched a series of boats cast off from the shore. Papyrus sailboats, wooden fishing boats and more barges floated across the wide expanse of water. The barges were loaded with goods—vegetables and livestock—for trade at the market in Thebes.

The city itself straddled the river. The sun sparkled off the tips of the many obelisks that stuck up from the skyline on the east bank in the main part of the city. Along the west bank, the city was oddly deserted. The people that had crowded around them on the road earlier had all left the road, boarding boats or taking one of the smaller roads that branched off and led to the small villages on the outskirts of the city.

"Where did everyone go?" Megan said.

"We are coming to the Necropolis," Diedrich said in a hushed voice. "It is not a place many people visit."

"What's a Necropolis?" Rachel said.

"The direct translation would be 'City of the Dead'," Claire said. "In other words, a cemetery."

Rachel went pale. "I don't like this. What if we run into some mummy come back to life and gone mad?"

Megan rolled her eyes. "You watch too many movies. I told you the *Book of the Dead* doesn't do that."

"Excuse me, we just escaped a giant snake that can kill by looking at you, so who knows what other crazy things are in this book?"

Megan sighed. "Good point."

Diedrich stopped them in front of a small temple. A few men and women, dressed plainly and with no jewelry — slaves — walked between the short, blocky structures that marked where people were buried. Many carried covered baskets into and out of the crypts.

"Come on, this way." Diedrich pulled his horse to the left, onto a road that led into the heart of the City of the Dead. "The valley is on the other side."

"This one." Diedrich stopped along the valley path, in front of one of the many rectangular openings carved in the base of the hills that rose above them like sleeping giants. "They all look the same," Rachel said, her voice trembling. "How can you be sure this is the right one?"

"Because of the cartouche above the door." He pointed to a series of characters inside a stretched-out oval. "That is her name. I recognize it from my father's notes."

Rachel's face went pale. "Do we have to go in right this minute?"

"We could wait until nightfall, Rach," Megan said. "You know, when all the spirits return to their tombs. I know the mummies will be glad to see you then."

Diedrich shook his head, his face serious. He obviously wasn't in the mood to joke.

"I do not think we should. Who knows where my father is."

Rachel flapped a hand at him. "We left him behind in Byblos. He doesn't know what the clue on the scarab said, and he missed us in Edfu, so he doesn't have any idea where we are." Her horse danced beneath her; it was nervous about being near the tomb, too.

"Diedrich, can you please ask this nag to stand still?" Diedrich dismounted and spoke to the animal in a series of whinnies and neighs. The horse shook her head and stomped the ground, but stopped moving her feet. He patted the mare's nose.

"Do you think we do not stand out?" he said to Rachel. "That no one would remember us? It would be only too easy for my father to ask if people have seen a boy that looks like him and a girl with red hair. He is nothing if not resourceful. Even if he did not find anyone who saw us, he knows the story behind the Ankh. He will be here eventually, if, though unlikely, he hasn't already come and gone while we were occupied with the basilisk."

Megan didn't want to think about the consequences of that statement. If Josef had already gotten the Ankh, or the next clue, all four of them were doomed to spend the rest of their lives inside this book.

"So, how do we get in?" Claire said.

"Come over here." Diedrich waved the girls to the opening and disappeared inside. Rachel, Claire and Megan dismounted and followed him.

A flight of stairs carved out of the rock led down to a door made of stone. The walls of the stairwell were painted in bright colors with images of Egyptian men, women, and animals. Above the door was the cartouche. Beneath that was a pair of blue-and-gold wings, outstretched to cover the entire width of the door frame. Between them was an orange-and-yellow circle.

"Winged sun disk," Diedrich said. "So that Ra the Sun God will look favorably on the soul within." He pushed on the door, grunting as he shoved the thick door open to reveal a short narrow passage. The air was cool and dry; the smell of incense wafted on the air. Torches kept the gloom of the darkened corridor at bay. They flickered in the breeze from the open door.

Rachel jumped, frightened by her own shadow as it danced across the wall next to them.

"Where do you think they keep the mummy?" she said in a hoarse whisper.

"In a great glass case along the wall," Claire said with a straight face. "So you can see it up close, when you tour the tomb on school trips."

Rachel gasped. "Really?"

"No, not really, you dolt. It's in a sarcophagus in the burial chamber. Inside three coffins, if I'm not mistaken. So, stop your bleating."

Rachel wiped her brow and sighed with relief. A second later, she screamed.

"What now?" Megan said.

Rachel pointed at the floor. Huge, hairy spiders crawled along the corridor. They scuttled away from the intruders and into the shadows.

"Heart of a lion," Diedrich said with a laugh and a shake of his head. "You can face a basilisk but not a spider?"

Rachel scratched the back of her neck. "They surprised me, alright?"

An opening appeared to the right. They stepped into a large square room filled with treasure. Gold statues sat atop carved wooden tables, and a set of ornate gilt chairs stood against the back wall. Another table, long and narrow, was laid out as if for a banquet—plates and goblets, decanters of wine and piles of food vied for space on the table's top. In the very center of the room stood a golden chariot.

Rachel whistled. "No wonder people were into tomb robbing." She lifted a necklace from a box on the floor next to her. Emeralds sparkled in the torchlight. "What a haul."

Megan gave her a reproachful look. "Put that down. It's not real anyway, remember?"

As Rachel reluctantly put the necklace back she caressed a small, beautifully painted statue-like figure.

"And what's this? It's a pretty little knickknack."

"It is a mummified cat," Diedrich said nonchalantly.

Rachel yanked her hand back as if the statue was hot. "A what?"

"Cats were revered in ancient Egypt as guardians of the underworld. Important people often had their favorite cat mummified, placed in its own sarcophagus, and buried with them."

Rachel backed away. "I told you. Mental. Absolutely barking."

"That's enough, Rach." Megan said. "The Ankh should be here somewhere. We need to look for it."

"How do we know it's here?" Claire said. "We never found out where Sir Gregory discovered it."

"What do you mean?" Diedrich said.

"The Crown of Zeus," Megan explained. "Sir Gregory wrote in his diary about the place he dug it up in Greece, and recreated the place in the book. We figured out where to look for the Crown because we knew where it was supposed to be."

"But you do not know where the Ankh was found," Diedrich said slowly. He looked at the ceiling. "If it is really here in the tomb, I think it would be in the burial chamber." He glanced at Rachel. "Probably inside the sarcophagus. The queen would have wanted to be buried with it."

Megan furrowed her brow. "But the real Nefertari's tomb was dug up, and the Ankh wasn't there, or else your father wouldn't have come here looking for it. He'd already know where it was. Wasn't that the point of his expedition in the first place? To find some prince who had it?"

Diedrich rubbed his chin. "True, but I have never been sure that was not just a cover. What if it really was in Nefertari's tomb, and Sir Gregory got to it and dug it up before anyone else? Look, the clue led us here. And the line about leading us to life tells me we will find it here. If I were to look anywhere, the burial chamber is where I would start."

He marched out of the room and turned right. Megan grabbed a reluctant Rachel and dragged her along. Claire followed in their wake.

"Here's a question," she said. as she crunched a spider beneath her foot. "If the Ankh gives eternal life, and the real Nefertari actually possessed it, why did she die?"

Megan stopped short. "Good point. Like I said, I'll bet it's not here. So, we're probably looking for another clue." Diedrich hadn't heard what she'd said, or else ignored her, and continued down the corridor toward the back of the tomb.

"Bloody wonderful." Rachel yanked her wrist free of Megan's grasp and backed up, right into Claire. "I'll just wait outside."

"That might not be a bad idea, Rach," Megan said. "Go out there and stand watch. In case Josef Hemmlich, or anyone else, shows up."

Rachel's mouth dropped open. She looked from one end of the corridor, toward where Diedrich had gone, to the other, and the door to the outside.

"N—never mind. I'll come with you."

Megan smiled sweetly. "What made you change your mind?"

"I'd rather face a mummy than a crazy man."

Diedrich waited for them in the burial chamber, which was at the very back of the tomb. It was not as large as the treasure room, but the contents were no less valuable. In the center sat a rectangular stone casket. It was plain, without painting or decoration.

"Where's the gold-mask thing?" Rachel said. "Like the one I see in all the photos of King Tut?"

"If she has one, it will be on the mummy itself, in the innermost sarcophagus," Diedrich said. "Which is also where the Ankh—"

"I don't think the Ankh is in there," Megan interrupted.

He paused, then sighed. "Okay, tell me."

Megan told him about the conversation in the hallway. "So, if she had it, she shouldn't have died, right?"

Diedrich sat on the edge of the casket and rubbed his temples. Megan could only imagine what he was thinking.

"I guess it doesn't matter." He looked tired. "Ankh or another clue, either way, we should probably look in the sarcophagus first. We will have to find a way to lift the lid. It's not like Osiris's box. This must weigh a few hundred pounds."

"What is all this written on the walls?" Rachel asked.

Three of the walls of the chamber were covered with long columns of actual writing, not pictographs.

"This is Hieratic," Diedrich said. "Not as easy to read as hieroglyphs." He studied it for several minutes. "The *Book of the Dead*."

"Oh, yeah," Megan said. "I remember your father said they copied it onto the walls of tombs."

In the center of the fourth wall was a large painting. Megan was drawn to the image of a man wearing a loincloth. He had a dog's head. The collar he wore was painted in bright stripes of color. In the center, a real, oval-shaped blue jewel was set into the wall.

"How pretty." She reached up and touched it. A small slot opened beneath her hand.

"More secret openings," Claire said. "Can you see inside?"

Megan peered. "Not well. It's too dark. I think there's something in there, I just can't tell what."

The hole was very deep. She put her hand into the slot, then her arm up to the elbow. Her fingers brushed something that felt like a rolled-up piece of paper.

"Feels like a scroll or something," she said. "I can almost reach it."

Her arm was now entirely inside the wall. The paper scooted away to the very back of the slot. She extended her fingers as far as they would go. She felt something else, something hard. It must have had a sharp edge, because it bit her.

"Ow. That hurt."

"Megan?" Claire said. "You all right?"

"I think so." Megan grabbed the paper and pulled her arm out. A small red dot of blood perched on the tip of her index finger. "It doesn't look bad." She put it in her mouth and sucked on it.

"What does that say?" Rachel pointed to the paper in Megan's other hand.

Megan unrolled it and wrinkled her brow. "This doesn't make any sense. 'Before eternal life, you must pass through the Gates of Death.'"

Megan's head felt heavy. She let go of the scroll with one hand, and it snapped shut. She leaned on the edge of the slot, and the scroll rolled back to where it had come from.

"Megan, what's wrong?" Diedrich reached out and grabbed her by the elbow to steady her.

"I feel dizzy." The room spun before her eyes. Rachel and Claire's faces changed from concerned to upset. Megan sat on the cool stone floor. Her face was damp with sweat, and her arms broke out in gooseflesh.

"You look terrible," Rachel said. "Come on, we need to get you out of here."

Diedrich tried to lift Megan, but she slipped and fell from his grip. Her vision blurred.

"I can't see you," Megan said, her speech slurred. "I'm so cold." She was suddenly terrified. *What's happening!*

Her friends' voices called out to her, but they sounded very far away. She closed her eyes and slipped into darkness.

# CHAPTER 17

*Go To the Duat, Have Your Heart Weighed, They Said.*
*It'll Be Fun, They Said.*

MEGAN COULDN'T BREATHE. SHE GASPED, REACHING FOR ANY TINY BIT OF air. It felt like she was drowning — her lungs burned as she struggled to breathe. After a few rapid, shallow gulps of air, the burning stopped.

She lay on something warm and comfortable. She rolled her head to the side. Wherever she was, it was almost completely dark. Diedrich, Rachel, and Claire were gone.

*Did they just leave me here? Ugh — what happened? My head hurts.*

Megan sat up, and her head swam. Her eyes adjusted to the dim light, and she got a better look at her immediate surroundings.

*Uh-oh.*

To her right was a large black lake, its surface still and glassy. Small waves lapped at the shore, but they hardly made a sound. She couldn't see anything else. Warm, light-colored sand stuck to her hands and the backs of her arms and legs. If she hadn't been in a strange place, in the dark, the lakeside might have been very pleasant, just like a thousand days she had spent with her mother and father when she was little, when they would leave the city behind and spend all day in the bright sunshine and fresh air, eating a picnic lunch her mother had packed.

The memory gave her an unexpected twinge of loss, and bolstered her determination to figure out where she was and get home.

The last thing she could remember was pulling a piece of paper out of the hole in the wall of the tomb. She looked at her empty hands. Her head cleared, and she started to panic. *How did I get here? Where was here? Where are my friends?*

She struggled to keep her imagination from running away with her and concentrated on her current situation.

Megan stood and brushed the sand from her body. Turning in a circle, she narrowed her eyes to try and see a little better, hoping for inspiration to strike about which way she should go. The lake and the shore were inside a huge cavern. The dark rock walls seemed to have their own golden inner glow, allowing her to see. There was no exit.

"How do I get out of here?" Her voice bounced off the walls until it faded away.

As if in response, the water stirred. Megan backed away, afraid of what might emerge from the depths of the inky surface. She stood as far from the shoreline as she could and looked around for something that could be used as a weapon. There was nothing, not even a piece of driftwood.

She went back to watching the water.

A boat cut across the glossy surface in absolute silence. Like the walls, it gave off a soft golden light. She tried to see who was inside, but could only make out a tall shadowy figure standing in the prow.

The boat ran ashore, the hull scraping on the sand with a quiet hiss. Megan was awestruck. The low, curved vessel was made of gold, and encrusted with amethyst, jade, and onyx. The front was shaped like a great bird—a long, slim neck rose above the prow, ending in an elegant, sleek head with a long beak and large, round ruby eyes. A pair of golden wings stretched their feathers along the boat's sides.

A man, tall, thin, and dark-skinned, stood in the prow of the boat. He wore a long, bright-white robe that shimmered. His head was bald, but he had a long, thick braided beard. On his head sat a tall crown with a red disk in the center.

Megan, unexpectedly, felt no fear of the strange man. "Who are you?"

He looked down at her from the boat and gave a brilliant, beaming smile. "I am Ra."

Megan pulled her brows together. *Where have I heard that name before? Diedrich? He's told me so much stuff I can't keep it all straight anymore.*

Something told her this man would be able to help her. "Am I supposed to go with you?"

Ra nodded slowly and held out his hand. There was a moment when Megan wondered if she shouldn't be wary of this stranger, that it was another trap. But as soon as she slipped her hand into his, all thoughts were gone, and she felt nothing but peace, like she was floating.

She stepped into the boat and sat on a golden bench that stretched across the center. There was no one else with them, and no apparent source of propulsion; neither oars, nor sails, not that there was a wind to fill them.

As Ra waved his hand, the boat slid back into the water and turned around. They crossed the lake as silently as before. Megan watched over her shoulder as the shore slipped behind them.

Then, she saw nothing but more water and the cavern's walls as they glided along. Ra did not move from his place in the front of the boat.

"Where are we going?" Megan asked.

He didn't turn, nor did he answer her. She got the distinct feeling she would know soon enough, and maybe she was better off that way.

It felt like hours had passed when she spotted something up ahead — they had come to the far side of the lake. Another pale beach lay ahead, and beyond it was a pair of enormous double doors. Megan gasped in wonder. The doors matched the boat — made of gold and jewels, the bird in flight engraved across the front.

Her throat grew suddenly tight with unnamed fear. She wasn't sure she wanted to know what was on the other side of those doors.

The boat stopped so smoothly Megan wasn't certain they had reached the beach until Ra turned and looked at her. His face was serene, and his peaceful smile calmed her nerves as he helped her out and onto the beach.

"Am I supposed to go in there?"

Ra nodded.

"Well, uh, thanks for the ride." She gave a little wave. "I don't suppose you could tell me what I'm supposed to do once I'm in there?"

Ra, still smiling, shook his head. He made a deep bow, and with another wave of his hand, the boat slid back onto the lake and out of sight.

Megan faced the giant doors, her chest tight. She tried to take a deep breath but found it wasn't happening. With a hand that shook, she pushed one of the golden doors. It yielded easily to her touch. She stepped through, and into a long, white, brightly-lit hall with high ceilings and columns of gold.

"I'm in freaking Oz," she muttered. "When I get to the other end of this hall there'll be a giant green floating head and a man behind a curtain." She knew on some level that wasn't what she would find, but the thought of something familiar and harmless helped to calm her down.

Her footsteps echoed in the vast space as she walked the length of the hall. The walls were trimmed in gold, and lined with pedestals holding jewel-toned vases filled with palm leaves and strange, bright flowers. The hall was more beautiful than any room in the manor, or even the palace of Byblos. This was by far the most magnificent place she had ever been in.

She approached the end. A curved gallery of seats, like bleachers in a gymnasium but polished and elegant, stood on both sides of the back wall. A low-backed, golden chair sat on a dais between the two sections of seating. On the floor before the dais was a large gold ankh.

Megan stopped in front of it and bent over to see it better, but she couldn't tell if it was painted on the floor or inlaid. She straightened up and stepped forward.

No sooner did her foot touch the ankh than a cold wind blew over her. *Uh-oh. That can't be good.*

A booming voice sounded, not from one place but all around her.

"Who comes to the Hall of Judgment?"

Megan froze. Only her eyes moved as she searched for the source of the voice. She didn't know what to say, but the voice demanded an answer.

"Uh, me, I guess."

The wind blew again, accompanied by a cloud of shimmering silver dust. It swirled like a little tornado and settled on the chair. A man wrapped from neck to toes in white strips of cloth appeared out of the dust. On his head sat a tall golden crown with a disc in the center, not unlike the one Ra had worn. In one hand, he held a blue-and-gold-striped crook, in the other a long stick with strands of blue and gold beads hanging from the end. They were crossed over his chest.

"Are you ready to be judged?" he asked.

Megan felt the blood drain from her face. She gave an involuntary shudder, and her lips felt numb. That was a loaded question if she'd ever heard one.

"What do you mean?" she mumbled.

Beside the man appeared another figure. This one she recognized from the wall of Nefertari's tomb—a man with the head of a dog. In the gallery seats beside her, more strange-looking beings materialized. Like the dog-man, many of them had human bodies but the heads of animals—Megan saw a cow, a cat, a ram with curled horns and…

A falcon. She gasped, overcome with both awe and terror.

These were the gods of ancient Egypt. She had a very bad feeling about where she was.

"Please, sir," Megan managed to squeak out to the man on the throne. "Where am I? Why am I here?" *It can't hurt to ask, right?*

The man looked down at her, and his face was not hard but kind. Megan thought he looked a little sad.

"You are in the Duat, the place where all souls come to be judged."

"Souls?" Megan gaped at him. "But I'm not… dead." She thought back to the tomb and looked down at her right index finger. There was no trace of the small red dot. "Am I?"

There was no time to think about it, or ask further questions. The dog-headed man clapped his hands, and a set of golden scales, easily as tall as Megan, appeared between her and the man on the throne. Then the dog-man—Anubis, Diedrich had said his name was—came down from the dais and took Megan by one trembling hand.

"It is time for the weighing of the heart." His voice was low and gruff but not cruel.

Megan was speechless. She tried to comprehend what was happening to her, but rational thought was too difficult. She stood in front of the scales, her mind blank.

The man on the throne was Osiris. The name flashed across her thoughts. He was the god of the underworld.

Now, he bowed his head, and on one of the scales' gold plates appeared a long blue feather. If the scales dipped under the weight of it, it was imperceptible to human eyes.

"The feather of Ma'at," Osiris said. "If your heart weighs less than the Feather of Truth, you shall pass into the Underworld."

Megan snapped out of her fugue state.

"But I don't want to pass to the Underworld." She fought the urge to run, screaming, from the Hall. "I'm looking for the Ankh of Isis. That's all I want—to find it and take myself and my friends home."

Anubis smiled, and it was a strange sight—all of his sharp canine teeth showed. Megan almost found it funny.

"You must be proved worthy."

Megan's hands shook, and tears streamed down her face. This couldn't be happening.

Diedrich's voice raced through her thoughts, telling her the story from the *Book of the Dead.* She knew what would happen if she proved unworthy. To Osiris's left, a terrifying creature appeared. It bore the head of a crocodile, the body of a lion and the rear end of a hippopotamus. She remembered its name—the Ammut. If her heart was heavier than the feather, it would be fed to the beast, and her soul would never pass to the underworld. It would wander the world aimlessly forever.

"This isn't real, this cannot be real," Megan mumbled. She closed her eyes, hoping the nightmare would end, and she would wake up still inside Nefertari's tomb or, even better, back in the Library or, even better, her own bed.

She opened her eyes, and the hall remained.

*I'm still inside the book, aren't I? This is another of Sir Gregory's tests, it must be. I'm not really dead, just playing a part. Like Claire and Harriet did when they were Andromeda.*

She hoped that were the case, but if so, where were her friends? She still didn't know how she had gotten here from the tomb, or even where *here* was.

Behind her, there was a loud bang. She spun around. Josef Hemmlich pushed open the doors of the long hall and strode toward her. He wore a look of utter triumph.

"What are you doing here?" Megan said. "How did you get past Diedrich, Rachel, and—"

"Your friends and my misled son are no longer a problem," he said with a cruel sneer. He swept his gaze over the assembly of gods, one eyebrow arched high. "This cannot be—the Hall of Judgment?"

Megan said nothing—she was too busy thinking about what he might have done to her friends. *If he's hurt them, I'll… I'll… She didn't know what she'd do, actually. She was in no position to help anyone, not even herself.*

Anubis took Mr. Hemmlich by the arm, the same as he had done to Megan, and brought him before the golden scales. Mr. Hemmlich eyed the bright-blue feather. He pulled his head back and looked up at Osiris.

"I must have my heart weighed?"

Osiris nodded.

Sweat broke out on Mr. Hemmlich's forehead in large beads. He was obviously nervous about what would happen to him once his heart was on the scales. Megan didn't blame him. Not one bit. It was odd, but she almost sympathized with him.

Osiris pointed the staff with the beads at Josef. "Let he who comes last be measured first."

Josef's face blanched. "Uh, oh, no, mighty Osiris, you honor me, but I insist the girl go first. It is only fair."

Osiris bent forward, leaned around the scales, and looked him square in the eye.

"My word is law. Let your worth be known." He made a circular gesture with his hand, and the staff was gone, replaced by a pulsating, red mound of tissue. Josef Hemmlich gave a feeble whimper, but seemed none the worse for having his heart removed from his body.

Megan thought she was going to be sick.

Osiris slipped the shiny, slick heart onto the empty plate. Josef Hemmlich's hands shook, his sweating growing more profuse, and on the scales his heart beat faster. Everyone in the gallery watched—Megan held her breath.

The scales tipped. The heart sank below the feather.

Mr. Hemmlich dropped to his knees, his head in his hands.

"No! I am pure, I am pure."

Osiris sat up straight. "The scales do not lie. Your heart is burdened with greed and evil. You shall not pass."

Anubis lifted the heart, and the scales rebalanced. He turned from Megan and Mr. Hemmlich, and with one deft move, threw the heart to the Ammut, who caught it neatly in his crocodile jaws. He chewed it viciously.

Josef Hemmlich's eyes filled with terror. He turned to Megan, pleading. "Please, help me. I'm… so sorry. I had no choice, you understand? I didn't mean to…"

Megan was moved for about a second. She could almost forgive him. But the weight of everything he had put them through was too much to forgive. The image of him hovering over Rachel, saber in his hand, ready to strike, blocked out everything else.

"You did have a choice, though. And this is the consequence of your choices."

Josef's expression shifted to one of malice. He glared at Megan. His arm shot out, and he pointed an accusatory finger at her.

"I may have failed, but do not think this is the end. I am not the last, Librarian."

Without warning, flames engulfed his body. He screamed in agony. Megan, rooted to the spot, watched in horror as his body melted away in front of her.

The fire vanished as suddenly as it came, and nothing remained, not even a pile of ash. The floor was unblemished, and there was no indication anyone had ever stood in that spot, let alone burned.

Megan put a hand to her throat; her whole body trembled violently.

"Please," she begged. "Let me return to my friends. I don't want to be judged."

"You have no choice."

Osiris raised his arm again, and Megan felt a sudden tightness in her chest. She sucked in a sharp breath — it was like someone sat on her. Then it was gone, and to her horror she saw another heart, this one smaller, in the god's hand. He placed it on the empty plate.

Time seemed to stand still. What would happen if her heart was heavy? She tried to think of happy things. Her father, and riding Thunder across the empty field at a full gallop. Hanging out with Rachel, Claire, and Harriet in the coffee shop after school.

Diedrich's face floated to the surface of her thoughts. His warm smile, and the way he had looked at her when they were alone in the garden. His face was replaced by her mother's. Megan was only eight, and she and her mother were at the zoo, seated on a bench eating ice cream. It ran down the outside of the cone and her hand. Her mother's laugh, like a running brook.

Megan smiled, despite her situation. That last memory filled her, lifted her up until she felt...

Light as a feather.

The scales tipped slowly, but the opposite way they had for Josef Hemmlich's heart. The feather sank.

Megan rubbed her eyes and looked again. The view had not changed.

Osiris's face broke into a wide grin. "Your heart is filled with joy and love. You are worthy."

He snapped his fingers, and the heart disappeared. Megan felt the tightness in her chest again, and a tingling sensation from head to toes. An overwhelming sense of well-being and wholeness washed over her.

But she was still here, in the Hall of Judgement.

"Thank you, Great Osiris. Now, may I go back to my friends? And may I have the Ankh of Isis, please, so we can all go home?"

The scales vanished. The gods gathered in the gallery disappeared in a whirlwind of silver dust. Anubis bowed deeply to Megan, and he also faded away.

Only Osiris remained.

He stood, the cloths that bound him straining against his legs, and gave a respectful bow of his head.

"Eternal life awaits you in the palace of the queen."

With that, he was gone, leaving Megan alone. She looked up at the white vaulted ceiling.

"Excuse me, how do I get out of here?"

No answer came. Megan turned and ran toward the doors. Maybe she had to go back out to the lake, and Ra would take her back.

Her strides slowed as she crossed the floor. Her feet grew heavy, like lead weights were attached to them.

She fell.

Megan put out her hands to catch herself, but they went right through the floor. Her body followed, and as she plunged into utter darkness. A terrible coldness enveloped her as she plummeted through the nothingness.

Megan screamed.

# CHAPTER 18



*A Bird-God Delivers the Most Obvious Message Ever.*

"I think she's breathing." Rachel's voice sounded like it was at the end of a long tunnel.

"Is she? Oh, please, Megan, breathe!" Claire's voice sounded watery, like she had been crying.

"Megan? Megan, can you hear me?" Diedrich murmured in her ear.

She tried to speak, but couldn't. Her lips and throat felt frozen. Her lungs seared again, the same feeling as when she'd woken on the shores of the underground lake.

*It must have been a dream. A crazy dream.* She struggled to speak. A low grunt was all she could manage.

"I hear you, Megan," Rachel said. "Come on, wake up." Her eyelids felt like they weighed a thousand pounds. Each. They fluttered, and she forced them open. Blurry faces hovered above her. Slowly they came into focus.

Rachel's hair hung down on either side of her face.

Megan sneezed as the ends tickled her nose. "Get your hair out of my face, please."

Rachel breathed a deep sigh of relief. "She's okay."

"I wouldn't say that." Megan put her hand to her forehead. Her headache was back. "Did anyone get the license number of the camel that ran me over?"

They were still in Nefertari's tomb. Megan lay on top of the stone sarcophagus, her head in Diedrich's lap.

"What happened?" she asked.

"There was a scorpion in that secret compartment," Claire said. "When you reached in to pull out the parchment, it must have stung you. You passed out."

"It was really weird," Rachel said. "You turned blue, and you stopped breathing. We thought you were dead."

Megan didn't want to frighten them, so she didn't say anything about what she had been through for the moment. She sat up and looked at Diedrich.

"Was your father here?"

He nodded. "He snuck up on us. We were busy trying to figure out what happened to you, and he hit me from behind. Turnabout is fair play, I suppose."

"Claire put up a heck of a fight," Rachel said. "She and I thought we had him, but..." She shrugged. "He had some sort of sleeping powder that he blew in our faces. When we woke up, he was over there." She pointed to the edge of the sarcophagus.

Megan leaned over and saw Mr. Hemmlich's body on the floor. His skin looked pale, and his lips and around his eyes were tinged with blue. On his chest lay the scroll Megan had read from just before she passed out.

"I figure he got stung, same as you," Rachel said. "He should wake up soon, then, too, right? Shouldn't we get out of here?"

The full weight of what had really happened crushed Megan. *How do I tell Diedrich? Will he even believe me? I wouldn't believe me if I hadn't been there.*

Megan bit her lip and shook her head slowly. The best way was just to do it, be straightforward.

"I don't think so." She told them what happened in the Hall of Judgment after all. "I guess it wasn't a dream after all, but another part of the book's spell. I... died." Her face softened as she looked into Diedrich's eyes. "Your father's not coming back, Diedrich. I'm so sorry."

Diedrich's eyes watered, but his face remained stoic, and Megan felt her heart break for him.

"It's all right." His voice sounded ragged, and he choked on the words. "He... uh... was not who I thought he was." He brushed the back of his hand across his eyes, then wrapped his arms around Megan and pulled her into a tight embrace. "I am just glad you came back safe."

"I'm sorry about your dad, Diedrich. And I hate to break up this heartwarming moment," Rachel said, not unkindly. "But we're still here. We don't have the Ankh, and we don't know where to look next."

Megan gave Diedrich another squeeze and sat up. "Osiris said something to me just before I came back. It could be the clue."

"Don't leave us hanging," Claire said. "What did he say?"

"'Eternal life awaits you in the palace of the queen'."

Rachel sighed and rested her forehead against the edge of the sarcophagus.

"I suppose this means we need to make another trip?"

Megan looked confused. "But isn't this the palace of a queen? Her afterlife palace, but still…"

"Or it could mean the palace at Thebes," Claire said. "I know the pharaoh's a king, but he's got a wife or two—"

"There must be a thousand tombs of queens in this valley," Megan continued, not really listening to Claire.

"Or what about what you said before, Megan? That Abu Simbel place?" Rachel said. "Where Nefertari's husband built that shrine thing?"

A smile broke across Diedrich's face. "Rachel, you're brilliant. Osiris must have meant his queen. The Queen of the Egyptian Gods— Isis herself."

"It is her ankh, after all," Claire said with a nod.

"Thanks for that, O Queen of the Obvious," Rachel retorted.

"And just where is the palace of Isis?" Megan asked as she spun around and slid off the coffin to the floor. "And can you tell me after we get out of here? I've had enough of this place."

With one last look at Josef Hemmlich's body, the four of them left the burial chamber and walked out the tomb's front door. Megan caught the look of utter misery on Diedrich's face as they pushed the stone door closed.

"He would have killed us all, even me," he said in a choked voice. "And for what—this thing, this Ankh?"

"Eternal life is a powerful temptation," Megan said.

She put her hand on Diedrich's shoulder. "He was blinded by it."

"He didn't deserve what he got," Diedrich said. "To die like that. He should have been able to come home and be turned over to the authorities." His expression turned cold. "But he was judged fairly, and he has paid for his actions."

Their horses were where they had left them, plus a fourth—Mr. Hemmlich's. The sun was well past midpoint in the sky; there wasn't much day left.

"So, where to?" Megan swung her leg over her horse's back and settled into the saddle.

"Philae," Diedrich said. "And we'll need to take another boat ride to get there. It's in the middle of the Nile."

Sweat from Megan's horse flew into her eyes and mixed with her own. She wiped it with back of her hand and gave the white horse a kick, urging her to go faster. They left the Valley of the Queens at a full gallop and headed south again.

Diedrich told the horses speed was needed, and they obliged. People on the road between Thebes and Edfu scattered as the four steeds raced along, leaving a cloud of throat-clogging dust in their wake. Even at that speed, it would take half a day to reach Aswan, the city where Philae was located. They stopped on the outskirts of Edfu just long enough to give the horses a short rest and some water, and then were off again.

The sun hovered above the western mountains when Megan and her friends charged onto the ferry dock. The horses' hooves stamped a rapid beat on the wooden planks that led over the water to the wide, flat, floating platform that moved between Philae and the western shore of the Nile. People stared at them, but all pretense of following local customs had been dropped — none of them wanted anything more than to get home.

"We need to go to the temple," Megan said. "Now."

The ferryman scoffed. "The last ferry to the temple was an hour ago. You cannot get there until morning."

Diedrich reached down and grabbed the man by the front of his dingy tunic. He swore in the ferryman's face. "Did you not hear her? You will take us to the temple, and you will do it now."

The man's face dropped. He bowed his head, but not before Megan saw his lower lip trembling. She had never seen Diedrich act like that, but she understood. They were all anxious and upset, but he was channeling his grief for his father into getting them home. She totally got it. There was a time after her mother had died where she had been angry at the world. Diedrich would need his friends, once they got home, to help him through.

"Right away," the ferryman muttered. In an instant, the ropes that tied the boat to the shore lay coiled in a corner and the island temple of Philae grew closer.

It was a quick trip. The temple and island were enormous, and took a good-sized chunk out of the middle of the Nile. Two confused-looking men stood on the island dock. When the ferry drew close, they grabbed the barge and tied it up.

"Thank you," Megan said stiffly. The ferryman had been rude to her, but that didn't mean she had to return the favor.

She clucked to her mount and led her friends onto the dirt path that led around the island to the front of the temple. Above them loomed a great stone wall that marked the perimeter.  A gate guarded the tip of the oblong island, and beyond it a flight of wide steps that led to an enormous courtyard, paved with flat, red stones. A series of columns ran down each side. At the far end stood a pair of pylons with a door between them, much like at the temple of Horus.

"This temple is set up a lot like that one," Diedrich said when Megan mentioned it. "I think they were built around the same time."

They dismounted and left the horses to roam freely in the courtyard. Megan gave the white mare a grateful pat on the neck.

"This is probably the last time I'll see you, girl. Thanks."

"She says 'You are very welcome'," Diedrich said, translating the series of whinnies and neighs the horse gave Megan.

"That's still super weird," Rachel remarked.

The four companions walked through the door, past the hypostyle halls, and into the sanctuary. The time for sightseeing had long passed.

The room was large and rectangular. The door they'd used to enter was the only way in or out. To the left and right, by the shorter walls of the room, were sunken stone pits. A fire blazed in one, and in the other a fountain.

Directly across from the door stood an altar.

"Isis," Diedrich said, his voice a little above a whisper. The goddess was portrayed as a woman with long, straight hair, seated on a throne. Horns sat upon her head like a crown, the sun disc of Ra suspended between them. On her lap sat a smaller version of the falcon they had seen at the temple of Horus.

Megan approached the altar. The Ankh wasn't on the statue itself, so she pushed on it with the hope of opening another hidden passage or secret compartment. No such luck.

"Just give it to us!" Megan shouted to the air. "We played your stupid game!" Frustrated and tired, she pulled a foot back and kicked the statue, and immediately regretted her life choices as pain shot up her leg. She swore loudly, her injured foot in one hand as she hopped up and down on the other.

"That was dumb," Rachel said. Megan gave her a rude hand gesture.

Rachel put a hand on her chest in a gesture of mock offense.

"And that was unnecessary. Just because you did something stupid, don't take it out on me."

"It's not here," Megan said to the near-empty room. Her head sank to her chest, and her shoulders drooped. She wanted to go home. It was all she could do now not to cry.

"Did you think he was just going to leave it out with a big sign that says 'Take me'?" Rachel asked, her smile sympathetic. "Come on, Meg, you know that's not Sir Gregory's style. We've got to work for it."

Megan spun around and looked at Rachel, her hopelessness and frustration turning to anger.

"I died. I actually freaking died! Did you forget already? I managed to come back from the dead. I've worked plenty. I've earned it."

She clamped her mouth shut and tried not to cry. *Why did I do that? I just got Rachel back, and now I'm trying to trash my relationship with my best friend? This book... what is it doing to us?*

"Okay, okay, I see your point." Rachel held her hands up in surrender. "You've been through it. I can't pretend to understand, so I won't. I know I was wretched to you before, so now we're even." She put her arm around Megan's shoulders. "Sweetie, we know it's here, and we'll find it. Come on, Meg. Don't give up on me now."

"Found it," Claire said.

She stood in front of the fire pit. She pointed to the heart of the fire.

"It's in there."

In the center of the pit, engulfed in flames, hung the Ankh. It hovered inside the fire, suspended in mid-air or held in place by the fire itself.

"Just how in blazes are we supposed to get it out of there?" Rachel reached toward the flames, but quickly pulled her hand back and sucked on the tips of her fingers. "No way to reach it without getting burned," she mumbled.

As if to make Rachel's point more clear, the fire shot skyward in a column of flame eight feet high, that covered the ankh completely.

"Great," Diedrich said. "Just great."

From within the pillar of fire rose a magnificent bird. Red and orange feathers, with a golden beak, and gold-tipped tail and wings, as if the fire had created it. The bird broke free of the fire and glided above them; it circled the room before returning to the fire pit to land on the stone rim.

"It's so beautiful," Rachel said.

"It's a Benu," Claire replied in her matter-of-fact tone. "A phoenix."

After her experience in the Hall of Judgment, Megan knew better. "It's Osiris."

The bird seemed to understand Megan. It nodded its exquisite red-and-gold head. Then it turned its sad, round black eyes on her, opened its gold beak, and began to sing. Never in her life had Megan heard anything so sad and beautiful. Crystal notes warbled into the still air — it was as if the whole world stopped to listen to the Benu's song.

Megan's eyes welled with tears. All the strain of the last few hours melted away.

Everything would be all right.

When the bird finished he sat silently, cocking his head in a curious way at the four young people.

Diedrich took a slow step forward and bowed deeply. "Thank you."

The bird nodded again, then launched from the stone rim and soared upward. It dove into the flames. The fire returned to its previous size — the bird was gone.

Rachel looked at Diedrich. "What was that all about? Did you understand it?" She slapped herself on the forehead. "Of course you did."

"I'm jealous," Claire said. "I've never heard anything so wonderful."

"What did it say?" Megan said. "And why did it leave?"

"It said, after it apologized to Megan, that in order to retrieve the Ankh, you must put out the fire." He shrugged. "I guess it left because its message was delivered."

"Well, now, why didn't we think of that?" Rachel rolled her eyes in exasperation. "Like we never would have thought of *that* all by ourselves. Thanks, bird."

"If that's all there is to it, let's just do it," Megan marched across the room to the fountain. "Um, one problem. There's nothing here to carry the water with."

Rachel searched the area around the fire pit. "Nothing here, either. We could scoop it up with our hands and carry it, but I don't think we'd get enough to put the fire out, even if all four of us did it."

"Besides," Claire added, "it's so far from one end to the other we'd probably have empty hands by the time we got to the fire."

Megan sat on the edge of the fountain and rested her head in one hand.

"We're missing something."

Diedrich sat next to her. "Why do you say that? There was probably a bucket here. Someone could have just taken it or moved it."

She shook her head. "If we needed a bucket, it would be here. It's a puzzle." She closed her eyes, thoughts swimming in her head.

*What's the answer?*

Megan, her face hot and throat dry, turned around and splashed some of the water on her face. It was cool and refreshing as it ran down her face and neck in rivulets. She scooped another handful and poured it in into her mouth.

Behind her, something sizzled. Megan whipped her head around. Rachel and Claire stared at the fire, then at Megan, wearing identical looks of shock.

"What happened?" Megan asked.

Rachel pointed at the fire.

"It was rather strange. The fire—uh, got smaller, for just a second. There was that sizzling sound, like someone dumped water on it. Then it came back, big as ever."

Megan's face broke into a grin. *Sir Gregory, you were a weird, clever guy.*

"I have an idea." She scooped up another handful of water and drank it. She heard the sizzling again, and Rachel's exclamation.

"There it goes again! Whatever you're doing, Megan, it's brilliant."

Megan grinned. "Diedrich, help me—start drinking and don't stop."

She quickly abandoned scooping up the water and stuck her whole face in the fountain. Diedrich followed suit. They both sucked up water as fast as they could until they needed to come up for air.

"I cannot drink another drop." Diedrich let out a long, loud burp.

Megan wiped the water from her face and chin. "Was it enough?" She turned around.

There was nothing left of the fire but a pile of wet, smoldering ash. A stone pedestal, which they hadn't seen because of the flames, sat in the center of the pit. And on top lay the Ankh of Isis.

"Good job." Claire reached across the pit to lift the Ankh from its perch.

"Don't!" Megan said. "Remember last time? We all touched the crown to make sure we all got out."

Claire pulled her hand back quickly. "Oops, sorry, I forgot. I don't want to leave anyone behind."

"Too right you don't," Rachel said. "Come on, you two, I don't really want to be here another second."

As soon as Megan and Diedrich reached the other side of the room, they all stood on the edge of the fire pit, circling the Ankh.

"Everyone ready?" Megan asked. "Remember, hold on as tight as you can. Don't let go, no matter what."

Diedrich took one of her hands and gave it a squeeze. "Ready."

"Ready," Claire said.

"I've been ready for three days!" Rachel chimed in.

"One, two, three."

Together, they reached up and grabbed the Ankh. A glow surrounded the artifact and their hands, increasing until it blinded them. The wind followed, the familiar hurricane-level sound blocking out everything else.

Megan was lifted by the shoulders, Diedrich's hand still in hers, holding tightly.

She plunged headlong into the middle of the light, where she concentrated on keeping a hold of both the Ankh and Diedrich. All sense of time and space was lost; there remained only light and sound.

The light that blasted Megan's eyelids slowly grew dimmer.

Like a slow-motion film suddenly going full speed again, she felt herself hurtle through space until she landed on a hard, wooden surface. As she opened her eyes, the floor of the Library welcomed her.

She caught her breath and quickly rolled out of the way. The last time they came out of a book, Rachel had landed on her. Diedrich fell in the spot she had occupied just a second earlier, and with Claire and Rachel following immediately after.

On the reading table, the red-gold cloth cover of the book titled *Ankh of Isis* closed with a *snap*.

# CHAPTER 19



"ARE WE BACK?" DIEDRICH LAY SUPINE ON THE FLOOR, STARING AT THE Library's ceiling. The starry night had been replaced with a sky full of pink-and-gold clouds. He, like all of them, once more wore his nightclothes.

Megan, who was on her belly, lifted her head.

"Yep." Pushing herself onto her hands and knees, she searched for the Ankh. She found it beneath a nearby bookshelf, not far from the *Book of the Dead*. *Where did that come from? The last time Megan had seen it, it was tied to their* horse's saddles, in the bag with the *Book of Thoth*. Megan scanned the floor but didn't see the other book anywhere.

Rachel and Claire stood and helped Diedrich up. "Everyone all right?" Rachel asked.

Megan, Claire, and Diedrich nodded.

Claire scooped up the *Book of the Dead*. "Come on, Rachel, let's go and put this away."

"But, Claire—"

"Come on, Rachel." Claire tugged at Rachel's pajamas, giving her a pointed look. The girls disappeared around the corner.

Diedrich scanned the floor. "Why did my father's body not…"

Megan laid a hand on his shoulder.

"Because he wasn't with us," she said gently. "If one of us hadn't been holding on to the Ankh, they would have been left behind, too. We would have been stuck, because once the artifact is removed, the book is… just a book. I think the *Book of the Dead* came back because it wasn't a person? Maybe. I don't know, magic is weird. I guess." She wished she had a better explanation, one that might make Diedrich feel better.

Diedrich nodded. Now that they were home and safe, Megan watched as the reality of what had happened came down on him. His chin and bottom lip quivered.

"We should have brought his body, at least. I could have, I do not know, carried him or something."

"I'm sorry," Megan said. "I didn't even think about…" There was nothing she could say. She knew the pain he was going through, and that he would have to face it in his own way. She put her arms around him, and he pressed his head into her shoulder.

Diedrich sobbed for several minutes, and Megan let some tears fall as well. Not for Josef Hemmlich, no. She cried for Diedrich. Though, she was sorry his father had died, maybe he hadn't deserved it. But he was Diedrich's father, after all. And now the world would never know what kind of person he really was. But she was not sorry that she and her friends were all safe from him.

*Is this what it means to be the Librarian? That the people you care about are constantly in danger or in pain? That you fight with them?* She wondered if it was really worth it, if these… things, these artifacts, were really worth protecting so fiercely, or if the cost was just too high.

Someone behind them cleared their throat. It didn't sound female. Megan turned her head and saw Bailey in the center of the aisle, hands behind his back. His face held a mixture of annoyance and curiosity.

"Bailey." Megan disentangled herself from Diedrich and wiped her eyes on the sleeve of her pajama top. "What are you doing down here?"

"It is almost dawn, miss. I am always up at this hour, to do my morning inspection. Imagine my utter surprise when I found the door on the landing standing wide open."

Diedrich turned toward the butler, his eyes red and swollen and his nose running. He sniffed and wiped his face with his sleeve.

"I'm sorry, I must have left it open. I was the last one through."

Bailey must have finally noticed their tear-stained faces, because his expression changed to one of genuine concern. "Miss, what has happened?"

Before she could answer, Rachel and Claire came back.

"We had some trouble, Bailey. Uh, well, Mr. Hemmlich was after the Ankh of Isis." She held up the heavy Ankh and showed it to him. "It was why he was really here in the first place."

"He knew about the Library?"

Megan wanted to say no, but when she thought about it, she couldn't.

"You know, I'm not really sure what he knew or didn't know, except that he did know about the Ankh." She proceeded to tell Bailey all that had happened with Mr. Hemmlich and their adventure inside the book.

Something occurred to her.

"Come to think of it, I wonder why he thought Sir Gregory even knew where it was in the first place."

Bailey did not seem the least bit surprised, but the butler hardly ever seemed surprised about anything. He pursed his lips as if he were thinking about something. He gave a brief nod and turned to Diedrich.

"I am most sorry for your loss, Master Hemmlich."

Diedrich, who looked a little more composed, gave a weak smile. "Thank you."

Megan pressed the long stem of the Ankh between her hands and twirled it. There was an uncomfortable silence.

"We should go to the vault now, and put this away."

"Of course. Follow me." Bailey made a crisp turn and walked off between the shelves toward the opposite side of the room. Megan, Rachel, Claire, and Diedrich followed. When they reached the center aisle, Bailey came to an abrupt stop.

"I would ask that only Miss Megan continue from here, please."

"Why?" Rachel asked. "I've been in the vault before."

"Yes, miss, I know. But if you would please wait here, we won't be long."

Rachel gave Megan a look that asked if she would be all right and did she want Rachel to come with her anyway? Megan gave a quick shake of her head. Bailey didn't do anything without good reason, so there must be one for his request.

She and the butler continued their journey between the long stacks that filled the huge room.

"Why didn't you want my friends to come with me?"

"Because," Bailey said, just loud enough for Megan to hear. "It is time that you, as the Librarian, learned to open the vault yourself."

"What? I can't do that!"

"You've more than earned the right. So, why in heaven not?"

"The vault is opened by magic," Megan said. "And I can't do magic."

Bailey waved a hand at her, as if brushing away a bug. "Have you ever tried?"

The question took her by surprise. "Well...no. I didn't know it was an option."

"You have as much potential as anyone else. Sir Gregory taught himself, remember?"

"Uh, well…"

"I learned to do it, and I am no wizard, I assure you. It's very simple, you'll see."

Megan tried to think of some other reason she shouldn't be able to open the vault, but couldn't come up with a single one. She had to admit the thought of being able to work magic, even a small bit, intrigued her more than a little.

*Finally, some perk to this pain-in-the-butt job.*

Her shrug didn't let on how excited she was. "I guess it couldn't hurt to try."

"That's the spirit."

They arrived at the far end of the stacks. Just like the opposite wall, this was covered by a rack of small, square cubbyholes, and Megan was reminded of the library in the temple of Edfu. This rack went to the ceiling—a ladder leaned against it to reach the higher cubbies—and ran the length of the wall.

Except for one place right in the middle. This space was empty except for a small carved-stone owl that stuck out from it at about Megan's head height.

"Now," Bailey said in a manner that said Megan's lesson had begun. "The spell to open the vault is very simple. You must place your hand on the owl's head and say *Pseudothyrum expositus*."

Megan lifted both eyebrows. "What?"

"*Pseudothyrum expositus*. It's Latin for 'show the secret door'."

"Ah. I'll have to remember that for my Latin class. So, that's all I have to do?"

"Not quite. Visualization and intent are the most important parts. With your mind's eye, picture the door already open. You must see it clearly, understand, or the words won't do any good. You also have to want the door to open."

Megan pulled her shoulders back and stepped up to the owl. She cleared her throat and put her hand on the smooth stone head. It felt cool beneath her fingers and slightly sweaty palm.

"Pseudo, uh… tryem…"

Bailey sighed. "Pseudo-thy-rum expo-sit-us. And visualize."

Megan closed her eyes and tried to remember what the vault door looked like when it was open. She saw the stones in the wall rearrange themselves into a narrow open arch in the wall. She willed the door to open. *Come on…*

"Pseudothyrum expositus."

Her hand tingled with a feeling like when she shuffled her feet across a carpet and touched something metal, except that instead of a quick shock, this tingle lasted several seconds. Megan yanked her hand back. The owl melted into the wall, and the stones moved around until they shaped the narrow-arched doorway she had seen in her head.

Megan stared at her hand, which looked no different or the worse for wear, and then at the open arch, eyes wide.

"I did that? That's so cool!"

Bailey chuckled. It sounded rusty, as if he hadn't laughed in about a decade or so.

"You have successfully activated the spell Sir Gregory put there, yes. Congratulations."

"Thanks."

"I don't suppose you need me to tell you to keep this part a secret, even from your closest friend?"

Megan nodded, still staring at the wall. "No, Bailey, I understand. I don't think she'd believe me anyway."

"Being the Librarian does have its drawbacks. Keeping secrets even from those whom you trust the most is one."

*Yeah, tell me something I don't know.*

Megan walked into the vault and stopped. Something about what Bailey said reminded her of what she'd been wondering earlier.

"Bailey, let me ask you something."

"Yes, miss?" Bailey walked into the vault and around Megan.

"Does anyone, besides the people you know of, know about the Library?"

The butler didn't turn, but answered in an offhand manner, "No, Miss, I don't believe so. Why would you ask?"

Josef Hemmlich's last words echoed in Megan's head. "Uh, no reason. Never mind." She didn't want to upset Bailey over what was probably nothing. If there were other people out there searching for the Ankh, well, she would jump off that bridge when she came to it.

*Everything had kind of gone off the rails at that point — we were dead, for cripes' sake. I probably heard him wrong anyway.*

She took a deep breath and shook off the feeling of unease that had come over her. *I just heard him wrong, or he was trying to make me nervous. Nothing to worry about. No one else will come looking.*

A series of shelves ran along the left-hand side of the vault. Each one had a small tag attached to the front of it. Written on each, in Sir Gregory's elegant handwriting, was the name of an artifact.

Most of the shelves remained empty, their contents inside the enchanted books. The Ankh of Isis's shelf was one of the first, nearest the door. Megan stood on tiptoe and put the heavy golden artifact in its place.

Another tag caught her eye as she lowered her heels to the floor.

"The Book of Thoth." The shelf was empty. "So, was the book we found in the basilisk's lair the real one?"

Bailey shook his head. "No. The real one was never found. Sir Gregory thought he knew the location, and made a place ready for it. But that expedition never took place."

"The one we found—"

"Was just part of the story, based on Sir Gregory's research into the real book."

Megan ran a finger over the label of the empty shelf, thinking. "What about the spell Diedrich read? He said he could talk to animals. That was real. I mean, he talked to the horses, at least he said he did. He definitely understood the Benu, who told us how to reach... Oh, I see. If nobody had read the spell, we wouldn't have been able to... but we figured out how to put out the fire by ourselves. The exact method, I mean."

"But the bird is what put you on the path, wasn't it?" Bailey gave a knowing smile. "You see, there was a method to Sir Gregory's madness. Each task had to be completed in turn."

"But what would have happened if Diedrich hadn't been with us? The spell was in ancient Egyptian."

"That's a good question," Bailey said. "To be honest, I don't know. Did you look at the book?"

Megan nodded. "The clue was in the back, in English. So, we could get to the next place, but..."

Bailey shrugged. "You said you figured out how to put out the fire by yourselves. I can't pretend to speak for Sir Gregory, but maybe the spell was for added effect. He did like a bit of drama."

"I guess that means that Diedrich can't talk to animals anymore."

"We can't be sure until he tries to speak to one, but if I had to guess, the spell was part of the story and ended when you came out of the book."

"I wonder if he'll be upset." She remembered the look on his face when he realized he'd never see his father again. *Probably not. He's got other things to upset him.*

They stepped out of the vault and back into the Library Megan waited for the doorway to turn itself back into the wall, but nothing happened.

With a puzzled look, she turned to Bailey. "Why doesn't it close? I can't remember how it closed last time."

"You must close it," Bailey said. "This will be your second lesson in magic." He stood behind her and spoke into her ear. "Raise your hand, palm outward. Visualize the wall, whole again."

Megan did as he said, her faced screwed up in what was probably a hilarious expression of concentration that she was happy her friends weren't here to see.

"Now, just wave your hand across the entrance."

She waved her hand and opened her eyes. The door was still there.

"Concentrate," Bailey said. "Pull the stones together in your mind. Want it to close."

Megan tried again, focusing every ounce of brain power she had on closing the arch. She opened one eye, and dropped her arm. "I can't do it."

Bailey patted her on the shoulder and gave her what she supposed passed for a sympathetic look.

"Don't worry, dear. With time, and practice, you will." He lifted his own arm, and after very little effort and the same gesture Megan had used, the stones knit themselves back into a solid wall, owl and all.

They walked through the stacks toward where they'd left Megan's friends.

"Bailey?"

"Yes, miss?"

"Why didn't Sir Gregory use the Ankh's power for himself? He could have stayed alive forever if he wanted."

Bailey turned and faced Megan with a wistful look. "Don't think he didn't consider it. Mortality and all its trappings — disease, old age, the slowing of one's body and mind — is something from which no man is immune." He took a deep, ragged breath.

"But in the end, Sir Gregory realized he didn't have the right to cheat death. That, eventually, his existence would become one of isolation and grief, and while he remained ageless, those close to him would move on without him."

"That's totally messed up." Megan nodded slowly. "I never thought of that."

Bailey gave a thin smile. "The young never do."

"Bailey, let me ask you something else."

She paused, glancing around at the shelves of books that surrounded her. "Do you think this, I mean, all of this…" she waved her arm around the Library, "…is worth it?"

The butler considered for a moment before he answered. "The things within these walls… could change the course of human history. For the good, or the bad. They need protection from both."

"Both?"

"People with the best of intentions often stumble down the primrose path to evil. If everything stays here, and stays safe, no one can corrupt them, unintentionally or no."

Megan still had mixed feelings about her role in protecting the Library, but Bailey's explanation helped her feel better about it. Rachel and she were still as close as ever, and they could shut the door on this horrible experience and get back to their normal lives.

It didn't make what Diedrich was dealing with any easier, though.

The girls and Diedrich were right where Megan and Bailey had left them. Claire and Rachel talked with their heads together, while Diedrich leaned against the end of one of the bookcases. His face was turned to the domed ceiling, watching the sky turn from pink to robin's-egg blue. He glanced at Megan and Bailey as they approached.

*He looks older,* Megan thought, *like he's aged years in the short time we were been inside the book.*

"How come no one knows we were gone?" Diedrich said. "We spent, what, three nights in that book?"

"Well, let's put it this way. When you read a book, there are a whole bunch of days in the story, right?" Megan said. "But you can read a whole book in one day. It's like that."

Diedrich didn't look like he quite got it.

Megan shook her head—she'd explain again later. "Come on, let's get out of here." She took his hand and led him to the door. Rachel and

Claire wore matched expressions of sympathy, but remained silent, falling into line behind them.

"If you would, miss, just close the door behind you. I will go and retrieve the Ankh's book and put it in its rightful place."

With a quick bow, Bailey turned on his heel and walked away.

Upstairs, the entrance hall was filled with soft light. Megan closed the secret door and joined her friends on the landing.

"How are we going to explain this to your dad?" Rachel said. "He's going to want to know where Mr. Hemmlich's got to."

Megan shook her head, closed her eyes and leaned against the statue of Athena. She didn't want to think about that yet, only savor this moment of peace.

"I'll figure out something." A sudden thought occurred to her. "What about you, Diedrich? What are you going to do now?"

Diedrich's face was pale and expressionless. He looked as if he were made of wax. He lifted his head from his chest, his gaze fixed on Megan. He gave her a bewildered look, as if he had been thinking of something else and was caught off-guard.

"I am, uh, going to call my mother, if that is okay."

Megan nodded.

He rubbed a hand through his hair, leaving it standing on end at strange angles. "She's in Switzerland. I will call her and tell her I want to come and stay with her. I do not know what I will tell her about Father, but..."

"We'll think of something," Megan said. "Right now, I think you should go and lie down."

"Yes." Diedrich's eyes blanked out again. He nodded. "Lie down. Rest. Sounds good." He walked, still in a trance-like state, down the stairs and toward the front door. Megan caught him by one elbow and spun him around. She pointed him in the direction of his room and watched him walk up the stairs and down the hall.

"He's in a right state, isn't he?" Rachel said.

"Wouldn't you be if you'd just lost a parent?" Megan said, and a familiar pain shot through her heart. "I think I lost three whole days after my mom died. It was like walking through a fog."

"What a tragedy," Claire said with a slow nod.

Megan puffed out her cheeks and held her breath for a second, then let it all out in a cathartic rush.

"Yeah, it is."

"Bright side?" Rachel said with a small, silly smile. "I'm totally going to get an A on my history paper."

"It's a pity your father had to leave so suddenly," Megan's dad said to Diedrich over breakfast. He picked up a forkful of western omelet. "Where did you say he went?"

Diedrich cleared his throat. Megan had come up with a good story and, after a few hours of blessed and peaceful sleep, walked Diedrich through it on the way downstairs to the dining room, where Maggie had a late brunch waiting for them. Megan had learned from Miranda, the head housekeeper, that Bailey had informed the staff about what happened in the Library, including the reason for Mr. Hemmlich's sudden disappearance.

"He got a call on his cell late last night," Diedrich said. His eyes remained on the French toast and sausages on his plate. His voice sounded cold, almost robotic. Megan hoped her normally clueless father wouldn't notice. "There was some emergency at the museum. He left so quickly, I do not even think he packed his things."

Megan's father nodded. "Ah, of course. I understand those things happen." But the look on his face said he wasn't quite certain what sort of an emergency at a museum would require leaving in the middle of the night, without even his son.

*It was the best I could come up with. I'll just have to make him believe it later. I hate to lie to him, but would he believe the truth? Poor Dad.*

Her father chewed slowly, and took a gulp of coffee. "You're welcome to stay as long as you wish, of course, Diedrich."

Diedrich swallowed. "Thank you, sir, that is very generous, but my mother is expecting me tomorrow. I will stay with her until it is time to return to school."

A few hours after brunch, Diedrich and the girls stood by the front door, where Claire and Rachel said their goodbyes.

"Good luck," Claire said.

"Keep in touch."

"Chin up," Rachel said. "It will be all right."

Diedrich gave each of them a hug. "It has been a pleasure meeting both of you."

Claire and Rachel left for home, and Megan and Diedrich hiked upstairs to pack Mr. Hemmlich's things. Miranda had offered, but Diedrich wanted to do the job himself.

"I think it will give this whole — ordeal — some solidity, some closure," he said sadly.

Megan understood. Her father had taken a year to go through her mother's things. His words echoed in Megan's memory.

*If I get rid of them, I'll have to admit she's really gone.*

Diedrich opened the closet and pulled out an array of suits, shirts, and ties, and dropped them on the bed. Megan opened the top drawer of the antique bureau and emptied out socks, handkerchiefs, and underthings.

Buried at the bottom, she found a small leather-bound journal. It looked very familiar, and she almost panicked before she realized it was not Sir Gregory's diary. Mr. Hemmlich's own initials were stamped in the bottom corner of the brown cover. There was also something else stamped into the soft calfskin.

"Diedrich," she said. "Come here for a sec?" She pulled the book out of the drawer and showed it to him. "Do you know what this symbol is?" she asked. It was like an upside-down horseshoe with little feet.

"It is the Greek letter omega," Diedrich said. "The last letter of the Greek alphabet. I do not know what it means to my father, but…" His face turned pensive.

"But what?"

"He had this same thing tattooed inside his left forearm."

Megan frowned. "I never saw a tattoo."

"He almost always wore long-sleeved shirts — and it was not obvious, the tattoo is small. He has had it as long as I can remember. Strange he had this same thing on his journal. He was never into Greece or Greek mythology, as far as I know. It was always Egypt he loved.

"I kind of thought him even having the tattoo was weird, since whenever I mentioned getting one he freaked out about me defacing my body." His face went slack, as if the memory of his father getting angry with him hurt.

Megan put the diary into the suitcase with everything else. She was curious about what it said, but decided she would let Diedrich take care of it. For whatever it was worth, she trusted him. Likewise with the pile of his father's papers — she still had the photos Rachel had taken anyway. She would keep them, just in case.

When they were finished, Bailey came and collected the two suitcases, a briefcase, and a garment bag they had placed in the hall outside the room.

"I will have these sent to your father's home," he said.

Diedrich nodded sadly. "There will not be anyone there to receive them. I will give you the address of a storage facility where you can send them. Thank you, Bailey."

It was time for Diedrich to leave. He and Megan were alone in the entrance hall, hands entwined. Silence hung awkwardly between them.

"Dad's right, you know." Megan felt her face get grow hot. "You could stay. It's not like we don't have the room. If you really wanted to, I'm sure you could even transfer and go to school here. There's St. Bart's, St. Agatha's brother school, not far from here. We could ask your mother."

Diedrich shook his head. "No. I really have to go. The sooner I get away from here, the sooner I can, you know, move on."

An arrow to the chest would have hurt less, but Megan didn't let it show.

"You really want to get away that badly? I totally don't, you know, blame you."

Diedrich shook his head. "Not from you, just from this place. I am sorry." He leaned down and kissed her cheek, while a thousand butterflies swooped around in her stomach. She and Diedrich stood there, holding hands in silence.

The front door opened, and Bailey stuck his head inside. "A-hem."

Megan and Diedrich jumped apart.

"Everything is prepared. We must leave soon in order for you to catch your train." He looked at Megan and winked. She wondered what that was all about. "I'll wait by the car." He pulled the door closed.

Diedrich ran his hand over the back of his head and sighed.

"Time to go."

"Text me when you get to your mom's? Let me know you got there all right?"

"I promise. Listen, Megan, I, uh, I'm really going to…" He let the rest drift away, his cheeks turning red.

Megan pulled him into a tight embrace. "I'm so going to miss you, too."

Two weeks later, Megan bounced into the breakfast nook. As she sat, she draped her dark-blue school blazer over the back of the chair, and grabbed one of Maggie's scrumptious corn muffins. Her father sat in his usual place by the window, his face covered by the paper.

"Ready for school, Megums?"

"Uh-huh."

"Don't talk with your mouth full, dear. It's rude." The top of his paper flopped over, and he snapped it up straight. "Hmm. Would you look at that."

"What?"

"Herr Hemmlich's gone missing."

Megan choked on her muffin. She grabbed her teacup and took a gulp of hot liquid to wash down the cake that had lodged in her throat. "Really?"

Her father's head peeked out from behind the paper. "You all right?"

Megan nodded. "Muffin went down the wrong way. What happened to him?"

Her father laid the paper on the table and squinted at the article.

"Apparently, he got lost in the desert. He went off into the Valley of the Kings, alone for some reason, sometime last week. No one's heard from him since." He looked up, confused. "Now, why would he do that?"

"Who knows, Dad. Maybe he wanted to scout things out before the expedition. Or he got a lead on what he was looking for — that lost king's tomb, or whatever — and he couldn't wait."

"Perhaps. Odd thing, though. I hope he turns up. I'd hate to lose him as a client."

"Yeah, that would really suck for you."

Megan said goodbye and walked to the front door, where Bailey was waiting to drive her to school.

He bowed his head. "Good morning, miss."

Megan tilted her head to one side and gave the butler an inquisitive look. "I heard the most interesting thing this morning, Bailey."

"Really, miss?"

"Yes, it seems that Josef Hemmlich has gone missing. It was reported he went into the desert alone and never returned."

Bailey pushed his lower lip out and nodded. "That is interesting. Do they have any idea of where he might be?"

Megan moved in close to the butler. "No, and I'd like to know how the newspapers came by that story."

"How would I know that, miss?" Bailey's face remained unchanged as he opened the front door for her. "I am but a humble butler."

"Yes, Bailey, and I'm the Queen of Egypt."

# ABOUT THE AUTHOR

Once Upon a Time, Christine Norris thought she wanted to be an archaeologist, but hates sand and bugs, so instead she became a writer. She is the author of several speculative fiction works for children and adults, including *The Library of Athena* series, *A Series of Curses* series, and several short stories in anthologies like *Gaslight and Grimm, Grimm Machinations, Other Aether,* and *An Assembly of Monsters.* She is kept busy on a daily basis by her day job as a school librarian in New Jersey. She may or may not have a secret library in her basement, and she absolutely believes in fairies.

# A Curse of
# Time and Vengeance

## by Christine Norris

### A Steampunk
### Sleeping Beauty Story!

Lost Time Is Never Found Again… Or Is It?

Christmas Eve, Philadelphia 1884. Henry Rittenhouse has bided his time long enough. Armed with a poignant gift, he heads for Sophie Weber's house with designs on entwining both of their lives forever more.

But capricious is the object of his love, whom he catches clad as a boy, shimmying down the drainpipe from the attic. Rather than making his declaration, Henry finds himself on a merry chase suddenly turned tragic as Sophie vanishes, with no trace left behind to find her.

A note delivered soon after betrays the truth: In an act of chilling vengeance, Sophie has been snatched away by Alexei Faber, her father's mortal enemy, trapped inside a machine where she will stay, frozen and asleep, for a hundred years.

Desperate to save his love, Henry gets tangled up with an unusual trio pursuing Faber on a mission through… dare he believe?… time. Henry must not only find a way to save his love, but help stop a plot that could unravel history.

## https://especbooks.square.site